MW00341421

OLD KING

ALSO BY MAXIM LOSKUTOFF

Ruthie Fear

Come West and See

OLD KING

A NOVEL

Maxim Loskutoff

W. W. NORTON & COMPANY
Independent Publishers Since 1923

Copyright © 2024 by Maxim Loskutoff

All rights reserved
Printed in the United States of America
First Edition

For information about permission to reproduce selections from
this book, write to Permissions, W. W. Norton & Company,
Inc., 500 Fifth Avenue, New York, NY 10110

For information about special discounts for bulk purchases, please contact
W. W. Norton Special Sales at specialsales@wwnorton.com or 800-233-4830

Manufacturing by Lakeside Book Company
Editor: Tom Mayer
Assistant Editor: Nneoma Amadi-obi
Project Editor: Dassi Zeidel
Copyeditor: Dave Cole
Book Design: Beth Steidle
Production Manager: Delaney Adams
Jacket Art Direction and Design: Derek Thornton

ISBN 978-0-393-86819-7

W. W. Norton & Company, Inc., 500 Fifth Avenue, New York, N.Y. 10110
www.wwnorton.com

W. W. Norton & Company Ltd., 15 Carlisle Street, London W1D 3BS

1 2 3 4 5 6 7 8 9 0

For Dave

We have a true king, he lives behind the mountains . . . Before him hang a hundred thousand veils of light and darkness . . .

—FARĪD-UD-DĪN ATTĀR, *THE CONFERENCE OF THE BIRDS*

OLD KING

The University of Illinois at Urbana-Champaign, May 1976

Security officer Henry Leck stared down at the misaddressed package. He lifted it to his ear and gently shook it. It had a dense weight. The contents hardly rustled. Curious, Henry looked around. The computer lab was mostly empty. The mainframe banked against the far wall hummed loudly. A magnetic tape drive made a soft clicking noise. Across the room, a student worker fed cards into the teletype machine. Henry set the package down, unsure of what to do.

Purple Eugene O'Neill stamps checkered the corner. The receiving and return addresses were written in spidery block letters. The package was intended for a psychology professor at Boston University but had been returned, due to his no longer teaching there. The return address was the computer lab where Henry stood. He didn't recognize the handwriting. None of the lab techs nor faculty had claimed it. He tugged at the belt of his uniform, annoyed and intrigued by this task, which seemed outside his job description.

Henry found a pair of scissors by the line printer. Fitting his large fingers through the eye rings, he slowly cut the taped ends, wanting to be able to paste them back together if he found something personal. He pulled the paper apart. Inside was a wooden box a foot and a half long and ten inches wide. Henry felt a pulse of trepidation. Who sends a wooden box? The lid was snugly fitted with a steel clasp. It looked like a tiny coffin. The wood was unsanded and fresh, clearly handmade. Ponderosa, Henry thought, sniffing. He recognized the sweet pine smell from camping trips to Montana with his dad as a boy. He set the scissors down, remembering his father, who had died earlier that year. Sighing, he folded the paper packaging over to look again at the return address. It surely hadn't come from the lab.

Carefully, he unclasped and lifted the lid.

White light flashed before his eyes, then a bang, and heat seared his arm. He leapt back and looked down, horrified, at the wisp of flame amid the blackened components of the bomb. His wrist was purple-red, smoking. The skin on his hand bubbled. A gash ran across the center of his palm where a piece of metal shrapnel had slashed to bone. Panicked, Henry swatted at the flames. The shock faded and he felt pain, scorching pain. The smell of smoke and his own burning flesh brought tears to his eyes. He looked around for help, and found only the stunned eyes of the student worker cowering by the teletype machine.

DUANE

According to most accounts, the early West
was a primitive, dangerous, and lonely
place offering a life full of hardship that
mainly attracted the single man, and [the
town of] Lincoln was no exception.

—GOLD PANS AND SINGLETREES,
A HISTORY OF THE BLACKFOOT VALLEY

1

Duane Oshun packed his few belongings into his truck, drove to his ex-wife's house in Fairpark, on the outskirts of Salt Lake City, parked across the street, and sat staring at her door trying to figure how best to break in. He chose the side window, yanking off the screen and jimmying up the bottom rail with his pocketknife. He raised the lower panel and hooked his arms inside, then hauled his body in headfirst, squirming over the sill. Splinters pricked his stomach. He landed on his head on the carpet. His neck bent painfully and he cursed, rolling his long legs in over him. He found himself on his back on the carpet, breathing hard. The sudden rush of familiar smells made him dizzy: Tracy's perfume, Hudson's dirty clothes, egg scraps left in a frying pan on the stove. Duane raised his head and looked around.

The couch and recliner were shadowed mounds. The digital clock on the Betamax player glowed red. Duane remembered dropping his ballcap on top of the TV every day after work, adjusting the antenna to pick up a game. Now another man's hat rested there. The hat looked brand-new, with a red bill, blue crown, and white embroidery celebrating 200 years! above the call sign for a local radio station. Duane wiped his palms on his shirt and sat up, feeling like a cornered dog. What the hell are you doing here? he asked himself. Almost a year had passed since he'd been inside his own home.

A tattered stuffed donkey lay sprawled over the edge of a box of toys. Duane grimaced. He'd given his son the donkey for his second birthday, and the boy slept with it every night for two years. The fact that it lay over the edge of the box—full of toys Duane didn't recognize—meant it still mattered to Hudson somehow. Duane spent every Saturday with his son, but still felt he hardly knew anything about his life. Heavy with sadness, Duane stood. He walked into the kitchen. The microwave, a large, S-Series Touchmatic, sat in the center of the counter. The chrome finish gleamed and the chamber lit up when he opened the door. He slid it forward, testing its weight. Heavier than he remembered. A plastic plate rested inside. He took it out and spun it toward the trash can in the corner. "Shit," Duane muttered. His voice sounded hollow in the deserted kitchen. He unplugged the microwave and turned it around. The stainless steel magnetron gleamed on the back. Pressure-activated turntable. Top-of-the-line. He'd been so proud carrying it through the door on his and Tracy's first wedding anniversary.

A ball-peen hammer lay on the counter. Unthinkingly, Duane stuck the hammer in his back pocket and hefted the microwave to his chest. He paused for a moment and looked into the sink full of ketchup-smeared plates and cereal-crusted bowls, remembering a thousand breakfasts with his wife and son. Cursing again, he walked out to the living room. The microwave's cord tangled around his ankle and he tripped, banging against the wall and knocking Hudson's first-grade picture askew. Hudson appeared stunned in the photo, with a halo of green light around his head, as if the flash had overwhelmed him. Looking at the delicate features and nervous smile, Duane felt a stab of doubt. But Tracy had left him no choice.

The distant boom of a speed test on the salt flats jarred him into motion. He kicked aside a dump truck and set the microwave on the small mail-piled entry table. Some of the envelopes were addressed to Pete Russell. The bastard sure hadn't wasted any time. Grinning like a con man as he rounded the bases of their rec league softball game. Duane had the sudden urge to smash the microwave on the floor. Instead, he turned and lifted the cap from the TV. He took off his own cap—sun-bleached and oil-stained from a decade of use—and set it down in its place. Then he put the new cap on and opened the door. Sunlight streamed into the room. Duane took one last look: *TV Guide* lay open on the couch, more of Hudson's trucks were piled in the corner, a lipstick-stained coffee cup sat on the coffee table. Even with all the time that had passed, and knowing what he did now, part of Duane still thought of it as home.

Leaving the door open, he carried the microwave across the street to his truck. He scanned the neighbors' houses to make sure no one was watching. Ms. Tackett, the pain-in-the-ass ex–second-grade teacher who lived across the street, was usually in her living room, knitting and spying, but thankfully her blinds were drawn. Duane balanced the microwave on his thigh and opened the truck's passenger door. He blinked away the sweat stinging his eyes. It was hot for May in Utah; the first hot day of the year. Divorce papers lay in a manila envelope on the passenger seat. His name was written in black marker across the front in Tracy's familiar scrawl. "Sign these," she'd written below. He dropped the microwave on top, satisfied to hear the envelope crumple, then slammed the door shut.

He took off the new cap, smacked it against his thigh, bent the brim, and snugged it on his head. Glancing up and down the street at the familiar homes, he imagined his former neighbors laughing at him. Had they all known? Stupid, easy old Duane. Sometimes it made him so angry he wished Tracy were dead. That would be easier to explain than her cheating. He walked around the hood of his truck and folded his six-foot-four frame awkwardly onto the driver's seat. It seemed typical of his life that he couldn't afford a truck that fit him. He slotted the key into the ignition. The engine coughed roughly to life. He tapped the dash three times for luck, straightened the cap, pulled out, and drove north down the empty suburban street, leaving Tracy's front door wide open behind him.

A sharp pain jabbed his lower spine. At the first stoplight, he leaned forward and pulled the ball-peen hammer from his back pocket. He held it up in front of the windshield. Sunlight glinted off the small rounded head. Of course Pete would use a pussy little tool like this. Duane tossed it onto the floor. Tracy. *Tracy.* He saw her laughing in the backyard in front of the kiddie pool years before, holding baby Hudson on her hip, her wet dress clinging to her ankles. He smelled the skin of her neck and saw the ridge of her collarbone beneath the thin fabric. His wedding ring still shone on his left hand on the steering wheel. You sucker, he thought. You fool.

Interstate 15 took him north out of Salt Lake City. The top of the temple passed at eye-level on an overpass. Six white turrets, the angel Moroni blowing his trumpet. The trumpet's golden bell was angled up to the heavens and Duane could almost hear it through the open window—lonesome and shrill. Then the highway descended into fading strip malls. Red, white, and blue bunting was strung from lampposts and each used car lot was done up like the White House Rose Garden. Duane hadn't thought much about the upcoming Bicentennial, but now it felt cursed.

Cars waited at service stations. Horns honked for those at the pumps to hurry up. Another gas crisis. The snowcapped Wasatch Mountains loomed overhead. Traffic lessened and the city dissolved, replaced by sweeping ranchlands with the occasional house set far back at the base of the foothills. Cows wandered aimlessly among bales of hay. Sprinklers threw silver arcs of water over alfalfa fields. Duane drove with both hands on the wheel, his lips pressed together, his former life slipping away behind him. Don't think, he told himself. Just go.

2

Tracy Oshun, née Tate, soon to be Russell, waved to the pharmacist as she pushed through the glass door of the Fairpark Walgreens. Her back ached from standing behind the register for eight hours. Bright hot air greeted her, carrying the sharp smell of scallions from the China Buffet next door. Summer temperatures already? She shook her head. The weather seemed to be getting schizophrenic: weird balmy lulls followed by crazed, violent blizzards. She'd loved summer as a girl. Now it meant Hudson was home all day, and trying to get him to bed while it was still light outside.

But she had a wedding to plan. The thought made her smile. She drove home with the windows open, enjoying the heat and the faint smell of flowers. Pete had proposed to her in the rose garden on the Jordan River the previous weekend. None of the roses were blooming—the sticklike bushes hadn't even started to bud—but, when she remembered the anxious look on Pete's face as he dropped to one knee, the pain in Tracy's back faded. She'd been waiting for the proposal for almost a year, and held off on divorcing Duane until it came, knowing you couldn't give a man too many reasons. Now sunlight glinted off the small emerald-cut diamond on her engagement ring, and she felt a flush of pleasure running her finger over the convex shape. Life was finally starting to turn around.

Jordan Street cut west through the duplexes and subdivisions of Fairpark, and Tracy nodded along to a disco song on the radio, imagining her wedding dress. She'd been pregnant during her first wedding, and felt bovine and helpless in the custom-made maternity cut. Even then, she'd hoped to get another chance. She hit three green lights in a row before stopping at the Joseph intersection. A furniture store was being renovated on the corner, with two banners hanging above the door. One said CLOSED the other said GRAND RE-OPENING.

Most of the snow had already melted on the lower slopes of the Wasatch Mountains. Tracy tipped her head back and took a deep breath, relaxing into the unusual weather. It was going to be a long summer. Good. They deserved one. She turned onto Young Street and the familiar houses of her neighbors rolled by, Ms. Tackett's closed and shuttered like a bunker since she'd gone to Florida to visit her sister. A vacation. That was another thing Tracy deserved. Maybe in eleven years, when Hudson graduated from high school. She smiled bitterly at her joke, parked, gathered up her purse and keys, and noticed the open front door.

The shadowed rectangle of her living room was like a mouth, a cave. Its wrongness called out to the street. Fear froze Tracy. All kinds of drifters and criminals were moving to Salt Lake: drug addicts, bikers, hippies. Every day there was a shooting on the evening news. Sirens followed each other across the night. The world wasn't safe anymore, not even in Utah. She bit down on her bottom lip.

Whoever it was could still be inside.

Tracy sat back, staring. Without the radio, the silence of the warm afternoon tightened around her like a fist. One hour. One hour alone before Hudson got home, and this happens. She thought of driving to the Silver Dollar Bar, having a drink, and calling the police.

No. It was full daylight, and Pete could've left the door open his own dumbass self. It wouldn't be the first time. He'd forget the sky if you pointed him toward the ground. Tracy sighed. She'd never had any luck with smart men. She gently eased the car door open, flinching when it creaked, and stepped out. Crouching, she rounded the hood and peered into the house for any sign of movement. If someone came busting out . . . She stopped and took the small pearl-handled knife from her purse. She opened the blade, held it in front of her, and crept up the front walk.

The street smelled of dry grass and paint. A new duplex at the end of the block was getting a coat of primer. Pete had bid on the job, been undercut, and instead of fighting for it, considering how the lack of commute would've cut his gas costs, he'd gone to the movies for four straight nights until Tracy stopped bringing it up. She edged to the doorway shoulder-first, clutching the knife. "Hello," she called, ready to bolt, scream, stab. Nothing moved. She leaned into the shadowed living room, seeing Hudson's trucks, Pete's boots, the *TV Guide*. She stepped inside. The TV was still resting on the stand, as was the Betamax player. Maybe it had been Pete, rushing off to work, late as usual.

"Idiot," she muttered, closing the door behind her and tiptoeing down the hall past the toys and boots. The fear left her as she realized the house was empty. Breeze rustled the curtain of the open window by the couch.

Hudson's first-grade photo was slightly askew in the hallway. Tracy straightened it, noticing for the hundredth time a smudge of dirt on his freckled cheek. His blond buzz cut was framed by a wash of greenish light, like he was about to be beamed up to an alien starship. Who wanted a photo like that? Often she wondered about the people who were running the schools. The photographer had caught the delicateness of her son's features, though, and his dark blue eyes. She lingered. He was skinny for his age, and shy. The thought of him getting pushed around made her angry enough to tremble.

In the kitchen, sunlight streamed through the blinds. Tracy stopped in the doorway and immediately noticed the empty space on the counter. A dust ball and an old candy wrapper lingered at the back. It took her a moment to remember what had been there. She leaned forward, the knife in her hand, her small features drawn together in consternation. Who steals a microwave?

Duane. As soon as she thought the name, it almost took her to her knees.

"Dammit," she muttered softly. The knife slid from her hand and clattered onto the linoleum floor. He'd been so proud of that microwave. She remembered his grin as he carried it through the door on their first anniversary, all wrapped in store wrapping paper with a big red bow.

The divorce papers couldn't have been a surprise, could they? They'd been separated for a year. Pete was living with her, for chrissakes. But Duane was a sufferer. He always had been, since the day they met, and he was even more so now. Aging like a flower: drooping. She turned and leaned against the doorjamb, the tension leaving her arms.

Wiping her eyes, Tracy slowly crossed the kitchen and sank into one of the plastic chairs by the table. She looked down at the knife on the floor. Sunlight glinted off the handle. She should have written a longer note. Often, her compulsiveness got her into trouble. It was how she'd gotten pregnant with Hudson when she was eighteen, and how she'd started her affair with Pete. Glancing back into the living room, she noticed the open window. The thought of Duane wriggling his long body through the narrow gap made her smile briefly. Poor Duane. The world didn't quite fit him. She spread her fingers on the table and looked down at the chewed skin around her orange-painted nails.

Compulsively, she flicked away a crumb, then saw the plastic plate on the floor by the trash. The sight hardened her. She'd spent eight years picking up after Duane, feeling like she was running away from something rather than toward it. She regretted sneaking around behind his back, but she deserved some happiness, didn't she?

A red sedan pulled into the driveway next door, her neighbor Eileen coming home with her fancy briefcase full of papers. A paralegal at a cheap law firm, she acted like Perry Mason. Tracy looked up at the clock. Four-fifteen. She stood and smoothed the front of her shirt. Then she retrieved the knife from the floor and snapped it shut. She needed to buy a new microwave before picking up Hudson. Pete wouldn't notice if it was a less expensive model.

"I'm sorry," she said, to the kitchen air, and then she shut the living room window and walked back outside, closing and locking the door behind her.

3

At dusk, Duane crossed the line into Idaho. He ate a cheeseburger in Idaho Falls—sitting alone at a picnic table, hardly tasting the overdone meat, staring across the empty parking lot at a long, low twenty-room motel. Oilskin curtains covered the windows. It had a seedy look, as if the occupants had been there a long time with nowhere else to go. He wondered if this was the kind of place Pete had taken Tracy. Hurrying to draw the shades, knowing Tracy had to be back before Duane got home from work. . . .

Duane didn't get back on the interstate, finding instead a series of ranch roads that wound north into the Bitterroot Mountains. He left the windows open, even well after dark when the piney air carried the cold sting of snow. The moon rose. The mountains and their snowcapped peaks turned to ghosts. Branches rustled, reaching toward him, offering up his failures.

Only twenty-nine, he'd already lost a wife, a son, and his home. He still couldn't believe Tracy had sent the divorce papers. After all they'd been through. With a son between them. . . . Her affair, the year apart, that was one thing. This was so final. The duffel bag with his few belongings was squeezed behind his seat. He reached back and touched the side, feeling the shape of his favorite boots. It was most important at a time like this, he figured, to just keep going.

Exhausted, he drove in a kind of trance, feeling continuously swallowed by the mountains. His right arm rested on the microwave. The trees around him seemed to grow, becoming more gnarled and ancient. Past the town of Salmon, the road rose steeply in tight switchbacks. Duane pressed down on the accelerator, rattling around the curves. Trees blurred by the road, then suddenly they were gone, and snowbanks leaned over the shoulder. The chairlift at Lost Trail Powder Mountain swung silently. A faded blue sign welcomed Duane to Montana, THE TREASURE STATE.

Duane would have settled for a warm bed, but even through his exhaustion he felt a buzz of excitement. He tried out the word. "Montana." It sounded like a benediction. Already the mountains were wilder, more powerful. The road dropped and the trees began again. It was after midnight. Duane turned on the radio. Found only static and the occasional crackling burst of a preacher.

The guardrail ended on the long straightaway coming down the northern slope into the Bitterroot Valley. The rocky ground on the shoulder plunged away into an inky sea of pine tops. A slight contraction of Duane's bicep, and the little truck would've glided obediently into the darkness. The microwave and divorce papers and ball-peen hammer tumbling through the air beside him.

Silver reflectors winked by the roadside. The yellow lines in the center snaked to a single thread, constantly separating itself as he neared. A white-tailed buck leapt up the embankment in two bunched, powerful strides, and a large sign shone in the headlights, welcoming him to the Bitterroot Valley, WHERE JESUS CHRIST IS LORD. In his exhausted state, Duane felt a kinship: his own heart crucified.

His eyelids sagged. He swerved, nearly going off the road. He had to stop. A washboard dirt track led beneath a stand of birch trees to a row of campsites along the shore of Lake Como. He parked beside a picnic table. A canoe was moored on the dark water below. The truck's motor ticked as it cooled. He patted the dash three times. "Thanks, old girl." His dim reflection in the rearview mirror looked older than he remembered beneath the brim of the new cap.

Through the windshield, the stars were veiled by clouds. He took the hat off and tossed it onto the passenger seat. A gust of wind rustled the branches around him, revealing the sliver of moon. The mountains were new to Duane but familiar in their indifferent splendor. He stared up at the hooked white finger of the tallest peak. It seemed to beckon him into the wild, away from his wife and son, away from his old life, toward a silent and ruthless immensity. A place where he might lose himself completely. Too exhausted to think anymore, or even crawl into the truck bed, he rolled over onto his shoulder, wedged his long legs against the stick shift, and went to sleep.

HIGH IN THE ROCKY MOUNTAINS the next morning, two hundred miles from the Canadian border, a bearded man on a bicycle crossed the highway in front of Duane's truck. Half asleep, Duane had to slam on the brakes. The tires screeched; the little truck jolted forward, then rocked back and clanked on its axles. The cyclist swerved. His glaring eyes were dark brown above dirt-smudged cheeks and an unkempt beard. His face was owlish, with thick brows set over a blunt Slavic nose. A metal-framed backpack leaned over his head, giving him the humped form of a mendicant in the shadow of the pines.

Duane reached for the window crank, ready to apologize, but the man had already righted his bike and was pedaling furiously into the forest on an unmarked dirt road. The bike's chain squeaked with every revolution of the wheels. Scrap metal was tied to the basket and a plastic bag billowed behind him. The tattered straps of his pack flapped over his shoulders. Duane couldn't tell if he was a hippie, or a traveler, or an honest-to-God hermit.

The places people found to live always amazed him. As a kid, he'd snuck down to the hobo camp on the banks of the Jordan River near his house, staring at the tents and tarps, the little stoves and firepits, like another kingdom.

Duane pressed down on the clutch but remained in place, staring up the dirt road after the bicyclist. Something about the road captivated him. The narrow rutted lane seemed to lead directly into the heart of the wild, with a row of ponderosas towering like sentinels on either side. The night before, he'd dreamt of a steel-blue army of mountains, the bladed summits marching to the horizon. He found it miraculous that the trip had only taken one night. One night and you could leave everything you'd ever known behind. Staring into the shadows between the pines, he felt drawn in, and frightened also. He imagined building a cabin there, hunting and foraging for his own food. Was such a life still possible? A man alone in the wilderness? He reached into his back pocket and pulled out his wallet. A hundred and fifty dollars. Hardly enough for two months' rent, let alone a piece of land.

Duane shook his head, surprised at himself, and accelerated up the highway.

Three dead coyotes hung from the eaves of a dilapidated barn on the outskirts of Lincoln. Flies circled the corpses as they swung slowly in the breeze, and Duane felt a chill of fear. Behind the coyotes, a line of rusted-out cars led down to a sagging sheep shed on a wide, muddy creek. Smoke rose from the shed and a German shepherd on a heavy chain loped toward Duane's truck as he passed. After the ranch—and in striking contrast—a jewel-like white church appeared in the center of a wide, manicured lawn. Its swooping cantilevered roof looked like the prow of a ship. Duane eased off the accelerator and looked up in surprise at the dramatic eaves and glittering stained glass. Who built that? he wondered.

Lincoln only had one traffic light, blinking yellow above the Wilderness Bar. Tall pines dwarfed the buildings around it, and mountain peaks dwarfed the tall pines. Duane felt his eyes drawn ever upward. He took in the shops' names like they were exotic locales in a foreign guidebook: Wolf-Goes-for-Fire Trading Post, Ricky's Auto, the Wheel-In Tavern, Ponderosa Hardware, the Ponderosa Café, Lambkins Restaurant, the Lincoln Hotel. Dirt driveways curved to ramshackle trailers. A few old Victorians stood above these, property of the town's rich, he assumed, the mill foreman and hotel operator. All the shops clung to the highway, cowering against the encroaching wilderness. Shuttered summer cabins lined the bank of a surging creek. At the far end of town, a giant rusted teepee burner stood between the post office and library. An old man with stooped shoulders was sweeping the library steps. Duane rolled to a stop beside him and cranked his window down. "Anyplace I can get some gas?" he asked.

The old man squinted in at him. "Where you coming from?"

"Utah."

This seemed to satisfy the old man. He raised his stubbled chin to the north. "Ollie's place, past Hooper Park, but it don't open till noon on Saturdays."

A pall fell over the trees and buildings. Duane hadn't realized what day it was, let alone where he was going. Usually he spent Saturdays with Hudson. "Is there another town that way?"

"Great Falls. Ninety miles, though, and nothing in between."

Duane looked down at the needle of the gas gauge hovering over empty. No way he'd make it. He had to wait.

The old man hitched his suspenders and leaned forward on the handle of his broom. "That's a mighty small truck."

Shaking his head, Duane turned the truck around and drove slowly back through town, figuring he'd get some breakfast. The neon red VACANCY sign of the Alpine Motel flickered over the green metal roof of the Ponderosa Café. Duane parked and took a deep breath. The bottom of the empty pool was littered with beer cans, cigarette butts, and pine needles. He reached up, expecting to find the new hat on his head, but it lay on the seat beside him. He retrieved it from behind the microwave and fitted it on his head. Then he got out, hitched up his jeans, tossed an errant pepperoni-stick wrapper back into the cab, and walked to the diner.

IN THE BOOTH BY THE WINDOW, Duane could see from one end of Lincoln to the other. Soaring conifers grew in every clear spot, and congregated beyond the town in a mass that surged up the foothills. Fresh logging roads zigzagged through the greenery, and even though it was Saturday, Duane could hear the distant grind of machinery. He wondered what kind of people lived here. Maybe they were all scraggly mountain men who worked six days a week before biking home to their backwood compounds.

The only other customers were a pair of identical truckers in red flannel shirts sitting together at the counter. "It was pure, shit-ass luck," one said to the other. "I was tracking up on Strawberry Ridge and that elk near tripped over me." Their hairy forearms were mirror images beside coffee cups and plates of pancakes. Duane stared at them for a moment, wondering if exhaustion had warped his mind, before realizing the truckers were identical twins. He was fascinated by the perfect duplication of their features.

The waitress cleared her throat and Duane snapped his head up, embarrassed. She stood over him, seeming closer than wait-resses usually stood, smelling of pine and bacon grease. Silver streaks in her black hair shone under the fluorescent lights. She had wide shoulders and a stern, unlined face. Her sharp gold-brown eyes made his own feel hot and blinkered. The name JACKIE was stitched across her green apron.

"What can I get you?" she asked brusquely.

Duane looked around for a menu. "I don't know."

"Where you heading?"

"I . . . I don't know."

"You don't know what you want or where you're going?" Jackie raised her eyebrows.

"No, ma'am."

"Sounds like you're in for a long day. How about Canada?"

"Canada?"

"We get a lot of guys coming through here heading to Canada." Jackie tapped her notepad against her thigh. "Used to be even more during the war."

Duane shifted in his old denim work shirt, aware of his busted Levi's, his oil-stained boots. Did he look like a draft dodger?

"I've got a cousin up there, he says guys are waiting on the other side of the border offering logging jobs, mining jobs, you name it. And with the Canadian dollar you get more for your money."

The Canadian dollar? Duane rubbed his wedding ring worriedly with his thumb, trying to get his long legs comfortable in the booth. He didn't know anything about Canada except that his mother had gone to the rodeo in Calgary once, with a roper who left her at a truck stop, one of her many stories about how men had made her life turn out wrong. "Pancakes," Duane said, feeling pinned beneath Jackie's eyes like a landed fish. "I'll have pancakes and coffee."

Jackie shrugged and slipped her notepad back in her apron. The roar of what sounded like a jet engine started up outside, and a man in a cowboy hat rode by on an unmuffled four-wheeler with "1776" spray-painted on the side and an outsized American flag flying from the rear bumper. *Two hundred years.* Jackie shook her head in disgust. "Going to be a long summer," she said. Then she turned on her heel and disappeared into the kitchen.

AFTER HIS PANCAKES, fearing Canada's pull, Duane drove south from the Ponderosa Café to the strange, jewel-like church on the outskirts of Lincoln. He couldn't think of anywhere else to go to kill the hour before the gas station opened. Besides, churches were supposed to take in weary travelers, weren't they? He marveled again at the modern architecture of the swooping white roof. Next to the manicured lawn, the large dirt lot was edged on three sides by a forest of lodgepole pine. The contrast between the futuristic church and the dark, tangled growth of the forest struck Duane as surreal, like a spaceship landed in a national park. He parked as far as possible from the other car: a cherry-red Scout with HESRISN plates. Then he stared up at the three white crosses on the sculptural steeple and took a deep breath. "All right, God," he said.

Duane braced his hips against the driver's seat and wrapped his fingers around his wedding ring. He pulled. The gold band didn't budge. Duane pulled harder, feeling the skin bunch underneath his knuckle. The ring had been on his finger since Tracy put it on at their wedding, seven years before. She'd often taken hers off, leaving it on the TV or beside the bathroom sink, but he never had. Now it twisted but wouldn't come. "Shit," he said under his breath. He thought of the waitress urging him on to Canada, and felt even more frustrated. Levering his shoulder against the door, he pulled until the knuckle popped.

"Goddammit." Duane sat back in the seat, panting. A white-tailed doe stared at him through the windshield from the church lawn. He opened the truck door and the doe bolted into the woods. Duane kicked the door closed, watching her bound out of sight, the white tail sensual somehow, like the first bloom of spring. Duane muttered darkly to himself, thinking of all womanly things. He unlatched his tool case and found a tin of grease. He slathered a nickel-sized dab on his ring finger. Then he held his hand up over his head. He counted to a hundred, letting the blood drain. He thought of Tracy as he did, wanting the memories of her to drain away, too—the white lace wedding dress she wore on the shore of the Great Salt Lake, tailored to accommodate her pregnant belly, and how she'd looked to him like the Virgin Mother. It had come natural for him to worship her. He'd spent his whole life looking for something to believe in. Hudson's early healthy birth had struck him as miraculous, as had the baby's dark blue eyes.

After Duane lowered his hand, the ring slid off easily. He stared at the gold band in his palm. It hardly weighed more than a dime. He wondered how something so light could hold so much power. He remembered how proud he'd felt when Tracy put it on his finger, like he finally belonged. He lifted the ring to the sun. The band glittered, mythical, full of light. He didn't want to let it go. Impulsively, he put it in his mouth and held it on his tongue. The coolness faded and only the taste of metal and grease remained. He thought of swallowing it but was afraid the metal would tear up his insides. He stood in the sunlight, unsure of what to do, until the screen door of the rectory swung open.

"You need something?" the pastor called, coming out onto the porch in a clerical collar, khaki shorts, and moccasins.

Duane spat the ring into his hand and stuffed it in his pocket. "No."

"I saw you raising your hand and thought you might have a question."

"I'm just checking the oil." Duane moved around the truck's hood and fumbled for the latch behind the grille.

The pastor walked down the steps and across the lot. His sandy hair was shoulder-length and he had Jesus tattooed on his calf. He would have looked like Jesus himself were it not for his potbelly and a jagged scar below his left eye. He stopped a few feet from Duane and both men stared into the truck's engine. "You come up from Utah?" the pastor asked, nodding to the license plate.

Duane nodded. He didn't know what to make of the scar or the tattoo. He'd thought it was illegal for churchmen to have tattoos.

"Straight shot?"

"I slept a few hours in the truck."

"I once went straight from San Diego to Omaha." The pastor crossed his arms proudly. "Twenty-two hours. Only stopped for gas. I had a traveling ministry back then. Tent revivals. People think the sixties were just hippies and drugs, but there was a lot of holy spirit, too."

Duane nodded uncertainly. He'd been a teenager in Salt Lake for most of the sixties, and the only hippies he'd seen were hitchhikers by the freeway on-ramps.

"Brought your microwave along?" the pastor asked, peering into the truck through the side window.

"It's my wife's. My ex-wife's." Duane stopped. "I got it for her."

The pastor raised his eyebrows. "Well, it's a fine-looking machine."

"Top-of-the-line."

"I use mine more than the regular oven."

"Same here. I never understood why you'd spend all that time waiting." Duane smiled at this discovered kinship. He felt a tension in his shoulders dissipate, and realized he'd been holding it all morning, since nearly hitting the bearded man on the bicycle.

"I've got a Radarange in the rectory," the pastor said. "I always go for the originals. Only thing it won't do well is meat."

Duane nodded. "Perfect for the defrost, though."

"That's the truth. I'm Younger, Pastor Kim Younger." The pastor stuck out his hand.

Duane took it. "Duane."

"Well, Duane, what brings you to my church? You looking for work?"

"I'm just waiting for the gas station to open." He nodded down at the fuel tank. "I'm heading north."

"You going to Canada?"

Duane shook his head in irritation.

"That's all that's up there. If you're not going to Canada, you best stay here."

The suggestion caught Duane off guard. He stared at the pastor.

"I don't believe in chance," the pastor went on. "When a man washes up in my parking lot, it's always for a good reason." He pointed up at the white crucifixes atop the church steeple. "God brought you here." The assurance in his voice reminded Duane of the radio preachers his mother listened to, all hellfire and damnation. "You a Mormon?"

Duane thumbed a patch of rust on the carburetor and shook his head.

"Good. Son, you can't just drift around. You need a job. Now, you might not believe it, but this whole church is still heated with a wood furnace. A mean old cur down in the basement. She ate through five cords last winter."

"It's beautiful," Duane replied. "Your church, I mean."

Pastor Younger nodded gravely. "It's a hyperbolic paraboloid. The only other one is in Indiana. They built them back in the fifties, when people in this country still had vision." He gestured toward the woodpile in the corner of the lot. "All that needs to be split and stacked. You want the job?"

The idea of physical exertion appealed to Duane. It would help clear his mind, and maybe when he was done he'd have a better idea of what to do.

"Twenty dollars per cord. And you're welcome to sleep in your truck while you finish the job. Folks will probably start bringing food around, too. It's a small town; we take care of each other."

Duane nodded dumbly, feeling borne along like a twig in a current.

"Good." The pastor placed his hand on Duane's shoulder. "I know it doesn't feel like it now, but God has something planned for you. He always does."

4

The microwave's chamber light blinked on and the turntable began to rotate, then abruptly went dark. Jackie Irons leaned forward and peered through the door. The broccoli heads formed a lumpy green terrain in the white bowl. She clicked the power button. Nothing. She unplugged and re-plugged the cord in the wall socket and banged the side of the microwave with her palm. She turned the timer dial as far to the right as it would go. The chamber remained dark.

Shit. Jackie refused to cook. It was a matter of principle. She was on her feet in the Ponderosa Café all day, smelling bacon grease, sweating in the heat of the grill, and scraping chewed hamburgers into the trash; the last thing she felt like doing when she got home was dealing with more meat. Thus her diet consisted mostly of microwaved vegetables. Broccoli was her favorite. Tiny trees, she'd called them when she was a little girl. The microwave was only a year old, the cheapest model she could find, but still. She'd driven all the way to Helena to buy it. She remembered the short, chubby salesman at Kmart beaming at her above his blue vest as he pressed the cardboard box into her arms. "You sell me a lemon, cocksucker?" she asked, out loud.

Moonlight spilled through the kitchen window and pooled on the counter by the sink. Jackie turned the microwave around and squinted down at the four screws holding the rear cover over the steel magnetron. She looked around for some assistance: pot holders were stacked on a pile of unused cookbooks, car keys and cigarettes lay next to her purse on the kitchen table. She lived in the house where she'd grown up, a house her great-grandfather built, but still she didn't know where anything was. She rifled through the drawer beneath the telephone. No tools. It was hell to live with a man—she'd tried it twice—but sometimes one could be useful.

Muttering to herself about chain stores and salesmen, Jackie walked through the side door into her garage. Storage bins were stacked against the far wall, full of old clothes, books, her dad's fishing tackle. She reached into the top bin and pulled out a purple boa, holding the shimmering feathers up to the light. When had she worn this? A party, it must've been. One of Rita's, before she moved. Christ, they'd been wild then. Jackie dropped the boa back in the bin, missing her friend, one of many who'd left Lincoln after the Delaney Lumber Mill closed, taking the town's economy with it. Now the valley had rebounded somewhat with tourists and back-to-the-landers, but none of her friends had come back. She dug through a mound of bedding, her mind wandering to Rita's going-away party, when they'd danced all night around a bonfire in front of the old teepee burner. She dug deeper beneath the bedding and found a toolbox wedged beside an old transistor radio. Inside was a rusty Phillips-head screwdriver next to a matching set of wrenches. She wrinkled her nose and carried the screwdriver back inside. Her fortieth birthday was two months away—rust reminded her of rot, deterioration, decay.

Pictures of her nieces lined the hall. Three fierce black-haired little girls. They lived in Billings and Jackie made the trip several times a year, even though her sister's balding, toad-like, chiropractor husband stared at her across the table all through meals with a look in his eyes that was the same as drooling. If you can find one who isn't a reptile, Jackie thought, as she slotted the screwdriver into the top screw on the microwave's rear panel. She'd wanted children herself once, when she was married to Mason Carnegie, one of the valley's forest rangers. He'd shown up in Lincoln from California in the summer of 1969 with a truck full of books and plans to restore the wolf population in the Swan Range, and she'd fallen in love so hard she'd thought she'd burn out, like a dying star. Together they'd pulled traps along Monture Creek, torn down poison bait stations, and talked late into the night about what the new Endangered Species Conservation Act could mean for predators in the West. She'd thought the valley needed saving and they were the only two who could do it. Now she saw their years together as the last gasp of her youthful idealism. Her last two boyfriends had been drunks. The most recent, a logger with two missing fingers, had shoved her over a bureau one night, then acted shocked when she jammed a steak knife into his thigh.

The screws held stubbornly at first, then twisted free. Jackie lifted off the rear panel and stared at the microwave's innards. Her mother had been afraid of microwaves, thinking they gave you cancer, and refused to have one in the house. Now Jackie wondered if she'd been right. How the hell did they work anyway? What looked like a magnet was banked with a bladed stirrer over the power cord and capacitor, all wired together with copper coil. She could see how the stirrer spun and where the power went, but where did the heat come from? Did the little fan create some kind of nuclear, broccoli-roasting surge? She was afraid if she stuck the screwdriver inside she might nuke herself.

All this technology, but nobody knew how it worked. Jackie bit her lip. She had the vague idea the problem could be a blown fuse. "Nine times out of ten, it's a fuse," her father used to say. Jackie sighed. She still found herself reaching for her father's assurances, even a decade after his death. "This one, Dad?" she asked, reaching in toward one of the small copper wires. A spark shot up and the shock sent her reeling back across the linoleum.

"Bastard." She leaned against the counter, shaking her hand. Her legs tingled and her toes felt hot. She thought of getting in her car, driving over the pass to Helena, and dropping the microwave on the little salesman's head. But the Kmart would be long closed by the time she got there.

Leaving the kitchen, she went into the living room and collapsed on the couch. She stared at the dark TV. Her hand still felt tight from the voltage, but gradually her heart slowed. She stretched out her fingers, the heat draining away. She wondered who would have found her if she'd electrocuted herself. Darlene from across the street, probably. Fried on the floor with charred toes was not how Jackie wanted to be remembered. It was getting lonesome, this life. Even Rita was married now, down in Phoenix. Crazy Rita. She sent Christmas cards every year with her kids lined up in front of a saguaro cactus, a wreath tacked to its main beam. Jackie thought briefly of her regulars at the diner: Would one of them do for a date? She shook her head, smiling to herself in the moonlight. "Really fishing the bottom of the barrel, aren't you?"

She sighed again. Her great-grandfather was one of the valley's first settlers and married her Blackfoot great-grandmother, which gave Jackie her Native American appearance, but wasn't enough for tribal rights or blood quantum. As a kid, she'd been called Indian by the white kids and white by the Indian kids. Shouldn't she be used to being alone? Clearing her throat, Jackie got up and went back into the kitchen. She glared at the dismembered microwave, then took the broccoli from the chamber and found a jar of mayonnaise in the fridge. She stood at the window, dipped the stalks in mayo, and ate the broccoli raw, glaring out at the dark street.

5

Frost covered the truck topper's windows. Duane woke at dawn feeling like he was in a coffin. The first light filtered through so dimly that he figured he must have frozen and crossed over in the night. Then a sharp pain jabbed his shoulder—the ball-peen hammer had somehow ended up in the truck bed with him. Relieved he wasn't dead, Duane shook his chilled head and sat up. With the return of sensation came a desperate need to pee. He kicked out of his sleeping bag, tossed the hammer aside, unlatched the truck's lift gate, and dropped his bare feet onto the frozen dirt. The shock of cold nearly knocked him back into the sleeping bag. *Ho-ho*-ing to keep warm, he hustled to the edge of the woods and hopped from foot to foot as he freed himself from his long johns, then loosed a long stream of relief on the gnarled root of a Doug fir. Steam rose through the misty air. Sighing, Duane stared up at the treetops. He watched a star fade into the bluing sky and felt content for the first time since finding Tracy's divorce papers tucked under his apartment door.

When he turned, he discovered a tall, scrawny black steer staring at him from the center of the dirt lot. The beast was so emaciated that each rib stood out against its mangy hide like the rails of a ship. A huge letter c was branded across its shoulder. Its four hooves were planted menacingly in the dirt. A tattered notch was missing from its right ear, and the cheek below was scarred. It was a haunting, underworldly beast, completely out of place in front of the church's swooping white roof. Slowly, Duane raised his hands. "Whoa, boy," he said.

The steer snorted and lowered its head. Its eyes rolled, the bloodshot white giving them a crazed, demonic aspect. Duane had no experience with cows except from a distance. He was terrified. The steer lifted one hoof and stamped the dirt. Duane looked longingly at the safety of his truck. "I don't want trouble," he said, keeping his hands up. The beast watched him, remaining motionless until Duane stepped back onto the dirt of the lot, and then, as if its new territory had been violated, it made a deep lowing sound and charged. Its ungainly legs and bony body hurtled toward Duane. He screamed and sprinted toward his truck, oblivious to the sharp gravel cutting his feet, and dove headfirst into the bed. The steer's blunt forehead missed his heels by inches. The beast swung around and rammed into the bumper. Duane scrambled to the front. "Help!" he shouted, pressing his back against the front of the topper and drawing his knees to his chest. The steer seemed determined to get in, bashing and swinging its head around, causing the axles to creak.

The rectory door banged open and Pastor Younger appeared bleary-eyed on the porch holding an old Winchester rifle. "Git!" he called. "Git! You damned Carter cow." He raised the rifle and fired into the air. The cow pulled its head back and cocked its chin, as if evaluating how serious the pastor was about the rifle. It remained there, trapping Duane, refusing to move even when the pastor fired another shot. "You hold tight, I'm calling Mason. He's the only one who'll do a damn thing about these cows." The pastor disappeared inside before Duane could protest. Once he was gone, the steer rotated its black eyes back to Duane.

"Easy, now," Duane said. The steer snorted again. The sun had risen over the Lewis Range and a ray of light lit on its mangy haunch. The dry nostrils trembled. It lifted one leg, as if trying to climb into the bed. Never before had Duane been so close to an animal that so obviously wanted to hurt him. Generally he got on well with wild creatures—shooing flies instead of swatting them, freeing sparrows that got trapped in the screen porch of his apartment building—but in the steer's eyes he found no kinship, only a dim, malevolent spark, as if generations of slaughter had winnowed the animal down to its darkest essence.

Finally, after what felt like hours, a pale green Forest Service truck bounced into the lot. Peering through the melting frost on the topper window, Duane saw a stocky, bearded man driving with a cattle dog sitting alertly beside him in the passenger seat. The dog's ears were raised straight up like antennae and its head was cocked to the side in concentration. Black markings surrounded both eyes, standing out against the blue-gray fur of its muzzle. The man parked and got out. He had a tired, aggrieved look— the opposite of his dog—as if he were waiting to find out how the world would let him down next. His olive uniform was wrinkled and he limped on his right leg.

"Mason," Pastor Younger called, coming back onto the porch. "We got a mean one here. Trapped this boy in his truck."

"How the hell'd you get him so riled up?" Mason asked, taking a large tranquilizer gun from the truck bed and approaching slowly. He stopped beside the topper window and peered in at Duane.

"I . . . I was just taking a piss," Duane replied.

"You know how these Carter steers are," Pastor Younger said. "They're a menace. One near bit Deacon Floyd's finger off."

"You living in there?" Mason nodded at Duane's sleeping bag.

"Just since last night."

"They're mean, all right, I've just never seen one corner a man before." Mason raised the tranquilizer gun and turned to the pastor. His dog was still perfectly motionless in the passenger seat, staring at the steer in anticipation. "You want me to knock him out? It'll piss Preston off, but it's the safest way to calm him down."

The pastor looked pained. "Don't make me answer that, Mason."

"Well, it's not my job to herd that son of a bitch's cattle."

The pastor didn't respond.

Mason spat in the dirt. Then he turned toward his truck. "Oh hell, all right. Molly, *cow!*"

The dog, which had been so still before, shot from the truck like a bullet, streaking silently across the dirt, then skidding around the steer's heels, barking ferociously.

All this time, the steer had remained motionless, staring in at Duane, but when Molly nipped its ankle it kicked back its hooves and turned its head, bucking like a rodeo bull. Snapping fiercely, Molly herded the steer toward the highway, neatly avoiding the flying hooves, and driving it with her flashing teeth. When they neared the pavement, she ducked between the steer's legs, spun around, and headed it off, snarling, her teeth bared, never taking her eyes from the steer's, which now stood docile and frightened staring down at her.

Duane watched in astonishment. Mason grinned. "Good girl. Now *hold*," he called. Then he turned back to the pastor and Duane. "The two of you are about as much use as bent nails."

"I love all God's creatures, but sometimes I wonder if the Carters got their cows from somewhere else," Pastor Younger said.

Duane pulled himself to the front of the truck bed and fumbled around for his boots, too embarrassed to speak.

"No cattle in Utah?" Mason nodded at the truck's license plate.

"Not in Salt Lake," Duane answered.

"You might want to find another parking lot to live in, then. The Carter Ranch is just down the way, and those boys do not mind their cows. Or anything else."

Duane nodded, his face red. "I saw the coyotes hanging from their barn on my way into town."

A vein rose above Mason's temple and he clenched his jaw. "Yeah, that's them. I ought to string up one of their goddamn cows." He turned to the pastor. "You know I'm going to have to put one down someday."

The pastor shook his head worriedly. "Just not at my church."

MOLLY HERDED THE STEER down the highway and Mason followed in his truck. Then the pastor went back inside and Duane was left alone in the parking lot. The adrenaline faded and he turned to the woodpile—a daunting jumble of heavy rounds scored by knots and surrounded in thick, sweet-smelling bark. He saw the dark afterimage of the steer's head in the pattern of the knots, and the humiliation pushed away his exhaustion. Trapped by a cow. No way to start his time in Montana. It seemed more important than ever to build his cabin in the woods. Flexing his shoulders, Duane wrested the ax from the log where it was wedged and hefted the haft onto his shoulder. He selected one of the larger pine rounds and stood it up on the knee-high log.

"All right, now," Duane said, speaking to the ax. He hadn't split wood since high school, when he and his mother briefly lived in an apartment with a fireplace. He'd hated the repetitive chore then, and resented the fact that his classmates simply twisted a thermostat for heat. The sun was well into the sky and a chorus of birds erupted from the trees when the ax slammed into the wood. Duane badly missed the center, landing the blade an inch inside the bark. He worked the blade deeper, trying to chunk off the piece. Finally, he was forced to pry the ax free and try again. Duane re-centered and swung more softly, cursing to himself, landing the blade squarely in the center but only chopping an inch into the grain. He raised the whole chunk with the wedged head and slammed it down. After three more attempts, it split in two. Duane was already sweating, but the success awoke a feverish energy and he moved through several more pieces, slamming them down in violent succession, growing angrier each time, thinking of Pete as he did. "Like this, Pete?" he asked, bashing a piece into kindling. "Or this?" He made it through five rounds before the rectory door banged back open.

"Good Lord, man," Pastor Younger called. "Are you trying to beat that wood to death?"

Shamefaced, Duane set the ax down in the dirt and leaned the haft against the log. Sweat stuck his shirt to his back and he wiped his brow with the back of his wrist.

The pastor squinted at him in the sunlight. "Haven't you had enough excitement this morning? Why don't you take a walk and find some breakfast?"

Hearing this, Duane realized he was starving. He nodded and hurriedly gathered up the kindling. Then he cleaned up as best he could, rinsing his face in the creek and putting on a fresh shirt.

Jackie was sitting on the high stool by the cash register when Duane walked into the Ponderosa Café. "Not even a year I've had that microwave, and the damn thing crapped out," she said to the old man at the counter. "I put some broccoli in, set it to two minutes like always, it started going, then bam, dead. No reason for it. Shocked the hell out of me when I tried to fix it."

"That's how they make 'em nowadays," the old man answered, emptying a packet of sugar into his oatmeal, then placing the wrapper on a sizable pile of others beside his napkin. "They're designed to break. All made in China or Japan or some such." Blue suspenders hung limply from his scrawny shoulders.

"What do you know about China, living up in Hogum Gulch?" Jackie pointed Duane toward the same booth he'd sat in the day before and he dutifully shuffled across the linoleum toward it. "You got a library up there I don't know about?"

The old man grinned, showing off several missing teeth. "My

panning equipment used to last ten years. Now it's all plastic crap and I'm lucky if I get two." He dipped his spoon into the oatmeal and stirred.

"You having a problem with your microwave?" Duane asked.

"I have a busted, piece-of-shit microwave, is the problem I'm having," Jackie replied, coming over and leaning her hip against the booth by his shoulder. "You want more pancakes?"

"I've got a spare in my truck." Duane felt himself redden. "Microwave, I mean. I bought it for my wife, my ex-wife, on our anniversary, and I've got no place to use it."

Jackie looked down at Duane as if he were a new species, previously undiscovered. "You got your wife a microwave for your anniversary?" she asked. The old man coughed and raised his eyebrows.

"It's real nice," Duane said. "Top-of-the-line."

Jackie looked at him for several more seconds, then her face broke open and she laughed. The gales increased until her shoulders shook and she had to steady herself against the booth. "Oh Lord," she said, wiping her eyes.

The old man swung around on his stool, likewise wheezing. "My God, boy, I've lived in the woods for fifty years and even I know better than that."

A deep discomfort spread through Duane's chest, and he felt his cheeks go crimson. Why couldn't he have gotten Tracy diamond earrings for their anniversary like a normal man?

Seeing his discomfort, Jackie composed herself. "It's very sweet," she said, a corner of her lips still twitching. "Just not one of the anniversaries I'm familiar with . . . the microwave year." She glanced at the old man at the counter, who continued to wheeze helplessly. "But don't mind me, I've been married twice and I was lucky if either husband remembered our anniversary, let alone brought home new appliances. I'm honored you'd let me borrow such a special microwave."

Duane nodded curtly. He was starting to wish he'd never come to Lincoln at all. That he'd simply driven until he ran out of gas and hitchhiked the rest of the way to Canada. "I'm over at the church," he said. "You can pick it up anytime."

Jackie cleared her throat and smiled down at him. "Thank you." The hard edges of her face had softened in the wake of her laughter.

6

After her shift, Jackie walked north from the diner to the abandoned Glory Hole Mine. She took this walk almost every day
in the spring and summer, and liked it best when her footprints
paired with those of deer and fox in the muddy ground beneath
the curved awning of branches. The air was alive with the smell
of rain. Hardly anyone else came this way anymore, with the new
trails along the river and in the hills around Arrastra Gulch, but
her father had loved this walk, and now so did she. Jackie paused
by an old ponderosa and smiled at the thought of Duane's anniversary microwave, a tremendously large, chrome-finished appliance
that now sat in the back of her car. Even after a lifetime, she never
knew what to expect in Lincoln. Shaking her head in amusement,
she carried on.

At thirty-nine, she felt a shift within herself more dramatic
than the changing of the seasons. She'd entered the second half of
her life, and the desires from the first were falling away. Children,
a family, leaving the valley and finding some greater purpose in
the world—these plans shimmered in the distance behind her. She
wasn't sure yet what was up ahead, but she was ready to be done
with the time of constantly wishing for something more. Drops

of dew hung like jewels from the tips of willow buds along the creek. Spring finches sang back and forth in broken cadence. Jackie closed her eyes, enjoying the fresh air. In high school, she and her friends had come to the Glory Hole to drink, sitting on the rim and throwing their empties down into the cavernous pit. Now the place felt sacred to her. A portal to the underworld that held the valley's history, the crumbling network of mine tunnels unknown to the tourists and newcomers who came in greater numbers every year.

Her right hip pained her—a testament to twenty years spent working on her feet—and she winced as she lowered herself onto the same stump where she sat every day. "You're falling apart," she muttered. Soon she'd need the special, hospital-colored orthopedic shoes her grandmother had worn. The pit was sixty feet deep in bedrock and three hundred feet in diameter, a near-perfect circle in the midst of the trees. It had a lunar aspect, as if it had been created by a meteor impact rather than a consortium from Butte. The Glory Hole had only operated for ten years, in the 1940s and '50s, and never produced much of anything save debt for its investors. Jackie appreciated its futility. All the hole had to offer was itself, and the time, energy, and willpower that had gone into its digging. It felt like a part of the valley's mining legacy, and by extension her own: To dig and dig and not find what you're looking for. Two husbands, three psychics, one reiki master, dozens of self-help books. . . .

Years before, as a girl, sitting on this very stump on a winter's day, she'd seen the albino moose. It had emerged from the trees on the far side of the rim, as white as the snow and almost impossibly large, its humped back brushing the low branches. Their eyes met briefly, the red of the moose's burning into Jackie's memory before the creature disappeared back into the trees like the ghost of the wintry landscape itself. The moose had been an icon in the valley during her youth, used as a bogeyman by parents, and as a namesake by the White Moose Guest Ranch. When Jackie was a teenager, Vern Floyd shot it on Strawberry Ridge, and Jackie felt a tremendous sadness, as if a part of herself had also died—the little girl who spoke to coyotes and checked for baby owls in tree trunks. She and her friends snuck through the woods to Vern's hunting cabin to peer through the window at the taxidermy head, white and lifeless mounted above the fireplace, and she'd been so angry she had to look away. For years after, she'd wished for Vern's death and the deaths of all the other hunters in the valley, and in the early days of her marriage to Mason they'd talked about killing poachers as casually as they talked about the rain.

Today, the branches were bright green with new buds and nothing stirred between the trunks. Jackie sighed, thinking back across her family's history in the valley. Her great-grandfather had opened Lincoln's first general store after failing as a miner, realizing it was better to sell shovels than use them. The store was a success, but his sons preferred fishing to work. After he died in a pump-house fire, they ran through their inheritances on half-baked scams until Jackie's grandmother was forced to start a laundry business out of her home. The highway hadn't yet come to Lincoln during Jackie's childhood, and the town was almost entirely cut off from the world in the winter months. Only three telephones existed in the valley: one at the post office, one at the Company Ranch, and one at the Lincoln Hotel. The Lincoln Stage snowcat made a daily trip over Stemple Pass to Helena, sixty miles each way, to transport passengers and bring back mail and supplies. Jackie still remembered the magic of Christmas, when Mr. Didriksen dressed up as Santa Clause in the lobby of the old Lincoln Hotel and gave each child a present. During World War II, when Jackie was six and most of the men were gone, groceries were rationed in the mercantile and the Blackfoot Valley was a place out of a fairy tale, populated by women, children, and the elderly. "Let the wolves howl," her grandmother would say to her before bed each night. "Here by the fire you're safe."

As the sun sank lower over Stonewall Mountain, Jackie stood and slowly walked the perimeter of the pit. She measured her footsteps carefully, saying a prayer of gratitude with each one: for the electric fireplace that warmed her feet after her shifts without requiring chopped wood, for the swooping curve of the church roof, which her father had helped build, for the mountains and the trees and the Big Blackfoot River. . . . She felt herself to be a spiritual orphan, apart from the Christianity of most of the community and apart from the traditions of the Indians whose teepees had once filled the valley, so it was her practice to invoke this circle of protection around the pit of the Glory Hole Mine. She laughed at herself each time, yet she always came back. She stopped by the stump where she'd started and smiled to herself thinking of Duane and his microwave, picturing his long, hangdog face grinning as he carried it wrapped in a red bow through the door on his wedding anniversary.

7

Over the next two weeks, Duane's life fell into a pattern. Parishioners' baked goods at nine with the pastor, chopping wood—cleaving through each piece, solidifying a begrudging alliance with the ax, enjoying the dull ache of exertion in his arms—then heading to the diner for a late lunch. He made sure to be there when Jackie's shift ended. His persistence paid off the following Saturday when she invited him to walk with her to the Glory Hole Mine. During this walk, she told him stories of her childhood in the Blackfoot Valley: how the sheriff used to handcuff rowdy cowboys to trees after the Fourth of July picnic, the heyday of the Mike Horse Mine, when an entire separate town existed in Lincoln Gulch, and the last Salish Indians who erected summer teepees on the fields outside of town. She was a decade older than Duane, and her stories seemed to come from a time of myth. He hung on every word.

They took to walking together most afternoons. Dropping her off at her door, he'd look in at his microwave with satisfaction, as if some part of himself had infiltrated her life. He spent the rest of the evenings in the woods following elk tracks into the hills, returning with eagle feathers, bones, and sparkling chunks of quartz, the nicest of which he set aside for Hudson, imagining the boy's bedroom in the cabin he hoped to build. He spoke to his son on the pay phone outside the Wilderness Bar. The connection was always fuzzy with static and the boy was shy on the phone, so the conversations were brief and left Duane feeling guilty, haunted by the quaver in Hudson's voice whenever he asked when his dad was coming home.

Often Duane sensed the presence of animals around him at night, great lumbering shadows in his dreams. More than once he awoke to the rolling, bloodshot eye of the crazed steer. Tracks spotted the soft dirt around his truck in the morning: raccoons, deer, and one curious fox that returned time and again to shit on the woodpile, as if reestablishing its domain. Once after midnight, Duane was awakened by headlights pulling into the church lot. He rose on his elbow and watched a tall, slender blond woman hurry through the rain into the rectory. The lights blinked on, then off. Duane lay in his truck waiting for her to come out, but the rain pattering on the roof soon put him back to sleep.

When Duane finished splitting the first woodpile, Pastor Younger asked him to pick up a second load from Hutch Smith. Duane was in the process of stacking the split wood in the shed. This part of the job befuddled him. He'd attempt to fit in several pieces, find large gaps between them, try again, and discover he'd only made it worse. It was like some hellish life-sized puzzle and he was relieved by the excuse of another task. He brushed the splinters off his jeans and followed the pastor to his truck.

"She got enough horsepower?" Pastor Younger looked skeptically at the small blue pickup.

"She'll make it," Duane said. Back in Salt Lake, he'd loaded the truck so full at the lumberyard her frame nearly touched her tires, and she'd never quit on him. He turned the ignition, spoke reassuring words to the engine, "All right, old girl," and backed behind the church. Pastor Younger heaved the trailer hitch onto the ball and locked the coupler. Duane watched him in his side mirror, still unsure what to make of the man. The pastor was far less holy than the Mormon bishops Duane had known as a boy, with his tattoo and long hair and late-night female visitors, yet he acted with a seemingly divine providence, and thus far his advice had proven true. Duane felt invigorated in the mountains, and had come to agree there might be a reason for his being in Lincoln, particularly during his afternoon walks with Jackie. Maybe God had plans for men like him after all. The pastor rocked his weight down on the trailer to make sure it was secure. "Hutch's road is the first one on the left. No sign, but you can't miss it. His place is a mile in. You'll see an old sawmill out front."

A thrill of excitement ran through Duane. He remembered the road—the arrow-straight corridor between the pines that had mesmerized him after he nearly hit the bearded man on the bicycle. He'd been wanting to go back ever since.

"Hutch will talk your ear off," the pastor went on, "and he's got all manner of animals on his property, so watch out. If you're not back by dark, I'll send help." He rapped his knuckles on the side of Duane's truck and ambled back into the church, his right hand resting on his potbelly.

Still skittish from the standoff with the steer, Duane wondered what the pastor meant by all manner of animals. The morning was cloudy and cool; the white paint on the church shone with last night's rain. Duane had found an old tarp in the rectory basement and staked it over the split wood before the rain. He hoped Hutch had done the same with the load he was picking up. Waterlogged, it would weigh twice as much. He put the truck in gear and started slowly forward, getting used to the feel of the trailer.

The highway was empty save for a logging truck that roared past heading north. Duane watched the truck recede in the rearview mirror, imagining the driver heading on to Canada. Light misty rain began to fall, and Duane turned the radio off and listened to the familiar grumble of the truck's engine. He liked to listen to the engine as he drove, a habit that had driven Tracy—who always wanted music—crazy.

A pulse of trepidation slowed his approach to Hutch's road. He remembered the cyclist's dark, scowling eyes, and suddenly worried that the man might be waiting for him, wanting vengeance. One of Duane's former neighbors had shot his wife after an argument. A nice man, Duane had thought, a tire salesman. You never could tell. Duane flipped on his blinker and rehearsed an apology just in case.

The smell of wet pine needles filled the cab. The road was empty, silent. A gust of wind blew down from the mountains and the trunks around him swayed in unison. He leaned forward and peered up at the trees' crowns. They seemed to be arranged in formation, like an army preparing to advance. He wondered what the forest would look like in midwinter with drifts of snow between the low branches and needles garlanded in frost. Bumping over deep ruts, the truck tilted and the trailer clanked painfully. An invisible force seemed to reach forward and pull him in. The rumble of the engine was an intrusion, the only unnatural noise in the air. The trees leaned over the road, examining Duane as he passed. Taken objectively, these trees were no different from the ones he wandered through in the woods behind Jackie's house— ponderosa and lodgepole pines and the occasional Doug fir, forty to seventy feet tall, reddish trunks, clusters of green needles—but here he felt a communion, a collective history, as if this forest predated all the other inhabitants of the valley, and contained a deep, watchful intelligence.

The road rose steeply, then curved south before straightening in front of Hutch's property. Sure enough, an antique Farquhar sawmill, lovingly restored, stood in the middle of the yard, its red paint still glistening with rain. A double-wide trailer was set on a high concrete foundation at the back of a football-field-sized clearing. A pair of huskies leapt up on the porch and began to bark at

Duane's truck, straining at the end of their chains. NO TRESPASSING signs were nailed to two fence posts, but there was no fence, just an old coil of barbed wire, as if one had been started, then abandoned. Behind the trailer, Duane could make out a series of steel cages and a corral. A tree's-worth of log rounds were piled beside the saw-mill's mandrel, soaking wet.

The trailer's screen door kicked open and a small, wiry sprig of a man burst out, gesturing for Duane to park in front of the wood-pile. Hutch wore a .45 at his hip, had a three-day beard, and was in the midst of buckling up his belt. He was smaller than Duane had imagined, hardly over five-foot-five, but he took up more space than his physical body. Even at a distance energy fizzed off him in all directions. He moved in hoppy bursts, like coiled wire. He yelled for the dogs to shut up, tucked in his stained undershirt, and jumped off the porch. The huskies jumped after him, jerked back by their chains. "How do you expect to live in Montana with a little baby truck like that?" he called, jogging toward Duane. "You know what happens when one of those little trucks hits a Ford?" He nodded to the giant, lifted F-100 parked beside his trailer, then clapped his hands together, crushing an invisible soda can. "No survivors."

Duane opened his mouth to say hello, but Hutch kept right on talking.

"The Ford doesn't even know it had an accident. Just a lit-tle scratch on the fender. Jesus, how do you fit inside that thing? What're you, six-six?"

"Six-four," Duane said, straightening awkwardly in the misty air.

"Goddamn, I haven't seen a man that tall since I left Tucson. You big fellas can't take the wind up here. You see all these trees?" Hutch waved around the clearing to encompass the entire forest. "They're bunched up together because of that wind. I hear them moaning about it."

Bafflement overtook Duane. He'd never thought about how his height affected his ability to withstand the wind. He heard a slight buzzing in his ears.

Hutch leaned forward. "Jesus, boy, you okay?" He reached up and tapped Duane's forehead. "You a Mormon?"

Duane shook his head.

"Good. You know that's all religion is: Dust. Dust to clog your ears, dust to block your eyes, dust to choke your throat. Doesn't matter which one. I came up here to get away from all that, and now look at me, giving my wood away to a preacher."

Duane shook his head again, the only response he could muster. "How'd you find this place?"

"This place?" Hutch stopped and looked back at his trailer, as if seeing it for the first time. He swiped a bead of sweat from his forehead. His eyes were pale blue and had a manic, dancing light. "It found me. I was looking for a road with no one on it for my animals, and when I got to town and started asking around, the first person I met was Tom McCall. He had a contract up here, graded and skidded out the road—it goes another four miles up to Stemple Pass, I've got one other neighbor up that way, hermit-type—but when they started logging, everything went to hell. Equipment breaking down, accidents. Finally they had an anchor tree snap. It rolled the skidder into a ditch and killed the man inside. After that, Tom bagged the whole operation. He's been trying to sell off the land ever since."

"Is your neighbor the one who rides the bike?" Duane asked.

"Yep. Doesn't own a car, not even a baby one like yours. How's that for crazy? He snowshoes to town in the winter, three miles each way."

"I almost hit him on the highway."

"You're not the only one. Ted rides that bike like a madman." Hutch gestured for Duane to follow and set off toward the woodpile, talking all the while.

"You've never had any trouble here?" Duane asked.

"Trouble? Shit, I have trouble all the time. I've had trouble a lot longer than I've lived on this road. But we've got an understanding." He gestured to the trees. "I help out with the animals, and the place lets me be." Some of the animation left Hutch's body, like a spinning top that finally begins to drift. He pointed to the soaked rounds. "Take the whole pile. I might as well get in good with that fool pastor. It's a small town, you know." Hutch waved his hand. "Now I've got animals to feed, so I'll leave you to it. Just holler if you need anything." He turned and jogged back to the porch, disappearing inside the trailer as abruptly as he'd emerged.

Dazed, with half of Hutch's words still undigested in his head, Duane set to work. Spring sun broke through the clouds, warming his back and causing steam to rise off the wet rounds. He moved slowly, carrying one piece at a time, though he easily could have handled two. He wanted to linger in these woods, smelling the butterscotch scent of the ponderosas after the rain, and looking up at the clean white form of Ogden Mountain across the valley and the red-tailed hawks that occasionally winged over the horizon. He wondered what Hutch meant by an understanding. Would he be able to find one of his own? He imagined building a cabin up the way in a clearing among these same trees.

An hour later, when he was nearly done, Duane heard the slap of a screen door and a storm of yaps and growls erupted from the cages behind the trailer. It was feeding time. Duane listened as Hutch spoke to each animal by name, his voice receding, discussing their injuries, and when they might be ready to go free.

Curiosity overpowered Duane, and he left the rounds and crept around the side of the trailer after Hutch. He didn't want to surprise him, remembering the .45 he carried. The huskies watched him disinterestedly, used to his presence by now. Duane peered around the corner of the metal siding. Cages were lined ten to a side along a mowed grass corridor leading to the corral. Hutch stood at the end, speaking softly to a bobcat as he hand-fed it from a bucket. Astonished, Duane watched the forty-pound cat snap up the meat, flattening its tufted ears as it ate. A large coyote paced inside the nearest cage, limping badly on a bandaged hip. It sniffed the air and turned toward Duane. Its lips slowly rose, revealing curved canine teeth. Duane pressed himself back against the trailer. He'd been taught that coyotes were dangerous, conniving animals, that attacked both cattle and humans, and he didn't want to startle it. The coyote stared at him silently, its eyes a striking pale blue that reminded Duane of Hutch's.

Hutch finished his conversation with the bobcat and walked past the corral. He lifted aside a large tangle of wire, revealing a path leading deeper into the forest. There were more cages hidden back there, Duane realized. Hutch disappeared from sight, still carrying the meat bucket. Skirting the coyote, Duane edged out from the trailer and cut into the trees after Hutch. He kept low, using both hands to steady himself against the rough bark. He felt like a child playing hide-and-seek. His heart pounded. Concealing himself in the shadows, he moved as quickly as he could.

A deep growl froze him. A huge cage, double the size of the others, more than twenty feet high, glinted in the sunlight ahead of him. Thick mesh cables held it in place and more wires were lashed around tree trunks for support. Duane dropped to his knees and crawled forward.

A young grizzly bear stood against the bars of the cage. Half upright, it held its bandaged front paw to its chest and extended the other menacingly toward Hutch, who stood outside the gate with the bucket of meat, talking to it in low, calming tones. "I feed you every day," Hutch said. "Why are you still trying to kill me?"

The grizzly waved the healthy paw, all its weight bunched back in its rump, ready to surge forward. Blood soaked the bandages on the other paw, and Duane could see above it where the bear had been chewing. He tried to imagine what kind of a trap had caught such a beast, and was briefly nauseated by the thought. The bear had to weigh two hundred pounds at least. Gold-brown fur covered the pronounced hump on the bear's back and cinder-block muscles rippled in its shoulders. Its two-inch claws darkened to amber at the base. It tilted its head away from Hutch, raising its ears along with the black tip of its nose as if it detected Duane hidden behind the trees. He remained there on his knees, dumbstruck, like a penitent before an angry god. The bear's nostrils twitched. Duane could tell the bear still had room to grow, but it was already massive, dwarfing Hutch, dwarfing even the trees. An impossible power flooded its movements, turning Duane's elation into a kind of wild, plunging panic, as if he'd come here to be eaten, having finally crossed the line between civilization and his dreams.

8

Jackie took no pleasure in going on dates in her hometown. She'd worked at the Ponderosa Café for over a decade, and she knew all the servers and staff at the other restaurant, Lambkins, as well. She told Duane—who'd been asking her out nearly every afternoon— that if he wanted to take her, it had to be in Helena. Thus, on the last Friday in May, she found herself standing in front of her bathroom mirror wondering what in the hell she'd gotten herself into, with only thirty minutes to get ready before he picked her up.

Foundation, blush, eyeliner, lipstick. She arranged them like a battalion on the front edge of the sink, steeling herself. What was she thinking? Duane was a decade younger and living in his truck in the church parking lot, for chrissakes. He'd tricked her with that microwave. It was always the tall, mournful ones you had to watch out for. But still, she thought as she unscrewed the cap of the eyeliner and held the brush up to the light, smiling to herself, it would be nice to get out of Lincoln.

The skin on her face was drawing in around the bones. She opened her eyes wide, then pressed her lips together, examining her face: the spiderweb wrinkles, the looseness below her chin. The teens and the forties were decades of makeup, both dreading and craving the familiar cloying scent. As a girl, she'd wanted to look like a woman; now, halfheartedly, she wanted to look like a girl again. She leaned forward, brushing her eyelashes upward in quick, sure strokes. "Thought you'd grown up, didn't you?" she said to her reflection.

Thinking of her youth, she was reminded of the Reiki master who'd passed through Lincoln in the early sixties, his flyers appearing suddenly on the bulletin board outside Food Town like dispatches from outer space. She'd met with him and he'd laid his hands on her. Told her of the seven chakras, the cleansing path, the third eye. . . . One night when her first husband, Rich, was out of town, he'd stayed over. At the time, she'd thought she'd be reaching higher planes by the end of that year. Now she remembered his teeth, which were overlong and overwhite, and had frightened her for a moment in the darkness.

She was still buttoning her dress when the doorbell rang. Duane filled the doorway in his hesitant, rangy way, his expression both hopeful and nervous. It was the first time Jackie had seen him without his red, white, and blue ballcap, and there was something endearing about his receding hairline, the sandy remains of his hair carefully flattened with gel. He'd worn a belt with a silver bison buckle, and tucked in his shirt—one of the ones with pearl snaps and deep stitching above each breast that reminded Jackie of rodeo clowns. His boots were freshly polished and he smelled overwhelmingly of cologne. She feared she might suffocate in the cab of his tiny truck.

"You look beautiful," he stammered.

This softened her and she nodded brusquely. "Let's get on the road and maybe we can make it back before dark."

Spring was in full bloom in Lincoln, and purple buds covered the rhododendron bushes in front of the Millers' house across the street. A rope swing hung lazily from their large ponderosa. Duane opened the door of his little blue truck and Jackie lowered herself in, trying to imagine how he fit in the bed under the top-per. Tucked in with his knees up, most likely. She could see his belongings piled by a sleeping bag and what looked like a tiny hammer. The cab had clearly been recently cleaned. A pine-tree air freshener hung from the rearview mirror and a red rose lay on Jackie's side of the dash. She decided not to say anything, but took the rose and held it in her lap, pressing the pad of her index finger on one of the sharp thorns and feeling herself blush. How long since a man had bought her a rose? Duane started the engine and navigated through town in nervous silence. They'd been walking together nearly every day, and he had no trouble talking then, but Jackie knew how men got when they had to comb their hair. She attempted a compliment. "You look nice, too," she said, carefully spinning the rose's stem between her fingers.

He turned red. "It's my first time going over the pass."

Jackie was surprised. Helena was the nearest town of size, and for most residents of Lincoln, herself included, some errand—haircut, bank, liquor store—was required every week. Complaining about it was part of the town lexicon: no one ever simply went to Helena, it was always that they *had* to go. "You talk to your son today?" she asked. She was fascinated by the fact that Duane had a child, unable to fit fatherhood into her image of him, and feeling an attraction because of it.

He shook his head. "He had baseball practice after school."

The sparkling blue of Flesher Lakes appeared between the trees east of Lincoln. Duane slowed, turning south over Alice Creek onto Flesher Pass Road. Newly hatched mayflies swarmed over the water and the air was fresh with the smell of life reemerging after the long winter. A canoe floated along the far shore, and a fisherman cast his line over the water. The image reminded Jackie of her father, who had often brought her here to fish, and she felt suddenly giddy, as if she might be reborn as well. "I'm glad we're doing this," she said.

"Me, too." Duane grinned.

The road rose out of the Blackfoot Valley, winding through ponderosa forest interspersed with old moss-covered miners' shacks slumping at the bottom of shaded draws. The foundation of what was once a rooming house for stranded travelers stood at the pass by the abandoned stage stop. Sunlight glinted off the windows of the fire lookout to the west. Snow runoff flowed down from the peaks through gullies; braids of meltwater glistened on the pavement. Jackie caught the brief view east to the Missouri River and remembered her childhood dream of rafting it like Huckleberry Finn. Then they descended to the ruins of Silver City and the Silver Camp Mine. Jackie craned her neck around to see her great-grandfather's old claim, just west of the lode vein. For her inheritance, her father had given her a four-ounce gold nugget. She was amazed the men in her family had kept it through all their years of unemployment and near-bankruptcy. Now it lived in her underwear drawer, wrapped in a padded bra.

Helena's first outbuildings appeared: a taxidermist, then a gas station, two motels, and a larger sporting goods store. In the distance, the copper dome of the state capital glinted green, topped by a statue of Lady Liberty. Helena was a small town by most standards, but for Jackie it had always been a sprawling metropolis. She'd gone to Helena High for a semester when Lincoln High was being rebuilt after the fire of '53, and hated every second of it, most of all the constant traffic: people and cars shuttling down narrow streets.

Duane mumbled directions to himself—which he'd clearly memorized—and soon they were pulling into the parking lot of the House of Wong. Duane parked under the corner of the pagoda-style roof and leaned forward to stare up at it happily through the windshield. "Looks just like the China Buffet back in Fairpark," he said, grinning.

Wong's was Jackie's favorite restaurant as a girl, when it was still in its old location by the Palace Bar downtown. It was the only non–steakhouse or hamburger joint within a hundred miles, and the high-walled green booths and ornately carved dragon above the bar had been for her the height of adventure. At the time, Montana still had an anti-miscegenation law on the books, and Jackie remembered her father leaving an extra-large tip, as if in apology to Jerry and Eleanor Wong, who worked discreetly together behind the order window. Now it was in a fancy new building and Jerry and Eleanor were long retired. She thought of explaining all this to Duane, but he was already out of the truck, coming around to her side to open the door, clearly flooded with relief at the familiarity of the restaurant.

"They had an early-bird special back at the China Buffet. Two dollars all-you-can-eat if you got there before six. Tracy and I used to go straight from work." He peered down at his watch. "We already missed it if they do that here."

"It's not a buffet," Jackie said, mildly irritated. "It's a sit-down place." She was curious about Tracy, the woman who'd had Duane's child, then left him for another man, but all of her recent dates—not that there were many—had devolved into conversations about exes, each horror story outdoing the last. "Let's try not to spend dinner in the past," she said.

Duane looked confused but nodded agreeably. Jackie paused before following him inside and looked up at the evening light on the Big Belt Mountains, their snow-helmet peaks and the pine trees that covered the foothills like fur. They were a gentler, more welcoming range than the Lewis, and even after a lifetime they had a way of looking brand-new.

A young freckled girl with red hair in a black kimono led them to a table below a pearled engraving of a heron taking flight. Duane pulled out Jackie's chair for her, tucked it beneath her legs, and stood beside her until she'd settled herself.

"Thanks," she said. "Not many men remember how to do that."

"It was just my mom and me growing up," Duane replied. "She taught me a few things about how she wished men were."

"Where's she now?"

Duane looked down at the carpet. "Still in Salt Lake. I don't talk to her much."

The hangdog expression began to make sense to Jackie. She'd known other mothers who tried to turn their sons into the partner they wished they had, and punished them for the deeds of ex-lovers. "I visited Salt Lake once," she said, opening her menu. "Didn't seem like a place human beings should live."

"It's just temples and strip malls," Duane agreed.

The waitress appeared, took their drink orders, and rattled off the night's special five-course menu: chicken subgum, chow mein, egg rolls, pineapple chicken, beef tomatoes, Wong's Special Fried Rice, and cookies, all for $3.50.

"I reckon I'll have that," Duane said excitedly. Jackie ordered the fireworks shrimp, her favorite, and a glass of red wine, giving the waitress a reassuring, service-industry-compatriot smile.

Drinks arrived and Jackie felt herself relax in the familiar room with the gold gilt ceilings and mirrored walls, the red tassels hanging like tailfeathers from the light fixtures. Duane settled in as well, spreading his legs and taking rapid sips of his beer while commenting on the molding. "How do you suppose they carve that?" he asked, pointing up at a roaring dragon head.

"Probably a machine now," Jackie answered. "But I've heard there are palaces in China where everything was done by hand. Millions of tiny details, like lace."

"I might like that, as far as a job," Duane said pensively.

"You carve?"

"I chop." Duane grinned. "But my arms are getting tired."

"You think you might move out of your truck at some point, too?" Jackie smiled.

"Oh, I might. I'd miss the mornings, though, deciding

whether to freeze to death or take a piss." Duane set his beer down and leaned toward her conspiratorially. "What I want is to build myself a little place up by Hutch Smith. You know his road?"

The stem of the wineglass was suddenly cold in Jackie's hand. She knew Hutch's place well, and the cages behind his trailer where he illegally kept wounded animals. Hutch was Mason's best friend in the valley, and the cause of much of the trouble in their marriage. After the two men met, they'd become inseparable, and Mason went from actions that were at least vaguely within his job description—clearing old traps and patrolling for poachers—to ones that decidedly were not: stealing legal traps and rescuing predators. He'd hidden these excursions from Jackie until someone cut the brake lines in his truck on the side of Stonewall Mountain and he shattered his femur in the ensuing accident. She remembered the blind panic she'd felt driving to the hospital in Helena, and how Hutch was already there at Mason's bedside, buzzing with self-righteous fury.

"There's something about those woods," Duane went on. "I can't stop thinking about them. It's like they're trying to talk to me." He blushed. "That probably sounds crazy."

Jackie narrowed her eyes and studied Duane. She knew from experience that newcomers to the valley often went through a phase where they thought the trees were talking to them and every sunset was drawn up for them special and all the deer came bringing personal messages. At the same time, he wasn't exactly wrong: the woods would talk to you if you knew how to listen, and the old growth below Stemple Pass did have a special power. "You're not one of these back-to-the-landers are you?" she asked. "Wanting to shit in a hole in the ground?"

Surprised, Duane shook his head.

"Because they don't usually last past Christmas. The winters here are no joke."

"I want a nice place, insulated, with electric heat and plumbing and a room for Hudson and maybe a little garden. I've got to save some money first, though."

If she'd been a betting woman, Jackie would have put his odds of achieving this dream at about five-to-one, but she hoped he would stay. He reminded her of her father, and in the afternoons she found herself looking through the diner window hoping his little blue pickup would pull into the parking lot. Not many men were truly gentle, and she was old enough to appreciate it when one came along. "I'll talk to Tom McCall for you, if you want," she said. "I know he's filling crews for the summer and he owes me at least one favor. You know how to work?"

"I know how to do what they tell me." Duane shrugged.

"That's all it takes. He might even give you a deal on land once he gets to know you."

"I'd sure appreciate that. I'm about through chopping wood at the church."

The entrées arrived and Jackie discovered that Duane's mother's lessons had not extended to the table. He ate from all five of his plates at once and used his fork as a kind of shovel and his knife as a plow, occasionally enlisting the spoon to corral a piece of pineapple or chicken that had escaped from his plate onto the white tablecloth. Watching him, Jackie ate slowly, conscious of not smudging her lipstick and keeping any little pieces of green onion from getting stuck between her teeth. She thought of her own dream of building a house with Rich out of high school, and how the reality of electric companies, water lines, and her first husband's laziness had sucked the joy right out of it. When Duane finished, his plates shone bone-white and he leaned back and sighed with accomplishment, as if he'd just put in a hard shift. Jackie couldn't help but smile. Secretly she loved the boyish parts of men, the moments when all the years fell away and they were purely consuming the world, as if all of its wonders were a playground made just for them. "Get enough?" she asked.

"Surely." Duane sighed.

———

AS THEY DROVE HOME over the pass through the long shadows of dusk, Jackie was surprised when Duane again brought up Hutch. His brow was furrowed in the dim light, something clearly weighing on his mind. "You know about his animals, right?" he asked.

Jackie nodded.

"I was over there picking up a load of wood and I saw all the coyotes and bobcats and whatnot in the cages behind his trailer, and then I saw him sneak off into the woods. I followed him, and he's got another cage hidden back there. A bigger one." Duane paused and glanced over at her.

Jackie's chest tightened. She'd suspected something. Mason had been irritable and nervous when he came into the diner that week, and Hutch's manic energy was in overdrive. He'd shredded half a dozen napkins to go along with his coffee the previous morning. She wondered what they'd found, and feared what might happen if they drew too much attention to themselves. Privacy was sacred in Lincoln, and a man's right to do what he wanted on his own land was fundamental, but a fine line was crossed when it came to anything that might threaten ranchers' livestock.

"It's got a grizzly bear inside," Duane finished.

For a moment, Jackie was too stunned to speak. Ten years had passed since she'd heard of a grizzly in the Blackfoot Valley. They were supposed to be extinct in the Swan Range, and on the rare occasion when one wandered over from Glacier, it was quickly captured and returned to the park. She remembered hunting parties going out to shoot cubs in their dens in her youth.

"Must have gotten caught in a trap. One paw is all bandaged up. It's huge, like . . . like a god."

Once the shock wore off, Jackie's mind raced. She tried to imagine Hutch and Mason smuggling the bear through Lincoln. How had they done it? A grizzly, even a young one, was an incredibly dangerous animal. Bringing predators onto Hutch's property was always a risk—no rancher wanted a coyote hospital in their midst—but a grizzly was another matter entirely. Grizzlies killed people, and they were endangered. Getting fired would only be the beginning. Both Hutch and Mason could go to federal prison. "You tell anyone else?"

"No." Duane shook his head. "I figured I shouldn't."

"That's right."

Chewing his lip, Duane went on. "I hate thinking of a bear like that all caught up in a trap."

Jackie nodded. Mason had told her awful stories of what animals did to free themselves. He said bears were some of the worst. They had the means to inflict as much damage on themselves as they did on their prey. She turned to Duane, watching his profile as they descended from the pass back into the Blackfoot Valley. "Just be careful and keep your mouth shut. People here like their privacy, and Hutch doesn't need any more trouble."

9

The green of the forest gave way to the hacking roar of the machines. For the first week in Tom McCall's logging crew, Duane cut road south of the freshly graded landing near Flesher Pass. Following the skidder into old growth, clearing away brush, pulling out stumps. Then hauling dirt, packing it down, watching a corridor form through the trees. Scarred rings of slash collected in his wake. It was violent work. The choke and whine of chain saws, splinters flying, branches groaning and snapping. The older loggers all had gruesome stories of injury: splinters through the eye, splinters through the hand, an escaped chain-saw chain slicing a man in two.

Sawdust worked its way into Duane's pores. His clothes smelled of sap, and soon his skin did, too. Little balls of sawdust fell from his ears, like he was becoming a tree himself. He hated the noise—it made his whole brain rattle—but liked the exertion, returning to his camp bone-tired and crawling into the back of his truck too exhausted to think.

The road they'd built connected to another, and they began to spread out into the forest. Tom had a government contract to clear-cut two square miles of former national forest on the far side of Strawberry Ridge, southeast of Lincoln. To the north, the Bob Marshall Wilderness covered over a million acres of roadless territory. Looking across at the Bob, Duane felt comforted that the carnage their crew was wreaking was minor in comparison to this untouched vastness, though he sometimes felled twelve trees in a day. The two buckers followed behind him to strip the trunks and then Dixon Sleepingbear drove the eighteen-thousand-pound skidder and used a winch to pull the eighty-foot lodgepoles six at a time across the forest floor to the landing.

While at work, Duane stashed his stove and cooler on the floor of the passenger seat in his truck. A little antler he'd found rested on the dash. It was a spike buck's first shed, and comforted him somehow. He'd mailed Tracy the divorce papers and thrown the ball-peen hammer in the river. His wedding ring was hidden under the floor mat; he didn't know what else to do with it. One of the church ladies had given him an old single mattress and he lined both sides with blankets to make a proper bed beneath the topper.

The nights under the trees were black. Duane had to practically touch his face to see his hand. He lay with his eyes open, feeling what it must be like to be blind, and listening for intruders over the distant rush of Halfway Creek. Rumors of spiked trees and sabotaged equipment spread from valley to valley that summer in northern Montana, and Tom was paying Duane extra to sleep at the landing. The Wilderness Society was rumored to be holding covert training in secret locations, and monkey wrenchers were making their way up from Utah and Arizona, having failed to stop the dams on the Colorado River. The year before, Tom had lost a full week of work and thousands of dollars when the transmission wires were cut in the skidder's engine and sugar was poured in its gas tank. He suspected radical environmentalists from California. Others thought it might be Mason or some other disaffected Forest Service man. In any case, Tom had given the crew instructions to shoot on sight if they saw anyone suspicious. Not having a gun,

Duane kept his hunting knife beside him in bed. Sometimes, when anxiety overtook him in the inky blackness, he walked out to the road they'd made and looked down its winding, rutted path. Even more than the clear-cuts, the road had transformed the landscape, and he felt its connective power. The trees would grow back, but this access would remain, an artery to the surging bloodstream of twentieth century civilization.

A LATE SPRING STORM brought a foot of snow to Lincoln in mid-June and halted all work. After they staked tarps over the machines, Tom drove Duane and the rest of the crew into town in the back of his lifted quad-cab, snow whipping around them, the forest transformed. Duane pressed against the wheel well with his jean jacket pulled up over his face. It was such a violent swirl that he felt like the whole world was being shaken, upended, as if God were a violent child with a snow globe.

The truck bounced and rattled over potholes and Duane feared he'd be thrown from the bed. He wished Tom would slow down. "Feels like I'm back in Saigon," Dixon Sleepingbear shouted, gripping the rail across from Duane, his wide features hidden by the swirling snow. "They'd shoot at you, but at least it was warm." He'd come home to Montana after two tours and operated the skidder like it was a Humvee behind enemy lines, whipping the wheel around and spraying mud. He was a tireless worker, stopping only to eat, smoke, or adjust the bandanna that held his long black hair in place. Duane was slightly afraid of him. He nodded his chin deeper into his coat and pulled the cuffs over his fingers.

Tom parked in front of the Wilderness Bar. The men tumbled from the truck bed and rushed inside, halting immediately to stamp off their boots and shake the snow from their shoulders in the warm gloom. It wasn't even three in the afternoon but the bar was packed, the faces barely visible in a haze of cigarette smoke. Loggers and workers from all over the mountain had come in to escape the weather. Vern Floyd and his construction crew, Mason and the other Forest Service rangers in their olive-greens, and a half-dozen bikers gathered around the pool table. Shivering, Duane pushed inside and was confronted, on the neck of a female biker, by the grotesque tattoo of a serpent coiled tightly around a naked man.

"See something you like?" she asked.

"No, ma'am." Duane turned away, and the bikers laughed.

On his first visit to the Wilderness, he'd encountered a woman in a wedding dress weeping because her new husband was making out with her mother in the bathroom, and ever since he'd brought no expectations to the long, dim, tobacco-stinking room. A stone fireplace was cemented over on the far wall. Old wrestling trophies lined the hearth. A jackalope was mounted over the poker table, its antlers casting pronged shadows on the green felt. Bubbled glass beer signs hung above a dusty altar of liquor bottles. A small bouquet of miniature American flags in a pint glass by the cash register was the only nod to the Bicentennial. Duane took the stool next to Dixon and watched cheap whiskey pool in shot glasses between amber ashtrays.

The rest of the crew pushed in around them, ordering beer backs and eating elk jerky from the jar on the counter. The muted TV over the bar showed a baseball game. The bartender, Liv, was a burly, stoic woman who wore undershirts year-round and had no time for idle chatter. She collected money and she poured. Dixon leaned over the bar toward her and cocked his hat back, revealing the pink line from his hatband across his forehead. "What's the warmest place you've ever been, Liv?" he said. "I know you're a world traveler."

"Butte," she said shortly, and the men laughed.

Behind them, Tom was glowering at Mason. "You call in this storm?" he asked, drumming his fingers on the bar. "Trying to fuck up my schedule?"

"Sure, Tom," Mason replied. "It's all part of our training. Weather control, top-secret CIA stuff."

"Shouldn't you be out there making sure none of your precious national forest trees get blown over? Sure be a waste if they did."

"Sounds like you need a vacation," Mason said.

Tom grunted. "What I need is one month of sunlight in this godforsaken valley."

Within an hour, Duane had drunk more than he was used to. Wind buffeted the walls and whenever someone new came into the bar, snow swirled in after them while they struggled to press the door shut. Through the window, Duane watched great drifts wash across the highway, obscuring the yellow lines and the lone traffic light. The Ponderosa Café was completely hidden, and he wondered if Jackie might get off early. After their date, he'd dropped her at her door and he could still feel the warmth of her hand squeezing his while her lips brushed his cheek, kissing him good night. The memory so excited him that he ordered another shot.

Dixon leaned back in his stool and told him about a place in the Yukon where they served vodka out of a man's toe.

"What toe?" Duane asked, trying to picture it.

"Some prospector who came in frostbit. They were two days from a hospital, so they chopped the toe off right there in the bar, and kept it ever since."

"But what toe?"

"The big one. Froze solid. They hollowed it out."

The description still didn't make sense to Duane, but his questions were interrupted by one of the bikers loudly telling a joke about three Indians and a light bulb. His friends around the pool table smirked and Dixon's face went cold. He turned his large frame on the stool.

"You like jokes?" he asked.

The biker stepped out from behind the pool table and tugged down his leather vest to show the corded muscles in his neck. "I like all kinds of fun," he said. Duane felt the room spin slightly and looked toward the exit, wishing he hadn't drank so much. Liv sighed and stepped back from the bar.

"I got a good one," Dixon said. "It's about your mother. I saw her last night. I called her a two-bit whore and she hit me with a bag of quarters."

The room went silent, save for the crackle of the muted TV, then Tom began to laugh, a rasping, sandpaper sound that boiled the tension in the room. The biker hefted a pool cue and Dixon lifted his beer bottle by the neck. The biker winged the cue at Dixon like a spear. Dixon ducked, surprisingly nimble for a man his size, and charged. The biker met him by the pool table, grunting and swinging. Everyone stood back until Dixon smashed the bottle over the biker's head, sending a gout of blood onto the green felt. Then the other bikers rushed in, joined by Tom and the loggers. Duane tried to scramble over the rail of the bar to safety, but a fist caught him in the ribs, sending him skidding sideways to the floor. When he regained his breath, the female biker with the neck tattoo was standing over him. She looked down at him—almost tenderly—then stomped his face with the heel of her boot. He tasted blood and felt the lights of his consciousness flicker. He crawled back behind the stools and dragged himself to the door. He was clawing at the knob when Sheriff Kima and his deputy pushed through.

"Any guns in there?" the sheriff asked, lifting Duane up by the collar and pulling his long body outside into the snow.

Duane shook his head, still fighting for air. Sheriff Kima—a notoriously temperamental bulldog of a man—dropped him on a snowbank and shouldered back through the door. Duane sat in the cold, tasting blood and feeling stunned and pitiable. Somehow sunlight was breaking through the clouds as the snow continued to fall, giving the day an even more crazed aspect. Gingerly, he prodded his nose. Nothing seemed broken. Why were women always so down on him? He heard shouting and breaking glass, and remembered all the times Tracy had called him stupid. He laughed suddenly, his face numb, adrenaline making his blood feel electric, glad almost to bursting to be out of Salt Lake. More glass smashed inside, and Duane pulled himself upright and lurched away from the melee.

A truck horn sounded in the blowing snow as Duane crossed the highway, and he felt the wind of a semi close behind him. Rattled, he stumbled to the totem pole in front of the Wolf-Goes-for-Fire Trading Post and leaned against the carved eagle at the top, looking back at the bar. He scooped up a handful of snow and held it against his nose. The bleeding stopped. Pain set in. Duane tasted the cold tang of snow mixed with the blood on his upper lip. The door of the Wilderness burst open and Sheriff Kima and the deputy marched out dragging Dixon between them, his hands cuffed behind his back, his legs kicking wildly in protest.

"This is how you treat a veteran?" Dixon shouted. "Can't tell a fucking joke?" He caught sight of Duane and spat blood in the snow. "You chickenshit. Tell Tom I quit. I'm getting out of this cracker town." The deputy shoved him into the back of the patrol car and Dixon flopped onto his back, kicking his feet out to prevent the deputy from closing the door. "Nothing you like better than locking up Indians, is there, you son of a bitch?"

The deputy cursed and Sheriff Kima came around the side and together they wrestled Dixon's flailing legs into the cruiser. The lights flashed and the vehicle slowly pulled away, leaving Duane alone in the blowing snow.

10

By the time Jackie left the Ponderosa Café, it was dark and the snow had already started to melt. She cursed as she picked her way across the wet, icy patches, holding a large Styrofoam container of chicken pot pie. The cook had insisted she take the pot pie, convinced she was getting too thin. "Everyone's got an opinion on my weight now," she muttered.

Duane was passed out in his truck in front of her house with the cab light on. Jackie paused at the corner and stared in at him. A bandage was pasted crookedly across his nose and one of his eyes was black. Dried blood stained the collar of his jean jacket. He'd wedged himself sideways in the truck's small front seat and had a large book in his lap, as if he'd been reading. His long features looked more mournful than ever with his busted nose. No one would ever confuse him for handsome. But what was handsome? Jackie sighed. Her first husband, Rich, was the best-looking man she'd ever met, and he was not worth one single solitary shit.

"Evening, Duane," she said, loudly, rapping on his window. He jumped, startled, and the book fell onto the seat, allowing Jackie to see the cover: *The Art of Japanese Woodworking*, checked out from the library. Duane glanced at himself in the rearview mirror, blushed, then fumbled for the door and stumbled out, stinking of whiskey.

"Evening," he said, trying to compose himself. "I must've drifted off."

"Right in front of my house. What the hell happened to you?"

"A woman kicked me," Duane said, reaching up to gently prod the bandage on his nose, as if he still couldn't believe it.

"What for?"

"Nothing. I was trying to get out of there. Dixon got in a fight."

Jackie had heard about the scuffle at the Wilderness. Half her customers that evening had come in with cuts and bruises, and Tom and the sheriff spent nearly an hour shouting back and forth about Dixon's bail.

"I got you something," Duane said. He leaned back into the truck and brought out a bottle of red wine that Jackie recognized as the third-cheapest available at Food Town. "As a thank-you for coming to dinner with me and . . . and all the service."

"The service?"

"At the diner, I mean."

"You're looking for someplace to stay, aren't you?"

Duane blushed. "I don't mind sleeping here in the truck. It's just too cold up on the mountain."

Jackie sighed and took the bottle from his outstretched hand. "You better come inside." She brushed past Duane and unlocked her door. Irritation and gladness battled inside her chest. She flipped on the light in the living room and saw the old magazines strewn across the coffee table, the dirty cup on top of the TV, and the underwear on the carpet of the hallway leading to her bedroom. "Why don't you open this while I tidy up?" she said, gesturing with the bottle as Duane came in behind her. "If you haven't had enough today."

"Getting kicked in the head has a way of sobering a person up," he answered, trailing her into the kitchen and taking the corkscrew she handed him. "She working all right?" He gestured to the microwave.

"Fine," Jackie said. "Does everything a microwave should. Beeps. Makes things hot."

"You've got to be careful of the capacitor. It fritzed out once when I slammed the door too hard."

"Oh, I'm real gentle with the door." Jackie dropped her coat over the back of a kitchen chair and returned to the living room. She gathered up her underwear and stacked the magazines into a pile, then paused to watch Duane try to extract the cork. He clearly had little experience with corkscrews, struggling to gain purchase with the sharp end, and eventually ripping the cork in half. He stared down at the remains, then violently stabbed the corkscrew back in. Jackie shook her head at the man looming in her kitchen with his bandaged nose and black eye. She briefly worried she was in the process of adopting a very large child. Finally, he managed to pop out the rest of the cork and fill two glasses to the brim. "To Montana," he said, handing her one.

Toasting her home state was like toasting air or water to Jackie, but she raised her glass and took a sip, letting the wine pool on her tongue. She wasn't sure if it was good, but she liked the way it puckered her taste buds. "You better let me take a look at that nose," she said, setting down the glass.

Reluctantly, Duane lowered his head and allowed her to peel off the crooked bandage. The cut was an ugly, jagged red line across the bridge in the tangible shape of a bootheel, and the bruise was dark, but there was little swelling and no more blood. Jackie ran her index finger gently down the side. "You'll be okay," she said. "It's not broken."

Duane nodded. "I figured it wasn't when it stopped bleeding so quick."

"You're lucky. Nearest hospital is in Helena," Jackie answered. "And you don't want to drive over that pass tonight."

"I thought I might have to go all the way to Missoula."

Together they moved into the living room. Jackie slipped off her shoes and tucked her legs underneath her on the couch, a habit she'd had since childhood. Duane looked around at the TV and magazines, then awkwardly sat beside her. "Real cozy in here," he said.

"Well, it's no pickup truck," Jackie said. "You wanting to build yourself a Japanese house?"

Duane blushed. "I just thought it looked interesting. Did you know they don't use any metal at all when they build? No nails, nothing. They join the whole house together with wood."

"I'd try one with nails first."

"I'm thinking about a lot of windows on the south side, to let the light in."

"You should put in a hot tub, too, if we're dreaming."

Duane nodded uncertainly. "That might be nice for winter."

"Winter, summer, it doesn't matter. Rita used to have one at her place. She'd have parties and everybody always ended up naked in that hot tub." Jackie took another sip, wondering why she'd told this to Duane. The parties had mostly been terrible. People worried about losing their jobs, drinking too much, Mason getting in fights.

"Rita?" Duane asked.

"An old friend of mine. She's down in Phoenix now."

"Your grandpa built this house, right?" Duane changed the subject, looking around at the plaster walls. The light fixture above him flickered, the bulb about to go, casting moving shadows across his face.

"My great-grandpa," she answered. "In 1904. He put in the first glass windows in the whole valley, except for the hotel."

"You ever think of building your own?"

"I bought land with my first husband, but he split before we even got the foundation dug. That ruined it for me."

"Where'd he go?"

"Spokane, last I heard. He ran off with my cousin. I haven't talked to either of them since."

Duane looked down at his hands. "I haven't talked to Tracy, either."

"Why would you?"

"I don't know. I just feel bad sometimes."

"What for? She ran off and now she's marrying someone else."

"Hudson, I guess." Duane shook his head glumly. "I'm not sure I realized how far I was going when I left." He looked pensively out the window, and Jackie saw how much he missed his son.

"You hungry?" she asked.

Duane brightened. "I could eat."

The large, chrome-finished microwave still looked strange to Jackie in her kitchen, dwarfing the other appliances. She divided the pot pie from the Styrofoam container onto two plates and stuck the first inside. Behind her, she could hear the faint whistling sound of Duane breathing through his injured nose as he sipped his wine. She tried to imagine Hudson—she'd only seen one small photograph of him—then her thoughts turned to what her own child might look like at this age. A pang of grief made her lean forward against the cupboard. "Mason and I tried to have kids," she said quietly. "It just never happened." She paused, staring in at the rotating plate in the glowing chamber, remembering those hopeful years. She had never defined herself as a mother, but the subject was a bruise that wouldn't heal. Sometimes she woke up in the night and felt the presence of a daughter, the pathway of a different life pushing against her own. "I still don't know if it was him or me."

"I'm sorry," Duane said.

After they ate, she and Duane sat side by side on the couch in front of the fire. They talked for a while about Duane's plans for his cabin, the monkey-wrenching that had gone on the summer before, and the old prospectors who still panned for gold up in Hogum Gulch. Then the hypnotic dancing of the flames lulled them into an easy silence. The crackle of the logs mixed with the sound of melting snow dripping from the eaves. Jackie felt her eyelids go heavy, and Duane's leg shifted into hers. Oh hell, why not? she thought, and let her hand fall open against his thigh. Soon his fingers slipped between hers. They were warm and callused, and she felt the bony ridge of his knuckle, familiar somehow, as if she'd known him in another life, or perhaps all men were the same in this particular bone. She thought Duane might kiss her, but the whistling of his breath steadied and slowed, and when she turned he was fast asleep in the firelight, holding her hand.

11

With the last of the equipment loaded out, the landing where Duane camped looked strangely empty. A large round clearing, the mud deeply rutted, the late spring snow long gone, piles of slash ringing the edge. No sign of the skidder or knuckleboom loader or Dixon's bellowing laugh. Tom had given the crew the long weekend off for the Fourth of July Bicentennial celebrations and cleared out most of the equipment. Duane's truck was the last remnant of technology. He looked wistfully at the anchor tree—a tall ponderosa with a curved trunk like a question mark—on which he pissed every morning.

Gingerly, he touched the scab on his nose. He knew he was lucky to have avoided more serious damage, but he still wondered why the woman had stomped on him. He'd woken up the morning after on Jackie's couch with only hazy memories of the fight. Had he accidentally bumped her when he fell along the rail, or had she detected something sexual in his response to her tattoo? It didn't matter, except the injury seemed unjust.

Ah well. Duane had the entire afternoon free. Jackie was working and he had no errands or chores before the weekend's parties. He decided to take a hike, something he had yet to do after three weeks at the logging camp. He made a cheese sandwich, filled his canteen with water, and set off. He walked away from the landing, skirting the clear-cut on a faint game trail into the forest. The Swan Range lifted skyward through breaks in the trees, Stonewall Mountain still white with snow. Duane picked his way down the draw along Halfway Creek. Double-crescent prints and piles of fresh droppings marked the places where deer had stopped to drink. Huckleberry, wild rose, red twinberry, and Oregon grape were in full splendor, their leaves bright and green, flowers blooming. The creek turned east along the face of Ogden Mountain and the landscape changed, opening up into a wash of tumbled granite boulders. Keeping one hand up to protect his nose, Duane scrambled across, ending in a field of bear grass. He stopped and looked back at the glacial till, wondering what forces had brought the huge boulders tumbling down, the tectonic plates and sedimentary layers. He felt a swell of emotion in his own heart, as it reflected the earth's, and was surprised to find tears in his eyes.

Wiping them away, Duane hurried on to Heavy Runner Rock. The huge flat promontory jutted out from the mountainside with a panoramic view of the Blackfoot Valley. Salish Indians had used it as a lookout a hundred years before, when Blackfoot raiding parties followed bison over the hills. Duane walked to the edge and looked down over the patchwork of ranches on the plain. The brown snake of the Blackfoot River twisted between them, heavy with snow runoff and surging at the steep banks. Ogden and Stonewall Mountains faced each other across the valley like two ancient brothers. Ogden was slightly taller, rising more than ten thousand feet, but Stonewall was more impressive, the jagged white turrets of its peak like battlements against the blue sky. In open places, Duane could see the whole of the mountainside sweeping down to the distant river.

The next tract of land to be logged was visible to the west. The trees to be taken were tagged with orange spray paint. Tom's contract was for four million board feet of timber and more than six miles of specified roads—a gut-wrenching amount of clearing. Dirt bikers were already using the new logging roads, roaring over bumps and spraying mud. Duane caught a glimpse of a neon-green fender in the distance, its motor muffled by the breeze. He wondered at how quickly the landscape could change.

The call of a raven interrupted his thoughts. He looked north, wondering which direction he should go. It was strange to see the cliff face above Deadman Draw up close. So often he'd gazed up at it in the distance from outside the Wilderness Bar and in the Food Town parking lot, the striations in the rock like long scratches from a giant bear. He knew that glaciers had formed this landscape thousands of years before, but at times he sensed a volition behind its features more intentional than a shrinking block of ice. He'd asked Dixon—who'd returned to work after Tom paid his bail—if he knew any stories of the creation of the valley, remembering the Paiute myths he'd learned in elementary school in Salt Lake, but Dixon shook his head in irritation, still angry at Duane for abandoning him in the fight. "You've got your own stories," he said. "Jesus and Elvis and all that crap."

Secretly Duane had tried to make up his own, imagining a jet-sized owl plucking trees from the forested floor of the Blackfoot Valley and carrying them in its talons up through the sky to feed the fire of the sun, clearing the great plain. The vision made him feel silly.

Up the trail, Duane found a waterfall tumbling over a rocky cliff into a deep pool in a clearing. The water was clear, and even from high above Duane could see the silver flashes of fish. Red and yellow stones formed a mosaic on the bottom. A huge flat moss-covered rock lay on the far side. The exposed roots of Douglas fir searched for holds on the boggy bank. Duane followed the steep muddy trail down beside the waterfall, clinging to roots for support. The mud slipped out from under his boots and he slid the last stretch, ripping his shirt. He propped himself on his back at the bottom, catching his breath and laughing through his throbbing nose. Mud caked his jeans and elbows. His back hurt. He laughed again. The pool was twenty feet across. Rainbows of sunlight sparkled in the mist where the waterfall crashed down.

Filthy with sweat and dust, Duane walked to the edge of the water and stripped off his clothes. Then he waded into the ice-cold pool. Sucking in his chest then aha-ing out his breath, he went deeper, up to his waist. Finally he sank all the way to his nose for a bone-seizing instant, scrubbing away a week's-worth of dirt. Every molecule of his skin came alive. Hooting, he thrashed out of the water, rubbed his arms wildly, and sat shivering naked in the sun.

The clearing was protected on all sides by the dense forest and the cliff. It reminded Duane of the enchanted places in the stories he used to read to Hudson before bed from an old book of fables he'd found on a job site. Secret gardens in magic kingdoms. The boy would cuddle up against his chest and listen raptly. Duane hated to think of his son going to bed alone—or, even worse, Pete reading to him. Dismayed by the thought, Duane took the cheese sandwich from his pocket and tossed the plastic wrapping aside. He chewed slowly, tasting little because of his clogged nose.

A solitary Doug fir stood out from the others on the far side of the clearing. A massive tree, its gnarled crown was flung across the sky. It was the biggest he'd ever seen, easily a hundred feet tall and five wide at the base. The thick, regal trunk was rod-straight and the upper branches looked like the roots at Duane's feet, reaching for purchase in the heavens. He set down his sandwich and approached the tree. The needles were a deep, shimmering blue and he felt humbled in the cool of its shade—a small furless animal at the foot of an old king. Dry brown needles carpeted the ground between the thick, knobby roots that split and buckled the earth. He reached out to touch the trunk and something sharp poked his toe. He looked down to see a crooked altar made of deer and rabbit bones.

Duane's breath caught. He stepped back. The small altar's bones were tied together with twine and arranged in three tiers, something menacing and disoriented in the construction. The ground around the base was blackened by rings of ash. Had someone been setting off fireworks? Fear seized Duane. His eyes flicked to the surrounding forest. He searched for shadows, any sign of movement, suddenly aware of his nakedness. He'd thought he'd hiked a long way, but who knew, maybe there was a road nearby or an encampment of some kind. The same monkey wrencher who'd sabotaged the skidder the year before. Several pieces of detritus Duane recognized from the logging camp lay atop the altar: a drill bit, a small piece of a tooth blade. Other pieces of sharp metal were strewn around in the dirt.

"Who's there?" he called.

The words echoed back to him. Squirrels chittered overhead. The waterfall roared. Duane quickly dressed, leaving the remains of his sandwich behind. The clearing had taken on a menacing character, no longer the enchanted garden. He scrambled up the cliff and paused, looking back across the pool in case someone was following. Then he hurried on, propelled by something deep and primal. Duane took the direct route across the clear-cut. The broken expanse stretched for a mile below Flesher Pass, shaming him as he struggled to jog across the churned mud, around splintered stumps and tangles of broken branches. He paused in the middle of the cut to catch his breath. No birds sang here, no insects whined around his ears. The landscape was so barren and lifeless that he could hear his heart beating. He put his hands on his knees. When he looked up, he saw movement in his peripheral vision. He ducked, crouching among the piles of slash, but it was only an elk, picking its way along the edge of the clear-cut toward the drainage of Halfway Creek. Relieved, Duane slowly stood.

The elk paused and raised its head. Eight tines rose from its rack, looking to Duane like more sky-facing roots. The animal was tall and noble, with thick brown fur around its collar. It sniffed the air with its black nose. Then it turned and stared directly at Duane. He looked back into the impassive brown eyes, feeling like he owed it some explanation for the wreckage he'd helped cause. The elk shook its rack from side to side, snorted, and bounded back into the trees.

12

"I don't know if you come to see me or the microwave," Jackie teased, watching Duane lean over and fiddle with the controls. The bandage was gone from his nose and the bruise around his eye had faded, so he no longer looked like a battered welterweight, much to her relief. He'd brought over a pair of frozen dinners and was attempting to heat them while she mixed a bucket of punch for tomorrow's Fourth of July picnic. The punch was mostly vodka, but it also involved chopping up melons, lemons, and oranges, a chore that annoyed her. "Shit-fire," she cursed, a spray of lemon juice stinging her eye.

The microwave beeped as Duane started the timer. He'd been preoccupied since he arrived, hardly commenting on her punch or the Bicentennial festivities already beginning in town, and now he chewed his lip before he spoke. "What do you think about all the logging we're doing?"

"What do you mean?" Jackie answered, leaning under the faucet to rinse her eye.

"I was hiking today, looking at all we've done and all we're going to do, and I . . . I don't know . . ." Duane trailed off.

Jackie dried her hands. She could tell the question was truly bothering him. "I think people need to cut down trees to put roofs over their heads, just like they need to hunt animals to eat. There's just too damn many people these days. If it were up to me, I'd rip out the highway and make them come on horseback like they used to. Then they could leave these mountains alone." She paused, feeling Duane's eyes searching her. "When I was a girl, it was all miners in Lincoln, then the lumber mill opened and it was all loggers, now it's mostly tourists. I don't know what will come next."

"So you don't think it's bad?" Again Jackie saw in Duane the lost boy trying to make sense of the world.

"No, I don't think it's bad," she answered. "I used to, and Mason and some others do, but now I see it as people just trying to get by. If you don't cut wood, someone's going to be cold, and if you don't want a lot of people freezing to death or going hungry, that's the way it is. Everyone thinks they deserve a comfortable life. And maybe they do." Jackie knelt and opened the cupboard by the stove, searching for the sugar. She was surprised by her own soliloquy; it was different than what she would've said five years before. When she was married to Mason, she'd believed that every remaining acre of wild forest in Montana should be protected, and the punishment for killing an endangered animal should be the same as for killing a person. Now here she was carrying water for Tom McCall. She shook her head and pulled out the sugar tin, dismayed to find several tiny pellets of mouse shit on top. Quickly, she brushed them off.

"That's good." Duane was visibly relieved. "I guess I'd never noticed when we were working and the whole crew was out there and all the machines, but today, with everyone gone, it was hard to see."

"You do tear hell out of a forest." Jackie poured two cups of sugar into the punch and stirred it briskly. "But trees grow back. It was even worse when I was a girl. No regulations at all. Big operations would come in and just raze miles and miles and then clear out. It looked like a war zone." She paused. "My dad worked just about every kind of job there is in this valley. Mining, logging, construction, running cattle, delivering mail. He never stuck to any of them until the post office, and we never had much, but it was always enough. I think there's something to that. You take just what you need to get by."

"He ran cattle?" Duane asked. "Never had any problems with them?"

"With the cows? No. But he wasn't much of a horseman. I think that's what retired him."

"I'd like to have met him," Duane said seriously, and Jackie smiled to herself, thinking she would've liked that, too.

After dinner, Duane dumped the foil trays in the trash and Jackie poured them both a glass of punch. They clinked the glasses together. "To two hundred years," she said.

"Seems like a helluva long time," Duane answered, taking a sip and coughing. "What'd you put in this?"

"Vodka. You're going to have to learn how to drink if you plan to stay on in Montana."

Duane took a longer drink and wiped his eyes. He breathed deep, as if coming to some decision, squared his shoulders, and stepped toward her. He set his glass on the counter and placed his hands on her hips. His fingers found their way beneath the hem of her shirt and began inquisitively exploring her waistline. Surprised by this sudden bravery, Jackie turned her shoulder into his chest, pushing him back.

"Half a glass and already you're pawing at me?" she asked.

Duane stopped, shamefaced, and Jackie felt a rush of remorse. She pulled him back toward her.

"It's all right. Let's just try not to make a mess of this."

Nodding, Duane leaned down and kissed her lips. His were chapped and clumsy, as Jackie had expected, tasting of vodka, urgently seeking hers each time she pulled away. The scruff on his chin scratched her cheek and she smelled the earthen, piney scent of his skin beneath his cologne. Slowly they turned in a circle and Jackie found herself pressed back against the oven. Duane had to lean way down to kiss her. His hands trembled as he swept the bandanna from her hair and ran his fingers through the silver-streaked black, as if it were something he'd wanted to do for a long time. She pulled her head back and smiled up at him. "Bedroom," she said.

Duane stammered in agreement and turned red.

Outside, it was getting dark and the whining bang of the first fireworks sounded down the street. They'd be going off all weekend, Jackie knew. A great patriotic revel in the wake of Watergate and Vietnam. Here by the fire you're safe, she thought, remembering her grandmother's words as she led Duane down the hall to her bedroom. She closed the blinds and turned on the small lamp by her bed, casting a mellow golden glow. Lighting was the most important thing, Jackie knew, in a moment like this. She smoothed the comforter while Duane hung awkwardly in the doorway. He'd never been in her bedroom before, and she could tell he viewed the threshold as a significant frontier. "Come on." She patted the bed and sat down. Duane approached wide-eyed.

"I haven't been with anyone in a while," he said softly, sitting beside her.

"Me neither."

"Really it was mostly only my wife."

Seeing his expression, Jackie felt a wave of tenderness. "That's all right." She scooted close to him. She unbuttoned her shirt and shrugged it off her shoulders, then unsnapped her bra. Duane opened his mouth but no sound came out. Jackie touched his chest and could feel his heart beating all the way up through her arm. His fingers tugged helplessly at his belt buckle. "Slow down," she said.

Grinning with embarrassment, Duane stood and freed the

clasp, then shucked his jeans off his bony hips and raised his shirt over his head. He stood awkwardly silhouetted in the light from the hall. Jackie took off her own pants and held out her hand. She pulled his long body down beside her, feeling his muscles loosen with the palpable relief of being held. He sighed deeply. More fireworks exploded outside and the room was briefly bathed in green light. Jackie smiled, thinking of two hundred American years leading up to this moment: naked in her bed with a man named Duane.

"What's funny?" he asked.

"Happy Fourth of July." Jackie swung her leg across his hips and rose on top of him. Duane reached up toward her. He shivered and she took his hand and looked down into his blue eyes, which contained joy and grief in equal measure, all the things he'd seen and those he wished he hadn't, the inexpressible totality of a person's time on earth.

AFTERWARD, THEY LAY TOGETHER in the lingering glow of the summer sunset. One of Duane's long legs was still thrown across Jackie's hips. She felt a calm and building strength inside herself, like a wave drawing back from the shore. She thought of her life—who she'd been and who she'd become. She listened to her heart slow inside her chest, and studied the way her body had changed. Her wide strong hips, the small rolls of fat on her stomach, the purple veins and thickly corded muscles in her calves from two decades of carrying plates. Things she'd hated when she was younger. Now they held her together and connected her to the earth. To a force more solid than whatever changes came to the Blackfoot Valley; one that had been here before she arrived, and would be long after she was gone. Her body, her land, what the Reiki master had called her soul, she knew it only as home.

Duane rolled up onto his elbow and looked down at her. His

long face was quiet in the dim light. "It was a lucky thing for me to find this place," he said.

"It does have its vistas." Jackie thought of standing alone on the edge of the Glory Hole Mine, looking across at the white moose in the snow.

"It has you," he answered.

13

Fireworks exploded above the treetops across the Blackfoot Valley. Cascading shimmers of red, white, and blue sparks falling on the last pink glow of sunset on Stonewall Mountain. Followed by obnoxious, whining streaks as a new round was set off to burst over the horizon. Ted Kaczynski sat on a picnic table in the far corner of Hooper Park, tired, hungry, and alone. He rubbed his forehead, leaving red marks above his eyes, trying to force away the throbbing pain behind his temples. He'd spent the day hunting without luck on the far side of Stemple Pass, and then suffered the horror of the new clear-cut on his path home.

The Fourth of July festivities had drawn him into town. Fresh salvos of green and gold lit the sky above Lincoln High School. Screaming children ran across the playground on the far side of the baseball field with ketchup-smeared faces, waving miniature American flags. The detritus of the town cookout—folding tables, beer cans, paper plates—littered the outfield, and distant drunken voices shouted back and forth. In the seven years since building his cabin, Ted had come to know Lincoln's secrets. The parking lots where Pastor Younger and Joni McCall met for their late-night trysts, Ernie Floyd and Cecil Frazier coupling on the floor of Ernie's hunting cabin below the head of the albino moose, and Cecil's father, Bud, who rubbed shoe polish on his cheeks and pretended to be Blackfoot for the tourists who passed through his trading post in the summer. The town's picturesque face was a lie, hiding the rot at the core of every American community.

A parade of classic cars crawled up the highway. Ted saw the exact-model Chevrolet his father had driven during his childhood, freshly waxed, with the high rounded wheel wells and silver zephyr flying atop the hood. He heard the steady groan of the engine and smelled the exhaust. The flag-waving children sprinted over to watch. Drivers honked the horns and their wives waved handkerchiefs out the windows. A sweet cloying smell rose over the park. Ted sniffed. It took him a moment to place it above the exhaust: apple pie. Of course.

Darkly, Ted remembered his first season in the Montana woods. His only neighbor was Ed Youderian, a craggy old prospector as silent as the mountain. That summer spent building his cabin was the best of Ted's life. Youderian taught him rudimentary hunting and trapping skills, and on rare talkative evenings told stories from when game was plentiful in Lincoln—a ten-day stretch in his childhood when he and his brothers caught five hundred trout in the Big Blackfoot River. When winter set in, Youderian's family took him away to a nursing home in Helena, and Hutch Smith moved in with his barking dogs and constant chatter. Ted grimaced in the dusk.

A chill breeze accompanied the dark of night, bringing Ted deeper into his anger. The bomb had barely maimed the security guard. "Minor injuries" the newspaper had reported, blaming a disgruntled ex-student. Ted had hoped to blow off a hand or blind someone, at least. He'd been wanting to hurt someone for years. An M-80 exploded in the street and Ted was brought back to William James Hall as a sixteen-year-old freshman at Harvard, in the basement beneath the hot spotlight. "What do you believe?" the experimental study's interrogators asked. "What role do you want to play in the world?" Ridiculous questions to proffer to a teenager. The interrogators were solicitous at first, then turned hostile, tearing apart Ted's answers, berating and ridiculing him until he shook with helpless rage and hot tears fell down his cheeks.

And now technology was tracking him. New roads cut into the wilderness around his cabin, the hack and roar of logging machinery tearing up the earth. Computer labs, logging companies, marketing firms—the whole evil mechanism. The grocery store was more crowded every week and the high-pitched beeps of the new electronic cash registers were like needles in his brain. Cars full of tourists lined up at the gas station. There was no escaping the clamor, the idiotic celebration.

The parade ended and the children ran off across the empty road. Ted stood and brushed the dirt from his pants, trying to ignore the hunger pains gnawing at his stomach. The only work he'd had that summer was a brief stint clearing brush for the Company Ranch. He was nearly out of money. He considered writing his mother asking for help, and the thought made him angrier still. He imagined his parents sitting in the backyard of his childhood home in Chicago, squinting to see these same colors through the smog.

Moving quickly down backstreets, Ted saw license plates from as far away as Michigan, where he'd gone to grad school, the most miserable years of his life. Tom McCall's shiny new pickup was parked on the corner. Ted slipped the hunting knife from his belt and stabbed the front tire, wrenching the blade through the inner lining. He grinned at the hiss of escaping air. Then he skirted the west side of town, glimpsing the church's swooping white roof in the moonlight and a crowd of revelers gathered on the lawn. The women wore low-cut blouses and their cheeks were flushed from alcohol. Ted felt heat rise in his chest. He gritted his teeth and turned south on a game trail away from the streetlights, moving quickly in the darkness, his feet instinctively picking their way over roots. He pushed past a sapling and a branch snapped back and hit him in the face. Furious, he turned and kicked the offending trunk, cursing until it broke. Breathing hard, he continued on.

After another mile, he saw the faint glow of Hutch's trailer through the trees. He kept well back in the woods, not wanting to wake the huskies, whom he hated for their barking, and made his way to the massive cage hidden in the forest. Ever since he'd seen Hutch and Mason sneak the bear onto Hutch's property he'd been coming back to see it every night, captivated by the animal's ruthless power. Up close, the bear was a reminder of the true nature of existence: harsh, uncaring, immense. Ted paused. He could hear the *thud* of his own heart. The bear was the first real killer he'd ever encountered. He wanted to be a killer.

Unsettled by the fireworks, the grizzly paced back and forth, limping on its bandaged paw. It stopped and stared into the darkness, leaning its great head back to sniff as Ted approached. Ted felt the small hairs rise on the nape of his neck. He had to force himself to keep moving, so strong was the instinct to turn and run. "Hello, old friend," he whispered. The bear shifted its weight and leaned forward to watch him through the bars. Moonlight glinted in its small golden eyes. Its nose twitched. For the first time, Ted could tell it was nervous. Frightened, even, of the inexplicable explosions in the night sky. It growled and swatted at Ted like he was a bothersome appetizer.

"I would have brought you something," Ted said apologetically, showing the bear his empty hands. "I didn't eat today, either." The bear stared at him. The labored intensity of its breath was audible for a moment in the silence between explosions. Then silver sparks showered the treetops and revealed its eyes in the center of its wide brown face. Two glimmering pools reflecting Ted's fear.

Chicago O'Hare International
Airport, May 1979

Edie Piñeiro was late. She dashed from the cab into O'Hare, through the terminal, across the mezzanine, and up the escalator with her suitcase banging against her knee. American Airlines Flight 444, the daily to Washington National, was scheduled to depart at 9:30 and it was already 9:10. Covering the library convention was the kind of crap assignment her editor always gave her, but if she missed the flight, she'd miss the convention, and then there'd be no assignments at all. Sucking air, she ran past the food concessions, the cocktail bars, and the numbered gates, until she found her own. The last passengers were filing down the jetway. "Is it too late to check this?" she asked, panting, as she came to a stop at the gate.

The red-haired stewardess smiled at Edie's discomfiture, quickly wrote out a claim tag, handed half to her, and fixed the other to her bag. "We'll make sure it gets there," she said. Edie noticed that her smile had the same forced, lingering quality as her ex-husband's, like a car stuck between gears.

Edie passed through the metal detector and onto the jetway. At the bottom, she paused to watch the conveyor belt carrying luggage into the cargo hold. Already most of the bags were inside, and she saw her suitcase along with a pair of airmail packages. One of the packages caught her eye. It was compact, the size of a shoebox, and she could tell that the sides were made from wood or metal—unusual for a piece of mail. The address was written in large spidery capital letters, visible even at a distance. Something about the package reminded her of the desperate, rambling letters her brother had sent home from Vietnam. She shook her head and boarded the plane.

Takeoff was smooth, and Edie leaned her forehead against the window to watch the suburbs of Chicago give way to the southern end of Lake Michigan. The patchwork of towns and farms blurred beneath her and Edie began to doze. She was nearly asleep when she heard a loud thud below in the cargo hold. At first she thought a piece of luggage had fallen, and hoped it wasn't hers. Then she smelled something acrid. Edie blinked her eyes open, looked around, and was horrified to see smoke streaming from the rear of the cabin. The woman beside her screamed. Men shouted back and forth, straining against their seat belts as they half rose to turn toward the smoke. The red-haired stewardess ran down the center aisle with her hand over her mouth. "Stay calm and remain seated," another stewardess called from the front of the plane. The smoke billowed forward, obscuring Edie's vision. She coughed, feeling a wild rush of panic. Her mind replayed the recent string of airline hijackings she'd seen on the news. It can't end this way, going to a library convention, she thought. Immediately she realized how ridiculous this protest was, as if death cared for an instant where she was going.

An oxygen mask popped from the panel above her seat. Edie stared at the dangling yellow cup and plastic baggie. Then she snapped into action, fitting the mask over her nose and mouth, pulling the rubber straps behind her ears, and turning to help the woman beside her. The red-haired stewardess ducked inside the cockpit and slammed the door.

The captain's voice crackled over the intercom. "Please put on your masks and assume crash positions. We've been cleared for emergency landing at Dulles. We'll have you on the ground in twenty-five minutes." Crash positions? Edie wanted to scream. Twenty-five minutes was an eternity. Couldn't they land in a fucking cornfield? The plane was on fire. She was shocked to find herself nesting her head between her folded arms. She braced against the back of her seat, knowing it would do nothing to save her.

In the strange, private intimacy of breathing between her knees, she was reminded of the hours she'd spent hiding from her brother as a girl. He'd been unpredictable and violent when they were children, and often tormented her. She'd stopped speaking to him as soon as he left home. She never responded to the disturbing, ink-blotched letters he'd written her *from Vietnam. Had he known he was going to die? She hoped not. Edie remained motionless, not wanting to disrupt whatever fragile equilibrium held the plane in the sky.*

Over Dulles, the plane began to descend, shuddering as the landing gear disengaged. The descent seemed endless, but finally, when Edie was sure she could take no more, the wheels hit the tarmac hard enough to jar open the overhead bin. Several bags spilled out. One bounced off Edie's shoulder and she raised her head, coughing and crying, oblivious to the pain. The brakes roared. The plane slowed. Memories of her brother were replaced by those of afternoons in Lincoln Park with her mother. The woman beside her raised her head and looked around the hazy cabin, her face insectile in the yellow mask.

A hysteric giddiness settled over the passengers. They had been spared. The terrible thing for which they were so unprepared had not happened to them. Edie's heart slowed. Then she froze. An elderly wrist dangled from the seat rest in front of her. But the man had merely passed out.

The plane skidded to a stop. The front and rear doors opened, releasing clouds of smoke. Wiping her eyes, Edie stood and joined the crush of passengers pushing for the rear doors. Midday sun shone on the tarmac—the most beautiful pavement Edie had ever seen. Ambulances, fire trucks, and a fleet of press vans waited at the bottom of the airstairs. Cameras flashed, momentarily blinding Edie. Firemen and paramedics ran past her. Women cried loudly. She moved away from the scrum and retrieved her notebook, sure there was a story behind the near-catastrophe. The smoke still streaming from the cargo hold caught her eye. There was something off about it, reminding her of fireworks and the Fourth of July. What was it? Edie stopped and stared, and then it hit her: The smoke was green. Deep, verdant, inexplicable green.

MASON

How shall I know when it is time to throw
bombs?. . . when the very last wolves
on this continent are trapped and caged
for captive breeding (as the remaining
Condors were, not so long ago), will
it finally be time to throw bombs?
Or will it be too late?

—ANONYMOUS,
EARTH FIRST! WILD ROCKIES REVIEW

14

High on Silver King Mountain, Mason trailed Hutch through the dense underbrush. He watched the older man carefully, as he always did. The only time the manic tension left Hutch's body was when he was tracking. He was silent and loose, his slight, wiry frame bent forward, one hand drifting over the leaves. He paused, gauging the early afternoon sun. In his friend, Mason saw all that he wanted to be: attuned to nature, driven by a deep inner purpose, unafraid. It frustrated him that he'd spent the last decade trying to become what the older man simply was.

"Listen." Hutch raised his hand. Mason stopped. Sure enough, over the rustle of the spring breeze and the roar of Landers Fork Creek in the canyon far below, came the faint *clink* of metal on metal. The sound made Mason's ankle throb, imagining the snap of metal teeth. He never understood how exactly Hutch found the wounded animals. Tracking was part of it, certainly, and Hutch often joked how much easier it was to track trappers than animals, but there was more to it than that. They could be driving for miles down an unmarked dirt road and suddenly without warning he'd tell Mason to stop, and discover a badger in a snare not fifty yards away. Life in Montana had cracked the foundation of Mason's rational upbringing. At boarding school and Dartmouth, he'd been taught the primacy of the scientific method: Only what could be observed and measured was real. Watching his friend, he saw intuition, magic. It was like Hutch could sense the suffering of animals on the wind.

The *clink* of metal grew louder as they descended into the draw. Mason favored his bad leg, searching for footholds on the steep decline. The doctor at the hospital in Helena had set the bone improperly after Mason's accident, leaving him with a permanent limp. At the bottom of the draw, a foot-wide current of snowmelt threaded down to the creek. Mason's boots sank in the soft mud. House-sized granite boulders, exposed by torrents of meltwater, lined the sloping sides. Lichen covered the boulders' faces, and gnarled, opportunistic bushes grew from crevices. The first spring flowers bloomed on the south slope. Picking his way through the mud, Mason saw animal signs all around: jumbled tracks, scat, a tuft of fur caught in a wild rosebush. It was obvious why the trapper had chosen this place: every kind of animal came here to drink. Ahead, on the edge of a copse of aspen, Hutch froze and drew in his breath. "You're not going to believe this," he murmured, as Mason came up beside him.

The wolf was black. As black as the charred trees on the opposite ridge, the kind of dense, impenetrable black that swallows light, a shadow inside a shadow. Big, too, a four- or five-year-old male, 130 pounds at least, the biggest Mason had seen. Separated from its pack, or packless, one of the rare loners that sometimes wandered down from Canada. Mason's jurisdiction covered nearly four thousand square miles, including the entirety of the Blackfoot Valley—an impossible expanse to patrol—and he was often astonished by what he saw. Before coming to Montana, he'd thought of the West as a dwindling dream, the last slivers of wild country in desperate need of protection. What he'd discovered was immensity. Overwhelming in its scope and power, and when he looked into the wolf's yellow eyes, he had the same teetering feeling he had looking north into the Bob Marshall Wilderness, as if he might be swallowed up and emerge as some primitive version of himself, naked and fighting to survive.

The trap was an offset design, with a small gap between the steel jaws to allow blood flow to the wolf's caught paw. This prevented the paw from numbing and the animal from chewing it off. Companies had the audacity to market such traps as humane. But the wolf had chewed, and bone showed through the matted fur and blood. The sight sickened Mason, even though he'd seen it dozens of times before.

"It's okay," Hutch murmured, carefully removing his rucksack and inching forward with his right hand extended to be sniffed, as one would to an unfamiliar dog. "We're not going to hurt you." The wolf pulled its lips back from long white teeth. Its yellow eyes were wide, frightened, yet still they held the implacability Mason had come to associate with the forest. Processing without judgment, only the calm evaluation of what was danger and what was food.

Slowly, Mason unslung the tranquilizer gun from his shoulder, calculating the dosage in his mind. Since the wolf was so large and fairly young, it needed a heavy dose, but too much of the sedative combination could kill it. Too little, and it would wake up in the back of the truck. He opened the gun case, removed the proper dart, and loaded it in the chamber. Then he straightened, lifting the gunsight to his eye.

"Wait," Hutch said. Hutch was now in the center of the clearing, only a few feet from the wolf. He crouched down, his hand still raised, and gazed at the animal the way Mason's mother had looked up at Christ crucified on the cross during Sunday Mass at their parish in Charlestown. Prayer, devotion, sacrifice—for Hutch, wild animals were God. The wolf was so still it hardly seemed to breathe. All around them the woods were silent, paused, like the space between breaths. A tingle ran down Mason's spine. Slowly, Hutch turned, and there were tears in his eyes. "Go ahead," he said.

Standing back so the force of the fired dart wouldn't cause injury, Mason braced the tranquilizer gun against his shoulder. The wolf hardly seemed to know he was there. Its attention was fixed solely on Hutch in its own kind of communion, but as soon as Mason's finger touched the trigger it turned, and the light in its yellow eyes was so strong that for a moment Mason froze. He thought of his own dog, Molly, waiting for him at home, and beyond her to the tens of thousands of years of canine and human interaction, first as predator and prey, then as allies, and now as pets, or fugitives like wolves and coyotes trying to escape extermination. Mason felt shame, as he often did, at being a part of the human race. Then he pulled the trigger.

The dart lodged in the large muscle behind the wolf's right shoulder. The wolf jerked and nipped at the pink tailpiece, but almost instantly its reactions slowed. It sat back and closed its mouth, looking confused. Then it tried to walk forward and keeled over. It shook its head. The long pink tongue moved within its mouth, searching for moisture. It blinked, still watching Mason, then slowly closed its eyes.

The two men approached cautiously, knowing an animal could appear to be knocked out, then snap awake for a last desperate attack. Slowly, Mason knelt beside the wolf. Its breath was shallow and regular. In sleep, it was somehow diminished. A humped form, a mounded rug, the tactile, kinetic menace gone. Mason studied the small scar below its eye, the missing patch of fur on its chest. Clearly it had been in fights—fights it should have won due to its size, though its solitude suggested it had not. Mason felt a pang of affinity and placed his hand on the coarse outer fur of the wolf's shoulder. He remembered his classmates in boarding school, their status determined by the carefully loosened knots of their ties, cliques of preening fools with no more to offer the world than the misplaced confidence that came from their last names. Mason had spent his youth alternately fighting them and wanting to be accepted by them. The only times he'd truly felt at home was on hunting trips in Maine with his uncle.

"Let's go," Hutch said, interrupting his thoughts.

Nodding, Mason straightened and pressed down on the springs on both sides of the trap, opening the jaws. Hutch pulled the wolf's leg free. Mason exhaled, feeling a palpable relief, as if a knot inside himself had been loosened. Hutch removed the folded tarp from his rucksack and the two men each took a side. They spread the tarp out beside the wolf, then dragged the animal onto it. Watching each other carefully, they lifted this makeshift sling. They'd rescued many animals this way, none more impressive than the two-hundred-pound juvenile grizzly they'd found on Strawberry Ridge three years before, and moved in unison, used to the awkward weight. They carried the wolf from the aspen copse and up the steep embankment, straining not to slip in the mud. Once they were back on the game trial, the going was easier and they moved swiftly back to Mason's truck.

A NEW RADIO COLLAR from the regional Forest Service office in Denver bounced between Mason and Hutch on the bench seat in the cab as Mason navigated down the rough, rocky switchbacks. The collars were part of a new initiative to track threatened populations, and ironically had arrived from the same address that once sent boxes of Compound 1080 for poison bait stations. Mason was fascinated by the collar and had been taking it with him wherever he went, fiddling with the antennae and receiver, testing its range, and teaching himself how to triangulate the signal's azimuths. It represented the agency's first timid steps away from extermination toward study. Mason was enthralled. With the data from the collar, he imagined being able to concentrate his efforts on high-use areas, clearing out traps and poachers, and creating a safe corridor for predators across the Blackfoot Valley from the Big Belt Mountains to the Bob Marshall Wilderness.

"I hope you're not thinking of putting that thing on him," Hutch said, reading his mind.

"Then we can track where he goes and how he re-acclimates. We'll know if something happens to him." He nodded back at the sleeping wolf lying under the tarp in the truck bed.

"Something's going to happen to all of us," Hutch answered. "You can't put a collar on a wolf. It's no dog. You'll turn all this into a zoo." He gestured to the wild landscape passing on the other side of the windshield.

Mason went quiet. He respected Hutch's opinion but couldn't stop imagining the possibilities. Selfishly, he knew he simply wanted to maintain a connection to the wolf. He hated that he never saw the animals they rescued again. He wanted to be acknowledged in some way. To be thanked somehow. Sometimes, when he was hiking, he glimpsed a coyote or bobcat and thought it recognized him, but he was never sure, and the animal always fled back into the woods.

The axle of the truck clanked against the shackles. Mason drove slowly, checking the brakes before every decline. He'd been a wary driver ever since his accident. He still didn't know who cut his brake lines. The Carters were the most openly vicious ranchers in the valley, but he and Hutch had made more enemies than he could count, and it could've been anyone, even the well-heeled foreman at the Company Ranch. Mason's predecessor, Walt Harwood, had written a grand total of twenty citations in his thirty-year career, and spent most of his time killing whatever coyotes he was asked to. When it became clear Mason wouldn't follow his example, the ranchers and trappers turned on him, joined by the old-time poachers. Mason always kept his state-issued .45 in the glove box.

Signs of an old logging operation lined the shoulder: blackened

slash piles, rusted pieces of chain, steel rivets. Plus the usual shotgun shells and broken glass. Mason retained his outsider's bereave-
ment at discovering litter in wild places. He'd grown up used to
the trash-strewn subways of Boston, but out here it struck him as
a heretical violation. If the wolf wasn't in the back, he would have
pulled over and cleaned up. Hutch leaned forward in the passenger
seat with his chin out like a hound, seeming to sniff the air, his pale
blue eyes dancing from side to side, scanning the horizon for the
trapper. They'd rescued hundreds of animals together, and were
keenly aware of the danger. Far below in the valley, Mason saw a
single twin-engine prop plane waiting on the Elk Trail Landing
Strip, where some of the larger ranches had supplies flown in. Sunlight glinted on its white wings.

"You ever see a wolf that big before?" Mason asked, to break
the tense silence.

Hutch shook his head. "I found a gray poisoned on the Missouri that was close."

"I didn't know they got that black. No wonder people are
scared of them."

"People are fools," Hutch answered shortly.

The switchbacks ended and they came to the plank bridge
over Landers Fork Creek. Slowing the truck over the rough-hewn
boards, Mason looked down at his watch: it had taken fifteen minutes to carry the wolf to the truck and thirty to drive down the
mountain. The sedatives would last for an hour, an hour and a half
at most. "We need to give him another dose," he said, pulling over.
"Be all kinds of hell if he wakes up in town."

Two doses were safe, but no more. Hutch nodded. "I'll do it."
He collected the syringe from the kit behind the seat, and both
men exited the truck. Mason didn't want to miss any opportunity
to see the black wolf. As a boy, he'd dreamt of living with wolves
in the Yukon, and when Hutch pulled back the tarp he felt the
same surge of excitement, though with sadness also, for he knew

the animal's existence would be a lonely one, pursued and harassed. Hutch laid his hand on the wolf's side and Mason watched the hand rise and fall. There was something otherworldly in the wolf's blackness. Most of the animals Mason dealt with were on the spectrum of brown or gray. He could sense the fear such emissaries of night had elicited in the early settlers, trying to survive in a landscape they couldn't control.

"Don't worry, this won't hurt," Hutch said, and plunged the syringe into the heavy muscle of the wolf's shoulder, opposite where Mason had fired the dart. It twitched, then went still. "Let's keep moving," Hutch said, pulling out the syringe.

"Something wrong?" Mason asked when they were back in the truck. Generally, after they rescued an animal, Hutch chattered nonstop with excitement.

Hutch pursed his lips and looked out the window. "It's just a feeling."

"About the wolf?"

Hutch shook his head. "No. Like something is wrong. I hardly slept last night. I've been chasing my own tail trying to figure it out." He ran his hand over his close-cropped gray hair and grinned. "Maybe I'm just getting old."

Mason himself was thirty-nine, a concerning and nebulous age. He was also divorced, living alone thousands of miles from his family, and spending most of his time with a renegade unlicensed veterinarian. Both men had arrived in Lincoln in 1969, during the summer of Woodstock and the moon landing. Mason as a newly hired ranger, fresh from a posting in the Sierra National Forest outside Yosemite. Hutch was fleeing from a series of confrontations with Animal Control in Tucson. He and Mason formed an alliance based on dreams of protecting the valley. Hutch through his animal sanctuary, and Mason determined to restore predators—and balance—to the Montana wilderness.

The tall log gate bearing the Circle C brand of the Company

Ranch passed on the right. The Company was the largest ranch in the Blackfoot Valley, totaling thirty-seven thousand acres with ten miles of Blackfoot riverfront, far more than any person should own. Mason slowed for the last two miles into Lincoln. Most days, he drove through town four or five times, due to his house and the ranger station being on opposite sides, but never did the mile-long stretch of buildings seem so long as when he had a knocked-out animal hidden in the back. Jackie had urged him to be careful, and he'd tried for a while, for her. A pang of longing gripped him as they passed the Ponderosa Café.

"Shit," Hutch said, pointing ahead through the windshield. "School's getting out."

A line of children in brightly colored backpacks waited below the blinking yellow traffic light in the center of town. Mr. Didriksen, the retired hotel owner and town crossing guard, stood with them at the curb in his orange safety vest, holding up a stop sign. Mason felt his hands go slick with sweat as he pressed down on the brake. The children filed in front of the truck, pausing to stare up at Mason through the windshield with the awed curiosity children reserved for all men in uniform. He drew his lips back into the rictus of a grin. Hutch, likewise grinning cadaverously, swiveled in the seat so he could keep one eye on the mounded tarp in back.

"Sure is a beautiful day," Mr. Didriksen called.

"Bluebird spring." Mason tipped his hat. The last of the children—a runny-nosed little boy in a red sweatshirt—dawdled, and Mason imagined the wolf erupting from under the tarp, leaping from the truck bed, and clamping its jaws around his neck. As soon as the boy was out of the highway, Mason shifted the truck into gear and drove on, letting his breath out in a *whoosh* while Hutch chuckled softly in the passenger seat.

15

With his beard shaved and his hair cut, wearing an ill-fitting department-store suit, Ted looked like an intense accountant. He sat beneath the TV in a bar outside the bus station in Rockford, Illinois, picking at the raw skin around his nails and trying not to let the fury show on his face.

Grainy footage showed Flight 444 on the tarmac, green smoke billowing from the front and rear exits, ambulances and fire trucks flashing their lights below the wings. A short, harried woman named Edie Piñeiro was being interviewed by a blond newscaster. "It was awful, terrifying. There was a bang and the oxygen masks came down. We thought we were going to die, but we didn't." Her disheveled face broke into a wide grin.

They had survived. All of them. Ted stared up at the screen in disgust, the ginger ale at his elbow growing warm. He'd spent a year designing the bomb, hand-made the altimeter using a modi-fied barometer, wired it painstakingly inside a carved wooden box, sealed it with layer after layer of epoxy, and traveled more than a thousand miles to mail it. All for nothing.

The bartender paused from drying a pint glass. "That's why I don't fly," he said, nodding up at the TV. He was a heavyset Polish man, his snub nose lined with the burst capillaries of an alcoholic, much like Ted's own father. "My car's broke down enough times that I don't trust no machine to take me up in the sky."

As if he had anywhere to go. Ted dug the nail of his index finger into the pad of his thumb. He wondered why people like the bartender didn't simply walk into traffic. He could see the shape of his life—pouring the same drinks, telling the same jokes, going home to his ugly wife, and staring at the TV for hours before doing it all over again. He'd be better off dead. Ted had felt this way himself in Ann Arbor in the sordid idiocy of the sixties, trying to teach calculus to drugged-out hippies, dismissed by his intellectually inferior peers, awash in a culture of incompetence. Listening to his roommates having sex through the walls, he was plagued by bizarre, uncontrollable fantasies. Suicide seemed like the only option. He even tested the beam in his room with a leather belt. But then he realized that if he was ready to die, he could do anything. He could kill someone else instead of himself. This idea saved him, sustained him through three more years of teaching as he set aside money to buy his land. Then he'd rid the world of the people he hated, the arrogant fools degrading the human condition.

Ten years had passed, and still he'd failed to remove even one. Smoke, smoke, and more smoke. It was green from the barium nitrate that he'd mixed with the incendiaries. All winter, he'd imagined a plane falling from the sky in a roil of flame and green smoke, the image replayed on every news station in America, showing the audience that their technology was not safe, the infrastructure would not hold. The green smoke was meant to be a rallying cry for the environmentalist agitators already blowing up dams and spiking trees across the West. A spark to light the fuse of bigger violence. Now here he was in a Chicago dive with two hours to kill before his westbound bus departed, and the plane was safely on the tarmac. He took a sip of soda, feeling trapped. He knew it was just a matter of time until the bartender continued their conversation. Then two days on a hard bus seat breathing recycled air before hitchhiking home from Butte.

Two women entered, accompanied by a rush of diesel from the street. They unshouldered their purses, set them on the bar, and sat down. Ted shifted his back to them and concentrated on the TV, further incensed by the cloying smell of their perfume. How had the bomb lit but not exploded? It didn't make sense. He'd packed in enough incendiaries to bring down two planes. It had to be the match heads. They were finicky, unreliable. He'd use something different next time. The bomb, the clothes, the trip—it had cost him nearly a hundred dollars. A huge sum on his thin budget. He'd spent the night before huddled on a bench in Garfield Park, too frightened to sleep, listening to junkies rant and moan. All he'd eaten that day was a hot dog.

The newscaster spoke of a mechanical malfunction. Ted listened in rising disbelief—his bomb was being covered up entirely, called an accident, a disaster neatly averted, a feel-good piece between the wall-to-wall coverage of the protests in Iran. They couldn't lie like this. Not after all of his work. But then, as if to mock him, the newscaster nodded her blond head and the coverage flicked back to shouting throngs in Tehran, American flags being burned in the street. Ted fingered the cuff of his shirt. It was stiff and starchy, bought on sale at the Kmart in Helena. He felt the same helpless rage he had as a child not far from here, undersized and at the mercy of dumber, larger boys. He wished desperately to be back in his cabin in the woods.

The bartender mixed vodka and soda in two glasses. Then he sliced a lemon into eighths with a paring knife. He squeezed a slice onto the lip of each glass and set the glasses on the bar in front of the women. "The Ayatollah," one of the women said. "They call him the *Ayatollah*, can you believe that?"

The bartender's eyes gleamed with piggish sincerity as he shook his head. Ted stared at the knife in the metal sink. He leaned forward and took a small sip of ginger ale. It did nothing for the gnawing ache in his stomach, nor his utter sense of failure.

THREE DAYS LATER, TED ARRIVED back in Lincoln. A fabric salesman had given him a hitch north from Butte in his station wagon. Ted retrieved his pack from the back and walked quickly across the wet pavement to Food Town. It had rained all night and most of the day, and now in the dusk large puddles reflected the waning light. His feet were damp and chill. A furious determination filled him. The spring storm had forced him to spend the night in the bus station, and his anger had grown over the course of those cold, buzzing hours, hunched on a plastic seat under fluorescent lights, subsisting on peanuts from the vending machine. Tired and sore, he felt as if he might explode, unlike his bomb, which was surely being dismantled in an FBI lab. He scanned the lot quickly, making sure no one was watching him. Then he jogged around the side of the store to the dumpsters at the back. He lifted the lid and rooted through the trash until he found a pound of expired hamburger meat.

Two crows watched him from a power line. Ted took the meat and an empty beer bottle deeper into the store's shadow, hidden from the street. Then he peered into the trees behind the store, in case one of the young mechanics from Ricky's Auto was smoking marijuana there, as they sometimes did. Nothing moved. Ted smashed the beer bottle on the pavement; the crows took flight. He pressed back against the wall and counted down from ten, making sure no one had heard. Then he knelt and used one of the shards to slash open the plastic wrapping on the hamburger. He pressed the rest of the glass down into the ground meat until it was completely hidden, then rewrapped the plastic and stuffed the package in his pack.

He kept to the woods hiking back to his road. It made the journey longer, but he didn't want anyone to know he was back in town. He was still wearing the starchy collared shirt and slacks and felt like a costumed clown. He'd spent much of his life in such a uniform, and had sworn never to go back. Fresh snow covered Ogden Mountain and filled the shaded ravines beneath it like wax from a melting candle. The vanilla-scented bark around him glistened red from the rain. Snapped twigs dangled from the lower branches. The crisp, springy smell the storm had left refreshed him, as did the silence. Arriving at his road, Ted kept to the shoulder, ready to duck into the trees at the sound of an approaching car.

Hutch's trailer came into view in the last light. Immediately the huskies began to bark. Their loud yaps shattered the stillness of the evening. Ted hated the sound worse than the jets that flew overhead or the logging trucks that rumbled past. He hated it violently for the way it interrupted his concentration and made him feel afraid. He'd always hated dogs, ever since a stray bit him as a boy. People had taken a perfectly reasonable animal—the wolf—and turned it into a toy, a sharp-toothed doll onto which to map their own neuroses. If it were up to him, all domesticated pets would be ground up into hamburger. He scanned the dark trailer for any sign of movement. A white dirt bike was the only vehicle in the driveway. Hutch was almost always out this time of evening, drinking with Mason at the Wilderness Bar. He wouldn't be back until ten or eleven. Steeling himself, Ted ran to the small shed at the edge of the driveway. The huskies' barking grew louder, accompanied by the clank of their chains against the deck posts. Ted leaned on the shed's cold metal siding and peered around the corner. The dogs were thirty yards away, straining against their collars, their pale blue eyes glinting like icicles. The rising moon lit the trailer's roof a milky gray.

Ted thought of the plane safely on the tarmac, the green smoke streaming from the front and rear. He imagined how quiet the road would be without the dogs. Perhaps his bombs were failing because of his inability to concentrate. So much of his life was predicated on distractions: tiny errors, fractures in logic. Six years of studying boundary functions had shown him how delicate the process of deduction could be. The package of beef was soft and heavy in his hand. He unwrapped it; the sour, overripe smell flooded his nose. The huskies' barking rose in pitch as they smelled the meat, turning to excited *yaps*. Their fur was bright white, the black around their eyes like a void. Ted took two steps into the yard and flung the glass-laced meat toward the dogs.

The barking paused. The larger of the two came forward and sniffed the beef. The smaller hung back. Ted waited, watching, until the larger lowered her snout and began to eat. As soon as she did, the smaller rushed forward to join her. The two of them gulped down the hamburger, tipping their heads back to swallow, their icicle eyes flashing. When they were done, they licked the juice from the dirt.

Ted turned and ran up the road, his pack bouncing on his shoulders.

Two headlights appeared before him and he dove into the trees, cutting his cheek on a chokecherry bush. He pressed himself down into the dirt, his heart hammering in his chest. Who was up here at this time of night? No one usually used the road after dark. His satisfaction was obliterated by fear. He couldn't be caught, not like this. A small blue pickup clattered past. In the dim light of the cab, he recognized Duane Oshun, the tall fool who'd bought two acres from Tom McCall up the road. He was planning to build a cabin across from Ted. Luckily, it had taken him two years to clear the land and dig a foundation, but a growing stack of two-by-fours by the pit suggested that he would soon start the frame. More people, more noise. Ted angrily untangled himself from the bush and trod the final mile to his home.

16

The next morning, Mason drove to Hutch's to check on the black wolf. Molly sat beside him in the passenger seat, her gray head raised, gazing through the windshield with a red bandanna around her neck in place of a collar. Mason drove with his hand on her back, mostly to reassure himself. She was almost nine and lately he'd begun to fear losing her. She was his first dog—a blue heeler and cattle dog mix rescued from the side of the highway in front of the Company Ranch—and it was hard for him to imagine life without her. After Jackie left, they'd bonded to such a degree that each could anticipate the desires of the other. She memorized new commands by performing the action a single time, waiting for his approval with her wise gray head cocked to the side.

Hutch's property was eerily silent. A foreboding silence, usually broken by the huskies' barking. Confused, Mason told Molly to wait. Then he jogged up the trailer's steps and banged on the door. No one answered. He checked the knob. It turned in his hand and the door swung inward. Immediately he saw the huskies, their long bodies stretched out, stiff and ghostly on the carpet. The coffee table had been pushed against the wall. An assortment of pill bottles and first-aid equipment covered the top. Hutch lay unmoving on the floor beside his dogs.

Fearing the worst, Mason rushed over to his friend and crouched beside him. He touched Hutch's neck, relieved to find a pulse. "Come on, now, wake up." He lifted the older man and held him in his arms, surprised at his frail weight.

"Who's there?" Hutch mumbled groggily. Mason realized he must have taken some of the animal sedatives himself. Not a fatal dose, thank God, but enough to knock himself out.

"It's me, Mason," he answered, holding Hutch upright. "I can't let you lie down. You might choke."

"My dogs," Hutch murmured.

"I know." Mason forced himself to look again at the two motionless forms on the floor. "What happened?"

"Poison." The older man's voice broke, and he stared up at Mason with childish desperation. "They did it to get back at me. At us." It was the first time Mason had seen such helplessness in his friend, and it frightened him.

"Just rest now," he said. "We'll find them. I'll . . ." He didn't know what to say. He'd kill them? He'd tear them limb from limb? Hutch began to drift, his eyelids sagging, his head heavy against Mason's chest. Mason leaned back against the base of the couch and stared at the window on the far wall, cradling the older man as if he were a child. He had to restrain himself from running out to his truck to check on Molly. Who could have done it? He knew they'd made enemies but this . . . this was evil.

THE PYRE WAS FOUR FEET TALL. A bristling mound of two-by-fours and brush topped by wood pallets. The two huskies lay side by side on top. Mason stood with Hutch beside it. His friend looked gaunt and worn in the morning sun. The sedatives had worn off, leaving him pale and confused, and Mason had fed him oatmeal to restore his stomach. Then they'd built the pyre with the help of Duane Oshun, Pastor Younger, and several Forest Service men— all friends of Hutch's—who were now arranged in a half circle opposite them. Mason's fury had grown steadily all morning. He

felt overwhelmed and embarrassed. He wanted to leave, find whoever had done it, tie them to the back of his truck, and drag them
through town. He glanced back at Molly waiting in the cab.

"They were like my children," Hutch said. His face was rigid,
his fizzing energy constrained into a terrible grief. The skin around
his eyes was bruised from lack of sleep and the gray stubble on his
chin trembled when he clenched his jaw.

"It was those goddamned Carters," a young ranger spat.

"I don't understand how anyone could," Duane said.

"When you see the damage a foothold trap does to a coyote,
nothing will surprise you anymore," another ranger answered.
"Some men don't mind letting an animal chew itself to death."

"Now's not the time for retribution," the pastor said, quietly.
"It's time to say goodbye."

The summer sun was rising toward its zenith and heat waves
shimmered on the horizon. Mason looked across at the Swan
Range. He tried to decipher the scope of the beauty and cruelty
contained within the Blackfoot Valley. He'd heard rumors of her-
mits who survived for decades in the Bob, emerging only in spring
and fall to resupply. Could he join them? Would he be better off?

"It spooks me to think of now," Duane said, interrupting
Mason's thoughts. "But I drove by on my way home last night after
dark, and I think I saw someone in the road."

All the men turned to look at him.

"I didn't get a good look. It was just a shadow and then gone. I
would've stopped if I'd known. . . ." Duane trailed off.

"Just one man?" Mason asked. He didn't trust Duane's memory or intelligence, and was less convinced than the others that it
had been the Carters. They generally used guns or knives to con-
duct their business, and by nightfall they were too drunk to leave
their ranch.

Duane nodded. "To be honest, I thought I was seeing things,
like a ghost."

A ghost. Mason shook his head in irritation. "You see a truck parked anywhere?" the young ranger asked.

Duane frowned. "No."

A buzz of agitated anger passed through the men as they told stories of the Carters, and Mason supposed this was how vigilante posses had formed back in the old days. The gnarled hanging tree still grew in Hooper Park. He remembered stories from Virginia City he'd heard when he first moved to Montana: gunfights and outlaws and cattle rustlers strung up by the score. Hutch cleared his throat. "Six years old, both of them," he said. "They say that's middle age for a dog, but it sure didn't feel that way."

The men went silent. Mason shifted his feet. He thought again of Molly. If someone hurt her, he reckoned he might burn the entire town to the ground. He touched Hutch's shoulder, feeling again the frailty of the older man's body. "You ready?" he asked.

In response, Hutch reached out and set his hand on the husky's side, just as he'd done with the black wolf. It remained there, motionless. He closed his eyes. The Forest Service men looked away, but Mason watched. The husky's body lay stiff and awkward, her limbs outstretched.

"They were like my children," Hutch said again. Then he took a matchbook from his pocket, struck a match, and dropped it in the brush.

Orange flame curled around the base of the pyre, lapping at the edges where Mason had poured gasoline, then sprang up the sides in a crackling roar. Smoke swirled up toward the sun. The flames grew, a *whooshing* heat that caused the men to step back. The pastor began to pray softly. "Our Father, who art in heaven . . ." He bowed his shaggy head so his chin touched his chest. Mason scowled at him. Secretly he disdained the pastor. The kind of hypocrite who played at being godly while running around with another man's wife. The men watched in silence as the bodies of the two dogs were consumed.

After the fire had died down, the pastor spoke softly to Hutch. "God's doors are always open."

Mason watched Duane amble back to his small blue pickup, wondering for the thousandth time what Jackie could possibly see in him. He was a long, wavering dipshit of a man, living in a rented trailer and scraping together a living chopping firewood. Now that he owned land by Hutch, Mason was forced to see him regularly, grated by his continued presence. The rest of the men drifted away and Hutch and Mason were left alone, staring into the smoldering pile. Hutch spoke softly. "All the other animals are fine. It's like they didn't even go back there."

"The wolf?" Mason asked.

Hutch nodded.

Mason turned this over in his head. The Carters almost certainly would've killed the wolf for its pelt, and probably all the other animals besides.

"I felt it coming." Hutch looked up with a stinging intensity in his pale blue eyes. "I felt it, but I didn't know what to do. I shouldn't have left them alone, I should have stayed here. . . ." He trailed off.

"Everyone leaves their dogs alone," Mason said. "This is evil."

He helped Hutch back inside, clearing a place for him on the couch in the living room. Looking around, he was disturbed by the squalor of his friend's home. Dirty dishes were piled high in the sink, flies looped around the overflowing trash, junk mail and coupon flyers covered every surface. Hutch dedicated his life to animals and barely remembered to take care of himself. Mason collected the pill bottles and first-aid equipment, wiped the blood from the carpet as best he could, and pushed the coffee table back to the center. "I'll bring dinner by tonight," he said.

Wearily, Hutch nodded, then closed his eyes. Mason gathered up the trash and carried it to the bin outside. Then he stood on the porch for a moment, breathing in the fresh air and looking across the valley.

IN THE HUNDREDS OF MILES of Mason's jurisdiction, no place bothered him as much as the Carter Ranch. They hung coyotes from
their barn like trophies, baited ducks on Monture Creek, and tore
hell out of the woods on their ATVs. The eldest brother, Cade,
was in prison in Deer Lodge for stabbing a man in a fight behind
the Two Dot Bar; the youngest, Billy, was a rodeo rider with a
torso full of knife scars; and the middle brother, Preston, was more
vicious than his two siblings combined. Everyone knew the Carters hunted and trapped year-round, regardless of season or tag
limit. They sold their coyote, bobcat, and mink pelts at the Wolf-
Goes-for-Fire Trading Post, and clandestinely supplied meat to the
roadhouse in Ovando.

Driving toward the entrance to their ranch, Mason left the
truck in second gear, going much slower than he needed to. He
tried to formulate a plan. He had the power to arrest Preston and
Billy if they confessed, but there was no way Sheriff Kima would
hold them in jail over a couple of dogs, particularly not Hutch's.
That left shooting them or fighting them, both of which had obvious downsides. Mason felt a deep exhaustion in his limbs. His
last fight at the Wilderness had left him with a concussion, afraid
to sleep for a week, and Preston was far more dangerous than a
drunken biker. Molly sensed his anxiety and rested her chin on his
arm. "We'll be home soon," he promised.

The Carters owned much of the land behind Hutch's property, including all of the gulch around Halfway Creek, where their
savage cattle gathered during storms. The Carter ranch predated
Highway 200, and the blacktop cut through the northeast corner,
a battle the family had lost but didn't consider over, much like
the Civil War. A Confederate flag flew beside an American flag
over the triple-padlocked gate. Idiots, Mason thought, his derision
fighting for control over his fear as he parked the truck. On the

south side of the highway was the old barn and the dirt driveway down to the main ranch house and sheep shed, on the north were Cade's two trailers, the windows boarded-up and lined with razor wire since Cade was sent away.

With Cade locked up, only Ma Carter, Preston, and Billy remained on the ranch, which totaled some twelve hundred acres, backing onto Forest Service land on Ogden Mountain, where they had a grazing lease. An assortment of Carter cousins and in-laws populated the surrounding woods, helping run the herd. Mason took a deep breath, removed the .45 from the glove box, checked the clip, and set it beside him. Then he leaned on the horn and waited.

Ten minutes later, he heard the roar of an engine and Billy Carter appeared on the back of a four-wheeler. Some of the tension left Mason's shoulders, and he clicked the safety of the pistol back into place. Billy was the youngest and least dangerous of the Carters. He had the preening arrogance of most bull riders, a weakness Mason hoped to exploit. Mason stepped out of his truck, folded his arms, and leaned against the hood. Billy scowled as he pulled up, his face shaded by a tall sugarloaf hat. He wore a gray sweatshirt sliced open at the sleeves, clearly a hand-me-down from one of his smaller brothers, secured around the middle by a shell belt. His torn jeans culminated in a pair of calf-leather boots, and his shotgun was racked to the side of the four-wheeler in easy reach. "What're you doing blocking our gate, Mason?" he asked.

"Preston in there?"

Billy shrugged. "Might be."

"Where were you last night?"

"Shit." Billy grinned. "You a cop now? You're talking like a cop."

"I'll come back with them if I have to," Mason bluffed.

Billy sneered, but Mason could see a hint of worry in his eyes. "What's this about?"

"I asked you a question."

"I was here all night with Ma, same as Preston. Two witnesses. Signed and swore."

Disappointment tightened Mason's jaw. He'd hoped the Carters were at the roadhouse or some other public place, with verifiable witnesses, not blood relatives. "Neither of you went anywhere else?"

Billy shook his head.

"You didn't take a walk over to Hutch's property?"

"What's this got to do with him?"

"Someone went onto his land and killed his huskies last night." Mason watched Billy closely to gauge his reaction.

Billy raise his eyebrows. "Killed his dogs?" he asked, swatting a fly off the brim of his hat.

Mason nodded.

"That's a mighty low thing to do," Billy said. "If we were going to kill something, it'd be one of those bobcats he keeps behind his trailer. Or maybe the wolf. Shouldn't you be talking to him about that, being a forest ranger and all?"

Mason felt his hands go cold. It didn't surprise him that Billy knew about Hutch's animals, but it worried him to hear the words out loud. Did everyone in the valley know? There were fewer secrets than he'd hoped. "What about your cousins?"

"Hell, I don't keep track of all them." The petulance in Billy's voice betrayed his age. He was barely twenty.

"You sure about that?" Mason set his jaw and looked into the boy's brown eyes.

Billy lowered his voice. "Maybe we should get Preston. He's more in charge of the day-to-day. You want to come down and talk to him?"

"I'm talking to you, Billy," Mason said.

The boy cleared his throat. "You've got a lot of nerve coming onto our property like this. I know you're from back East and went to fancy schools and all, but out here there's a lot of back roads for a man to get lost on." He paused. "You hear about that ranger up in the Cabinets last year? No one's found a single sign of him."

The threat bothered Mason more than he let on. He'd gone through wilderness first-aid training with the missing man, a tall, slow-witted Minnesotan, and they'd shared many interests, down to the worn copy of *Desert Solitaire* in their rucksacks. He stepped toward Billy, rubbing the knuckles on his fist. "I know you think it's the Wild West out here, but if anything happens to me, they'll stick you and your family so deep in a hole you'll wish you were never born." He glanced back through the truck window at his pistol, calculating the exact sequence of motions needed to pick up the gun, click off the safety, and level it at the boy's chest.

Billy narrowed his eyes. His boyish face was smudged with dirt below his hat. He looked at Mason disdainfully, revved the four-wheeler's engine, and turned back toward the ranch house, hidden at the bottom of the hill. "You tell Hutch if we've got a problem we won't come for his dogs, we'll come for him." He stood up over the seat in his roper boots and roared back down the hill, looking to Mason like some pretend, mechanized version of Billy the Kid. For a moment he wanted to shoot him in the back.

ON HIS WAY HOME, to calm his nerves, Mason stopped at his favorite spot on the Big Blackfoot River: a sandy beach on the bend where Halfway Creek emptied into the larger torrent. He let Molly out of the truck and immediately she dashed into the shallows, going just deep enough for the water to touch her chest, then sprinting out and shaking herself furiously in a wild flush of spray. She found a stick and flung it in the air, then pounced on it, gnawing at the end. Mason watched her, pleased by the way she entertained herself. He found a log on the sandy shore and sat watching the eddies in the roiling water. The current was still full from spring runoff, surging against the banks. Thick white clouds passed over the Swan Range like a slow and gentle army.

If it wasn't the Carters, who could have killed Hutch's dogs? The question frightened Mason. Not a month went by when he didn't find himself on an unmarked dirt road in his old Forest Service pickup, driving pell-mell toward who knew what, be it redneck poacher, survivalist encampment, ecoterrorist, or hippie cult. He'd chosen this work, but some days it didn't seem worth it—putting his and Molly's lives in danger to save a lone wolf, a lone grizzly. How long did the animals even last after they were set free? Mason worried it was only himself he was grinding down.

He picked up a flat red rock and held it in his hand. Then he flipped the rock over. He remembered his youth in the fifties in Charlestown, his parents' anxiety and resentment seething beneath the middle-class veneer of their daily lives. His life in the valley had taken on a darkness that reminded him of the long silences in his father's study; men frightened of nuclear war beyond their ability to express, clinging to the bars of their own cages. Visiting Hutch, he sometimes heard strange, distant explosions that Hutch dismissed as mining operations on the opposite side of the mountain, and he often found jumbled tracks deep in the woods. Molly came and lay beside him and licked the dirt from her paws. Mason held the rock for a moment more, then skipped it across the surface of the river, watching it hit the water and lift off again, pleased by this brief moment of flight, as if it could live there, a red flash suspended for all eternity.

17

Veteran postal inspector Nathaniel "Nep" Piper was led from the reception area of the FBI's Chicago office down to the evidence rooms in the basement by an attractive young woman in a pencil skirt. There she handed him off to Special Agent Wally Symes. The two men shook hands warily.

"Let's try not to muddle-fuck this up," Symes said.

Nep, a Christian, nodded curtly. "It was a piece of mail."

"And it crossed state lines. So here we are." Symes pushed open the door to the large fluorescent-lit evidence room. The room was as antiseptic and impersonal as everything else in the building. A black table ran down the center between the bare gray walls; tagged plastic baggies of bomb components were organized in numbered quadrants on the tabletop.

Symes nodded at the assembly. "Some amateur bullshit. Whole thing was made of wood and scrap, like you'd find in a junkyard. College student, maybe. Got dumped by his girlfriend. Mad at his parents. Read *The Anarchist Cookbook* and thought he'd give it a try."

"He nearly brought down a plane," Nep said, taking a notebook and pen from his pocket. He began to circle the table, jotting down notes.

"In bombs, nearly is the difference between something and nothing."

A wet, sour smell hung in the room. The chemicals that had been used to douse the fire, Nep guessed. He leaned over, looking at the batteries from the circuit. All the identifying marks had been carefully sanded off. Paranoid. Or careful, depending how you looked at it. The box and sealing caps were both pine, skillfully carved.

"Basically defused itself," Symes said. "The wood couldn't hold in enough pressure to blow. The cap popped off and started a campfire in the hold. Whole thing was damp, too, not sealed properly."

"Whose idea was it to keep it from the press?" Nep asked.

"Ours. No reason to cause a panic, or give copycats ideas."

The letters F C were carved into one of the surviving fragments. "Sense of humor?" Nep asked.

Symes shrugged. He stood with his chin thrust forward and an expression of irritated determination that suggested to Nep how the wrong men ended up, on occasion, in the electric chair. "Maybe. And take a look at this," Symes picked up a baggie of black powder. "Barium nitrate."

"What for?"

"We couldn't figure that out, either. It doesn't have any explosive qualities. Fireworks manufacturers use it to make smoke turn green."

"A message?"

"Who knows."

Nep stopped for a moment. Unconsciously, his pen drew an expanding swirl on the open page of his notebook. His mother still chastised him for his doodling, but it helped him think, and he often made connections along with the random patterns of his pen. He'd noticed a greenish tinge to the smoke watching the plane on the news. At the time, he'd thought it was the color aspect on his TV, or some synthetic from burning luggage. "Green," he said.

Symes nodded. "As a witch's tit."

———

NEP ORDERED A SAMPLE of barium nitrate and found it on his desk at his office in Evanston the next day. He called his mother and told her he'd be home late. Then he packed his briefcase, slipped the vial into his pocket, and drove north through Glenview to Lake Forest. He parked at the picnic area on West Lake. The narrow tip of the lake gleamed like hammered steel between the trees. He sat in the car for a moment wondering what he was doing. His mother got anxious when he came home late. She'd moved in with him after his father died the year before, and cooking dinner for him was one of her few remaining joys.

The June night was windless and cool, a rarity. Shaking his head, Nep buttoned his overcoat, took the flashlight from the center console, and got out. Black trees towered over the still water. The moon was a milky thumbnail through the shredded clouds. A small bulletin board by the trailhead warned against bonfires and poison ivy. After spending the entire morning going through the FBI's hundred-page list of radicalized college students and professors, Nep had been left with the nagging sense that he needed to get out of the city. Green smoke, wood, and the letters F and C: those were his only real clues. He felt himself standing on the precipice of something much bigger. The assassinations and protests of the sixties, followed by Vietnam and Watergate, had left so many people disillusioned with the government. The Postal Service was one of the last institutions they trusted. If more bombs were sent and people became afraid of their mail, it could shake the very foundation of democracy. Nep was glad Symes and his superiors had kept the bomb out of the press, but the story was bound to leak sooner or later.

The fresh air cleared Nep's mind. He was surprised, actually, that no one had sent bombs through the mail before. It was so much easier than hijacking an airplane or taking over an embassy.

The cement path passed through a picnic area with grills and tables organized neatly around a row of firepits. Loblolly pines grew close together, interspersed by the much taller eastern whites. He shivered as he walked deeper into the forest, noticing wild bergamot about to bloom. It was important to him to know things by their proper names. *Green and wood.* He touched the glass vial in his pocket. The beam of his flashlight played back and forth over the needle-covered ground.

After twelve years as a postal inspector, Nep was tired, deeply tired. His job forced him to look at the most terrible things: child pornography, snuff films, all manner of degradation. With a made-up return address, or none at all, a man could drop a package in a mailbox and walk away. And men did, time and again. He kicked a pine cone off the path and let his mind bounce along with it into the darkness. In some ways, the bombing case had come as a relief.

The bomber couldn't have known which flight the package would end up on, so it wasn't personal. It was a statement. But of what? Most recent acts of terrorism were Middle Eastern radicals fighting colonialism. Before that, it had been Black Panthers and Communists. Before that, anarchists. The green and wood suggested a more modern cause: the environment. As Symes had said, radical eco groups were springing up on college campuses across America from the ashes of the antiwar and civil rights movements. Nep didn't remember the world ecology ever coming up when he was in college; now in the wake of *Silent Spring* you could major in it. But did this really feel like the work of a college student? Angry kids were more likely to throw a molotov cocktail at a cop car than painstakingly carve a wooden bomb.

Nep had spent several hours the night before researching the Wilderness Society, the formerly austere organization founded by Bob Marshall and Aldo Leopold. Radical factions had split off from its membership and clandestinely held training sessions across the interior West. Could it be one of them, an older man, disillusioned by years of failure, turning to violence? The careful construction demonstrated a steady, determined rage, unlikely to burn out. Surely the bomber would strike again. It occurred to Nep, in a strange moment of clarity, that both he and the bomber were sharing the same frustration. The bomber wanted to be heard, Nep wanted to listen. FC. What did it mean? Flight crash?

The moonlight shimmering over the lake reminded Nep of his father, a quiet, impenetrable man who'd worked at the same accounting firm for forty years. Every summer morning, he sat silently at the kitchen table gazing out at the birdfeeder, where cardinals, robins, and goldfinches congregated in fluttering pageantry. Nep had spent his childhood searching for clues on how to please him; it was no wonder he'd become an investigator. He knelt on the edge of the rocky beach and gathered up a small pyramid of pine needles. Then he took the vial of barium nitrate from his pocket and poured the contents on top. In the deepening darkness, he struck a match. The needles crackled, burning yellow for a moment before flaring orange. Nep peered intently into the flames. The barium nitrate caught and a thread of green smoke curled skyward. It drifted up between the branches and dissipated in the crowns, as if it were being exhaled by the trees themselves.

18

Driving home, Mason slowed in front of the old Everett Ford homestead at the turnoff to Arrastra Creek Road. He thought, as he always did, of the strange story his realtor had told him when he bought the property next door. One evening at the turn of the century, Everett had climbed the tall ponderosa in his yard and refused to come down. His children got scared as night came on and went to find their neighbor. This man was likewise unable to get Everett down, so he found Everett's ax and chopped the tree down with Everett in it. The realtor told the story as if it were funny, so Mason assumed Everett had survived the fall, but every time Mason passed the weathered gray logs of the old homestead he wondered about this prior resident. Why had Everett climbed the tree? And why had the realtor emphasized that Everett's own ax chopped it down? For Mason, the story represented the valley's twisted, incomprehensible logic.

He drove past his house—a large, weatherbeaten old farmhouse with sagging shutters and white paint flaking from the trim—to his neighbor's to pick up Molly. In the two weeks since the killing of Hutch's huskies, he'd been leaving her on Clem and Suzy LeBlanc's farm every morning on his way to work. She could run with their two dogs and they kept an eye on her. As soon as his truck came into view, Molly began to bark frantically and charge back and forth along the buck-and-rail fence, kicking up dust. By the time Mason pulled in, she was in a frenzy of explosive joy, jumping and yapping. Some days he didn't feel he deserved it. Waving to Clem on his tractor in the field, Mason loaded Molly into the truck and drove home.

The doorknob was ancient and rusty and it took him several tries to turn the key. He hated that he'd had to start locking his door. What was the point of living in Montana if you couldn't trust your neighbors? Mason knocked the dirt off his boots in the entryway, went to the fridge, opened a beer, and turned on the oven. He took a casserole from the freezer and poured kibble into a bowl for Molly, added warm water and a little bacon grease, and sat at the kitchen table watching her eat, listening to the happy crunch of the kibble. He'd bought the house when he and Jackie were first married and planning for children. Now it felt much too big. Mason avoided the upstairs, where the extra bedrooms were, mostly limiting himself to the kitchen and living room. He knew his own depression and anger had caused Jackie to leave, but he still felt she'd abandoned him in a creaking house on a lonely road. Perhaps this was why Everett had climbed the tree. The realtor hadn't mentioned a wife. Mason thought of Hutch alone in his trailer, with no dogs even to keep him company, and dismissed his own self-pity. Others always had it worse. His father had made a point of teaching him that, driving him through the slums of Dorchester after the war.

The phone rang and Mason stood, hoping it was Hutch, but the line went dead as soon as he answered. He stared down at the receiver in his hand. Another message? Or simply a wrong number? Outside, long shadows reached across the deck as the sun set behind the mountains.

Molly finished eating and Mason walked with her into the

backyard. Mosquitoes whined through the evening air. Molly squatted to pee on the fence. Mason crossed the grass to his shed. A heavy padlock hung from the door. He swatted a mosquito from his cheek, fished the key from his shirt pocket, where he always kept it, and unlocked the door. A tangled mass of silver forms glinted inside. Traps, hundreds of them, piled on top of each other. Footholds, body grips, deadfalls, cages, and snares. They filled the small room. Some rusted, others shiny and new. They represented the sum total of Mason's accomplishments in Montana. If he couldn't maintain a connection to the animals he saved, at least he had these trophies of his exhaustive efforts scouring creek beds and mountain draws with Hutch. Thousands of dollars' worth. Enough, he hoped, to push some of the small-time trappers into destitution. No wonder they hated him. He wanted them to.

"Come on, girl," he called to Molly, closing and locking the shed and returning inside. He stopped by the stone fireplace in the living room, running his finger along the rough masonry, and thought again of his father. On school breaks as a boy, he'd loved to eavesdrop at the door of his father's study, aware of how adults changed their conversations when children were around. He'd been fascinated by anecdotes about cousins fighting on the Eastern Front, advances in political careers, and gossip from the Econ Department at Boston University, which his father chaired. But as he grew older, Mason's awe morphed into disdain. For all his worldly bluster, his father was a timid man, content at his desk and inside his own head. He advocated for the rapid growth and industrialization of the West without ever setting foot in the woods, preferring slippers and dinner jackets to any real travel.

Sinking onto the couch with the half-finished beer, Mason imagined a shaved and suited version of himself back in Boston, working at a law firm, like his brother, catching the train from the harbor to a glass-walled monolith downtown. Riding the elevator up to an air-conditioned office, flirting with the secretaries.

He tried to remember what had possessed him to come to Montana in the first place. A wild-eyed kid with an idea of the West as something to be saved. What he'd found were rednecks like the Carters who saw the entire territory as their birthright to squeeze for whatever meager resources it had left, and outside mercenaries like Tom McCall armed with government contracts clear-cutting everything. Tension had been building in the valley for years. The lawlessness reminded Mason of the western movies he'd watched as a boy. Lincoln felt less like a town and more like a collection of speculators, draft dodgers, survivalists, hippies, and crooks—men escaping from somewhere else. He looked across the room at his .45 on the dining room table, then down at his boots, which were stained with blood from an elk carcass he'd hauled off the highway that morning. Whatever shaved and suited Boston version of himself had once existed was now long out of reach.

The oven finished preheating and beeped. Reluctantly, Mason rose. Molly lifted her head and watched him but remained curled up on the couch. She was always exhausted after a day running with the two younger dogs at the LeBlancs'. He scratched behind her ears. "Don't you go getting old on me," he murmured, and walked into the kitchen. He opened the oven and set the frozen casserole on the rack inside. Then he retrieved another beer from the fridge and stood looking out the window at the dark trees, trying to guess how high Everett had climbed.

THE NEXT MORNING, MASON AWOKE hot and hungover, still in his jeans on the couch, with sunlight streaming through the picture window. Since Hutch had stopped joining him at the Wilderness Bar on Friday nights, and he didn't want to leave Molly, he'd found himself drinking harder alone at home. The temperature was already nearly eighty degrees, startlingly hot for a June morning in northern Montana. He rolled upright, cursing a crick in his neck, and stumbled out onto the back deck to pee. Molly followed him and ran off to perform her own morning ritual at the fence line. He squinted after her in the sunlight, his head dully aching. Back in the kitchen, Mason opened a beer and pulled a package of bacon from the fridge. He cooked the entire pound, tossing several strips to Molly and eating the rest himself—their weekend tradition. "Some kind of a cattle dog," he said, patting her head. Swallowing, she cocked her head and looked up at him, as if reassuring him she could still head off a steer.

A pungent aroma rose from her fur. Mason wrinkled his nose. "You stink. I guess I probably do, too."

In the backyard, he filled the old steel washbasin with water from the hose. He didn't allow himself the pleasure of a hot shower on hungover mornings. Gritting his teeth, he lowered himself into the ice-cold water, grunting at the shock. He forced breath into his lungs, reminding himself that the cold bath was the only way to clear his head, and vigorously scrubbed the dirt from his body. Afterward, he let his head fall back in the sun and enjoyed the tingling sensation spreading through his limbs. For the thousandth time, he ran through the litany of trappers and ranchers who had grievances against Hutch and himself.

A pair of crows harried a hawk in the Doug fir by the fence. Mason watched until his toes went numb, then he rose from the tub. "Your turn," he said to Molly. Dutifully, she allowed him to pick her up, flattening her ears and going rigid when her paws touched the cold water. He submerged her and kneaded soap through her fur, satisfied by the murky dirt that swirled forth. He could feel her ribs and muscles through her skin, the living engine that animated her body, and in her brown eyes he detected something more: a spirit, a soul. One of his great wishes was to speak to Molly, even just for an hour. "What're you thinking?" he asked.

"Hello?"

The unfamiliar voice startled Mason so badly that he jumped and spun around, banging his elbow on the deck rail. He'd barely managed to wrap a towel around his waist when Duane ambled around the side of the house with his usual dazed, sorrowful expression.

"Shit, I'm sorry." Duane froze, staring at Mason by the tub and Molly inside it, both dripping wet. He turned red. "I tried to knock on the front door, then heard you back here, so I figured I'd come around." Duane turned away and stared off at the fence.

"It's fine," Mason said through gritted teeth. Holding the towel firmly around his waist with one hand, he wrapped his other arm beneath Molly's chest and lifted her out of the tub. She shook herself vigorously—soaking him again with the spray—and stared up at him balefully, then jumped off the deck to greet Duane, sniffing his pants and wagging her tail. Mason watched the tall man kneel to pat her head. "Be right back," he said.

Dressing, he ran through his previous interactions with Duane, beginning the morning Molly had rescued him from the Carter steer when he was still sleeping in his truck in the church parking lot. Soon after, Duane had rented a trailer behind the hardware store from Vern Floyd, and now divided his time between the trailer and the land where he was building a cabin on Hutch's road, along with stints at Jackie's house. His son, a towheaded boy with a similar bewildered disposition, stayed with him during the summers. The only thing Mason found impressive about Duane was his height. He was useless when it came to conversation and had no noticeable skills, supporting himself like many other men in Lincoln by logging in the summer and performing whatever odd jobs he could find during the winter months. The particular, mournful helplessness he affected—which seemed to have a positive effect on women—irked Mason. He buttoned up his jeans and returned to the deck. "What brings you by?" he asked.

Slowly, Duane straightened, looking down at Molly fondly. "She sure is some dog," he said. "My God, I made a fool of myself that morning." He grinned sheepishly and shook his head. "Trapped by a cow."

"It was nothing." Mason pushed his wet hair back from his forehead. "She's a working dog."

"I'm not sure I ever thanked you proper. I might still be in there if you two hadn't come along."

The idea appealed to Mason. If Duane was still trapped in his truck, he wouldn't be sleeping with his ex-wife. "I've had more trouble with those cows in the past ten years than you can imagine," he said.

"Well, that's why I'm here," Duane answered. "The Carters, I mean. I've been thinking about who I saw in the road that night, and it's come to me that it must've been Preston."

Mason narrowed his eyes. "Before, you said it could've been a ghost."

Duane shifted uncomfortably and stuffed his hands in his pockets. "I know, but then I saw Preston yesterday in the hardware store, and it must've jogged my memory. I'm sure it was him."

The shape of the situation clarified in Mason's mind. Hutch had told Duane to come over and tell him this, believing a witness would force Mason's hand. He felt a new bitterness rise in his chest, that his friend would try to manipulate him this way, and that he'd allied to such a degree with Duane. "You'd testify to that in court, with all the Carters watching, under threat of perjury?"

The final word brought a confused look to Duane's face. "Perjury?"

"Lying under oath. You can go to jail for it."

"You think it'd come to that?" Duane lifted his faded, red, white, and blue baseball cap and dabbed a bead of sweat from his forehead. He looked worriedly down at Molly. His close-cropped sandy hair was receding from his temples and the skin above his hatband was blindingly white. "My son's coming up next week. I can't be involved in any mess."

"Well, it'll sure be a mess if it goes to trial." Mason didn't actually see how it ever would, but he took pleasure in Duane's discomfort, and was angry at the entire situation that had forced him into conflict with his closest friend.

"Ah hell." Duane shook his head forlornly. "Hutch said you'd appreciate this. He said you've been wanting Preston locked up for years."

"I have, but I've never railroaded anyone before and I don't intend to start now. Not even Preston Carter." Mason was surprised by his words. Even if Preston hadn't killed the huskies, the valley would be better off without him. Wasn't that what Mason had come to Montana to do? Put away poachers and protect the forests? And wasn't Hutch's friendship more valuable than some savage redneck?

"I do think it was him, though," Duane said. "I just didn't get a clear look. It was too dark."

"That's not enough. It won't be for the sheriff and it's not for me. You tell that to Hutch."

After Duane's little blue pickup pulled out of the driveway and disappeared down the road, Mason sighed and sat down on the edge of the deck. He squeezed his hands together and looked up at the sun high over Stonewall Mountain and the dark clouds amassing to the north. Storms came through quickly in the summer, transforming the sky, refreshing the landscape with violent wind and rain, and then passing on into surreal memory. The contrail of a plane made a white streak across the horizon. Mason wondered how many decisions he'd made in his life just to be different than his father. He'd hated the man's weakness, his tendency to stand back and let others do the real work. In doing the opposite, Mason seemed determined to make his own life hard. He smiled ruefully at this realization, ran his hand back through his wet hair, and tipped his face to the morning sun, trying to enjoy the warmth before the storm.

19

The two distant hikers—Duane and his son, Ted guessed—were following a game trail through Florence Gulch in the July sun. As they approached, Ted's suspicions were confirmed. Duane and the boy had been camped on Duane's property next to his partially framed cabin for the past week, and when Ted rode into town on his bicycle, Duane flagged him down to introduce him to Hudson. The boy spent hours sitting on the dirt bike in Hutch's driveway revving the engine. Generally speaking, Ted liked children little better than dogs, and the boy struck him as unintelligent and eager to please, like his father. Ted sighted the scope of his rifle on the boy's throat and followed him for several yards. He moved so jerkily in his sneakers over the rough terrain that a clean shot would be difficult. Ted touched the trigger with the pad of his index finger and let it linger, the gentle, insistent pressure a reminder of how easy it would be to take a life.

The satisfaction he'd felt after killing the huskies had faded. Encroachment around his home had worsened. Jet engines, logging trucks, and dirt bikes constantly interrupted his work. Duane's presence was another in a long line of indignities. The logging that summer had even come close to Ted's sanctuary, the clearing beneath the waterfall where he'd built his altar at the foot of the tallest Douglas fir in the valley, a tree he considered sacred. Often, sitting with his back against the trunk was the only place he could calm his mind. The thought of it being disturbed filled him with overwhelming rage.

Something brushed his cheek and he jumped, jarring the rifle from its position on a chunk of granite overlooking the gulch. He slapped his neck. Nothing was there, save for a faint, lingering tickle. Ted slapped himself again and cursed. All weakness vexed him, particularly mental weakness, like he'd experienced in Ann Arbor. Sexual depravity, paranoid delusions. He had no sympathy for the depressed and anxious, all the suicidal neurotics lining up for therapists and self-help gurus to root out their so-called traumas. If Ted could snap his fingers and eradicate modern civilization, he would. That would stop men from lying on their backs on couches moaning about anxiety. They'd be out hunting and killing and building shelter, as they should. The only true pleasure was the pleasure of survival, of emerging unscathed and dominant.

As if manifested by these thoughts, a grizzly bear appeared on the opposite ridge above the gulch. Ted smiled at seeing his old compatriot; he'd been watching the bear for three years, ever since their first encounters in the cage hidden behind Hutch's trailer. Ted had affection for its tremendous size and the obstinate way it treated its handicapped left paw, refusing to allow the old injury to slow it down, and sometimes turning and nipping at the offending foot for the way it dragged. He'd seen the bear take down a buck with ease, but it didn't like to travel far, and lived the entirety of its life in the woods around Stemple Pass. Tom McCall's new logging had destroyed much of its territory and Ted was not surprised to see it down here at lower elevation, closer to town.

Ted's affection turned to fascination as the bear changed course, cutting down through the woods toward the two hikers with its distinctive, limping gait—tracking them, Ted realized—its path destined to converge with theirs in a dense stand of jack pine where Florence Gulch emptied into the long draw below Stemple Pass. He wondered, with a thrill of excitement, if he was about to witness a mauling.

Three options presented themselves, and with amused detachment Ted considered each one. He could call out, warning Duane of the bear's presence and solidifying their friendship, which might prove useful if Tom and the sheriff came around asking questions about damaged logging equipment or dead dogs. Or he could shoot it, saving Duane and his son, and protecting himself, since the bear's increasing age and limited mobility would soon draw it to easier prey. This felt like a deep betrayal, one that would come back to haunt Ted in unforeseen ways, and he quickly ruled it out. The final option was to do nothing and simply watch. Let nature take its course. If Duane and the boy were meant to survive, they'd survive. If they were meant to be mauled, they'd be mauled. Ted smiled to himself and settled his chin on his hands atop the rock, with a vantage over the entire gulch.

The bear moved in surprising silence for its size. The wide paws picked softly through the forest, deftly avoiding branches even as the left front dragged. Duane and his son, on the other hand, seemed to step on every twig, crashing forward like tourists on safari. The boy lagged behind. He tripped over a stump and turned and angrily kicked the offending wood. Recalling times he'd done the same, Ted hoped the bear would rip the boy to pieces.

"You coming?" Duane called, stopping and turning. The bear also stopped, raising its black snout to sniff the air, seeming unsure of whether to continue. Come on, Ted thought, his fascination turning to a morbid desire. He'd watched coyotes tear apart rabbits and seen a hawk pluck a marten from a field and snap its neck, and each time nature's carnal savagery thrilled him. The way feeding became an act of power, a celebration of violence. Duane retraced his steps and Hudson rose from behind the stump. The two spoke—Ted was too far away to make out their words—then Duane shrugged and they turned back toward the mouth of the gulch. The bear's snout twitched as it looked after them.

Go, Ted urged silently. Get them. He was about to throw a rock to spur the bear on when he felt another insect on his cheek and flinched so violently that he cut his palm on a shard of rough granite. Cursing, he stanched the trickle of blood with his thumb and watched Duane and the boy leave the gulch. The bear ambled in the opposite direction, its broad shoulders rolling with each step, toward the cliffs at the foot of Ogden Mountain.

A pounding pain rose in Ted's temples and he squeezed his eyes shut. Failure, once again. He picked up the shard of granite and threw it as hard as he could into the gulch. For his entire life, he'd felt as if something alien were lodged behind his eyes. Doctors had prescribed a litany of painkillers and muscle relaxants. Nothing helped. Containing the pain left him exhausted. He spat on his hand and wiped away the blood.

Work on his next bomb was going slowly. He needed a more powerful explosive mixture and a more reliable detonator, and securing the necessary ingredients and shaving the aluminum powder for a malleable, C4-like substance was a painstaking process. He'd spent most of the past three months distracting himself by mapping out the territory east of his cabin and caching supplies in the hidden camps he planned to use if the authorities ever tracked him to Lincoln. He returned to one of these now, his headache worsening as the sun began to set.

A hollowed-out log served as a bed. He'd padded the cavity with old mattress stuffing—a perfect fit for his lean five-foot-nine frame. A tarp was buried behind the log to use as cover during rainstorms, along with an aluminum cooking pot. He dug out the pot, split kindling with his hatchet, and built a fire. Then he sat with his back against the log and heated a can of beans in the flames. Mosquitoes whined around his ears. He swatted at them, then took the small vial of catnip oil from his pocket and rubbed a drop onto both cheeks. The sharp, pungent odor filled his nose. Usually he enjoyed the smell, knowing it drove the bugs away, but now it intensified the pain in his temples. The mass behind his eyes seemed to have taken on density and shape. Muttering to distract himself, Ted ate quickly, then curled up in the log and closed his eyes.

HE WOKE IN THE DARKNESS before dawn with his head clear and a fresh sense of urgency. The summer was getting away from him. It was a brief, precious time when he could move free and far in daylight. He needed to restock on supplies for his bombs: batteries, chemicals, metal for shrapnel—whatever he could find. Ted stretched his stiff limbs. Moving quickly, he ate several pieces of venison jerky, packed up his camp, and made his way through the forest to the bottom of Deadman Draw.

The first sign of civilization was Ernie Floyd's hunting cabin at the mouth of Halfway Creek. The two-bedroom log structure had been built by a prospector in the 1920s for a wife who never came, and now Ernie used it with his friends during elk and deer seasons, and for his trysts with Cecil Frazier the rest of the year. Quietly, Ted approached in the first light. Plywood covered the windows and a padlock hung from the door. An old hatchet leaned against the wall. Ted set his rifle on the far side of the porch and tested the padlock. If he had to break in, he decided it would be better to trash the place. Make it look like teenage vandals.

Stepping back, he picked up the hatchet and swung it into the door. The old wood split with a satisfying crack. He swung again, splinters flying, and gouged a three-foot hole. Then he kicked the wood below it with his boot until it caved. He pulled himself in through the breach. His eyes took a moment to adjust inside the dim room. An old couch and bunk beds were arranged against the wall. Hunting magazines were scattered across the coffee table. Several tall candles and an empty wine bottle stood on the kitchen counter.

The only object of note was the huge white moose head hanging over the fireplace. Ted stared at the snowy fur and bright red eyes. He'd heard the story of the albino moose from Ed Youderian, who'd known the animal in his youth, and never forgave Vern Floyd for shooting it. The long snout penetrated halfway into the room, casting a shadow to the door and seeming to loom forward out of myth. It was astoundingly white. Ted felt he was facing a vision from a dream. Standing before its head, he longed for a spiritual connection, a sense of something greater—wasn't the animal supposed to be sacred?—but found nothing. Only emptiness and anger. He ran his finger along the cold pink lip.

Beginning in the kitchen, he opened every drawer and cabinet. He gathered up what he could use—candles, canned goods, lighter fluid, batteries, metal silverware, old nails—and brought them out to the porch. Then he destroyed what was left: smashing the coffee table, upending the stove, cutting the gas line, hacking through the cabinets. He urinated on the couch, as he imagined a drunken teenager would, and doused it in rancid cooking oil. He hacked up the bunk beds with such ferocity that sweat stung his eyes and his shirt clung to his chest.

When he was done, he stood amid the wreckage, panting. He felt exhilarated, like he had walking out of the University Health Center in Ann Arbor a decade before. Ted had made the psychiatric appointment after the increasing intensity of his sexual fantasies made him fear for his sanity in his fifth year, but in the waiting room he'd become so anxious and embarrassed that when he finally saw the doctor he lied and said he was frightened about the possibility of losing his student deferment and being drafted. The doctor condescendingly assured him that these fears were perfectly normal. Humiliated, Ted imagined crushing the doctor's birdlike neck. He thought how easy it would be to press his thumbs into the man's windpipe, squeezing his larynx, feeling him go limp, and feeling his own weakness and humiliation die along with him. The realization that he could kill gave Ted immense relief and satisfaction.

Grinning at the memory, Ted decided to send his next bomb to a shrink. He pictured flames engulfing the doctor, burning away his skin and features, and turning his office to a charred mausoleum. He looked up at the moose, feeling a tired kinship. The red eyes stared back at him blankly. Impulsively, Ted wrested the head off the wall and carried it with him out into the dawn.

20

"I thought it was a bear at first," Ernie Floyd said, as Mason peered in through the doorway at the wrecked cabin. "I might have gone on thinking that if they hadn't stolen all the cans and punched out the mirror in the bathroom."

"Jesus Christ, what's that smell?" Mason asked.

"They pissed on the couch." Ernie shook his head sadly. He was a short, portly man, wearing a hunting cap, gentler and more dignified than his father, with a bulbous nose, soft voice, and small hands that he tended to hide in his pockets. Mason knew about his relationship with Cecil Frazier and didn't care, which he figured was why Ernie had called him instead of Sheriff Kima. The unspoken assumption was that the cabin had been destroyed because of this relationship, and as such the sheriff would do nothing about it except share the joke with his deputies.

Mason covered his mouth with his hand and stepped inside. The level of destruction was shocking. Not a wall, not a surface, not one piece of furniture had been spared.

"They took the moose. That's the only thing my dad will care about," Ernie said.

"What else?"

"All the canned goods, the silverware, some candles. Other than that, I'm not sure. I never kept track of what-all was in here, but they went through every drawer."

Mason stepped over the broken coffee table. If it was meant to be a threat, or the work of high school kids, why had they taken canned goods and silverware? "You have run-ins with anyone lately?"

Ernie shook his head. "Red Boyer and the other guys at the auto shop make comments, but that's been going on for years."

"No way Red hiked his fat ass in here," Mason said.

Ernie smiled. "That's a fact."

"Well, someone has that moose," Mason said. "It's a hard thing to hide. We'll find it and then we'll know."

Ernie shrugged. "Maybe. But I've been thinking I should leave this valley for years. It might be time. There's a place in Missoula I can tend bar."

"Don't let them push you out," Mason said. "It'll pass."

"I'm forty-two and it hasn't passed yet. And with all these new faces in the grocery store. People are angry. . . ." Ernie trailed off. Mason had noticed it, too. It was the busiest summer he could remember, the escalating chaos and violence of the late seventies spreading even to Lincoln. Horns sounded under the town's single traffic light, sharply dressed couples with turquoise jewelry waited around outside Lambkins for a table, and cars lined up for the two pumps at Ollie's Gas. Sheriff Kima had arrested a man from California for slamming into the back of Mr. Didriksen's pickup, apparently in retaliation for driving too slow. Mason didn't know what was bringing them—if some glossy magazine had done a write-up on small-town Montana life.

"Everybody wants their piece before it's too late," he said.

"You ought to be careful, too," Ernie answered. "New people get the old ones riled up, and with all the tickets you're writing, they might decide you're the problem. My dad tells stories from

Prohibition, how if a deputy was causing trouble he'd disappear in the mountains and the bootleggers would blame the Salish and use it as another reason to run them out."

"That was fifty years ago," Mason said.

Ernie nodded up toward the craggy turrets of Stonewall Mountain bladed into the sky. "You think that's a long time?"

AFTER ERNIE HAD GONE, Mason hiked south into the mountains on a well-trod game trail, hoping to clear his head. All month, the phone in his small office in the ranger station had been ringing off the hook with anonymous tips of trap locations, trucks loaded with poached game, illegal furs being sold in Ovando, as if the killing of Hutch's huskies had opened the floodgates of a hidden war. On the other side came threats. Slashed tires on his truck, the bloody hide of a packrat nailed to the ranger station door. Even the young ranger who'd been so blustery after the death of Hutch's dogs had refused to come with Mason on a job adjacent to the Carter Ranch. Mason felt people avoiding him in town, too. Probably the same ones who called in the tips, brave when their faces were hidden by the telephone line.

Ernie's cabin was only two miles from Hutch's property as the crow flies. Could it all be related? Mason shook his head as he passed behind Ted Kaczynski's windowless one-room shack. The shack had a menacing quality even in the sunlight, and a sharp, fetid smell wafted up from the vegetable garden. Mason had heard that Ted was a Harvard grad, making him and Ted the valley's only two Ivy Leaguers, but it didn't seem likely. The man could barely afford groceries and spent all winter shitting in the woods. Mason hurried on, gaining elevation quickly, heading for the exposed cliff face below the peak.

The pines became shorter and more rugged. High-altitude trees eking out a meager existence in the stony soil among exposed chunks of granite. White tufted bear grass flowers bloomed above bunched, grassy stalks. Small purple asters dotted the ground of a muddy clearing. Crossing the channel of a creek, Mason saw a bear track on the shore. He knelt and placed his hand inside the blocky palm, noting the long claws. A grizzly. Could it be the same one he and Hutch had rescued three years before? Most likely. Grizzlies were rare in these mountains and other rangers had reported sightings that summer. Mason was irritated at not having seen it himself. He'd saved the bear, the least it could do was show itself. He decided to put the radio collar on the black wolf, Hutch be damned. Its leg had healed well and it was nearly ready to be released.

In a small clearing, Mason found a shallow cave with a firepit dug out in front of it. Who'd been here? he wondered. Hunters? Long-ago Indians? He imagined a pair of scouts huddled around a fire, cooking a rabbit, searching the horizon for signs of enemies. On a similar hike years before, he'd found an obsidian spear tip, nearly six inches long, which he now considered his most prized possession, and kept in a drawer along with his wedding ring.

The cool summer wind ruffled his shirt as he collected a bundle of sticks from the undergrowth and made a small fire. Rising sparks raced hot and red to the blue sky. He sat on a rock and warmed his hands. He'd brought a cheese sandwich and was considering how to grill it when suddenly the cracking bang of a gunshot broke open the day. He pitched backward off the rock. Scrambling in the dirt, he flopped onto his stomach, alligator-crawling into the woods. "Help! Don't shoot!" he yelled. But no pain came, and everything was silent save for the crackle of burning twigs and the thud of his heart. Desperately Mason felt around on his chest, sure that he'd been shot.

Gradually, his breath returned and he realized he was lying on his stomach in the dirt. He sat up and dusted himself off, checking his legs and arms. He was unhurt. Embarrassed, he scanned the surrounding trees. Shadows from the fire flickered on the trunks.

Nothing moved. He wondered if some out-of-season hunter had seen the smoke and taken a shot at him. Then Mason saw a piece of brass glinting amid the flames in the fire. He nudged it out with a stick and gingerly picked it up, tossing the hot metal back and forth between his hands. It was a shell casing. Live ammunition. Someone had left it buried in the firepit.

It must've been an accident. A hunter stamping out the flames in the morning and a bullet fell from his pocket. . . . But still, Mason couldn't shake the feeling that the bullet had been buried there on purpose as a booby trap. For the first time, he noticed the strange blackened rings on the ground around the edge of the clearing. He remembered the distant explosions he'd heard from Hutch's. He knelt and rubbed the ash between his fingers, sniffing the acrid scent. Something was wrong here, and it felt bigger than his mind could grasp. Perhaps Ernie was right: he should think about moving on, too. Mason hurried down the mountain to his truck, wanting to check on Molly, unable to shake the feeling of a malevolent, watching presence.

21

Downtown Urbana–Champaign was as quaint and charming as the tourism brochure had indicated. Nep drove slowly down the tree-lined streets, looking at the brick facades of the bookstores and coffee shops. College students wearing book bags walked hand in hand on the sidewalk. They seemed calmer and less agitated than the students he remembered from his own time at Northwestern, but perhaps it was a product of the warm summer sun. Nep had discovered the previous bombing by accident. Going through local campus newspapers searching for notices on environmental pro-tests, he'd discovered an article about a bomb exploding in the UIUC computer lab three years before, injuring a security guard. Immediately he'd called Symes, whose irritation had become almost apoplectic to conceal his embarrassment.

The former security guard, Henry Leck, now worked at an auto dealership on the east side of Urbana. A row of new Ford Broncos lined the front edge of the huge concrete lot with their rear tires raised on blocks. A blue awning above the showroom read DAVE WALLACE FORD. High-powered security lights were mounted above the awning. Apparently crime was rising here as well, or at least the accompanying paranoia. Nep had arranged to meet with

Henry on his lunch break. A few minutes early, he circled the block, taking in the strip mall architecture that now dominated the outskirts of every town in the Midwest. Red, white, and blue bunting hung from lampposts, but none of the businesses were advertising Fourth of July sales. Under the Carter administration, patriotism had become bad business.

The midday sun was hot and the air humid, without the faintest whisper of a breeze. Nep parked and sat in his car, feeling himself begin to sweat. He hoped that wherever Henry suggested for lunch had air-conditioning. Finally, a large young man in an ill-fitting blue suit emerged from the showroom. He moved with a burly, rolling confidence, and smiled broadly under his buzz cut when Nep got out to greet him. A wedding ring glinted on his left hand. He stuck out his right and Nep immediately noticed the scar: a curling pink gash wrapping around the palm all the way to his thumb. Taking the hand, Nep felt a stiffness in it, but all the parts seemed to work, and the fingers gripped his tightly. "I was lucky," Henry said, reading his mind, and holding up the scarred hand so Nep could admire it in the sunlight. "All it is now is a conversation piece."

"Probably helped you sell a few cars, too," Nep said.

"It sure has." Henry grinned. Nep followed the big man to a diner across the street. Henry squeezed into a red vinyl booth and drummed his fingers hungrily on the Formica tabletop.

"You're a football player, right?" Nep asked, recalling the detail from the campus newspaper article.

"Yes, sir. Four years varsity linebacker at Taft High, back in Cincinnati. We didn't have much of an offense, but boy, we knocked people around."

"I bet," Nep said. He'd avoided the football players in high school, and he had the sudden intuition that the bomber was a small man like himself. Explosives were a powerful equalizer.

"You know, it was funny when you called," Henry said, after

ordering a cheeseburger and strawberry milkshake. "I'd thought the investigation was over. Been almost two years since anyone talked to me, and now here you are, from the post office."

"Postal Inspection Service," Nep corrected.

"Right. I didn't even know that existed. Do you have a badge?"

"Of course." Mildly irritated, Nep took his badge from his pocket and laid it open on the varnished tabletop. A golden eagle crested the top, its wings extending down the sides around the blue logo of the Postal Service, with another eagle inside.

Henry whistled. "Double eagle. That's real nice. I guess I never thought about crimes in the mail, even though one nearly blew off my hand. What else do you get into?"

"You don't want to know," Nep said, returning the badge to his pocket and taking out his notebook, careful not to open to a page full of doodles. "You said you found the package on a table in the computer lab. Is that where returned mail was usually left?"

"Not really." Henry furrowed his brow. "It depended on the department secretary. If she was in, she delivered the mail to the professors herself. But when she was gone, the student workers sometimes left it there."

"Could someone else have gotten in and left it?" Nep asked.

"Sure. You were supposed to have a student ID to get into the building, but the doors were rarely locked."

"Did you notice anyone unusual hanging around the building that day?"

Henry shook his head. "I saw unusual things all the time on that campus, but nothing in particular that day. Really the box itself was the strangest thing, made of wood and all. It had this sweet piney smell that I remembered from camping trips with my dad out West when I was a kid. I was thinking about those trips when I opened it." Here Henry lowered his voice and leaned forward. "I know this sounds strange, but afterwards I took it as a sign. My dad had died the year before and it was like he was speaking to me, telling me I needed to shake things up and get my life moving. I quit being a security guard when I got out of the hospital and they hired me at the dealership after reading my story in the newspaper. Twice the pay, plus commissions. I met my wife Maddie on the showroom floor." He held up his wedding ring proudly.

"Where were those trips out West when you were a kid?" Nep asked, not interested in Henry's marriage, and unconsciously drawing concentric circles in the notepad.

"Oh, we went all over. Montana, mostly, but down to Wyoming and Idaho, too. My dad was big on the outdoors. We even had a camper trailer for a few years."

"Do you know what kind of wood it was?"

"Sure, ponderosa pine. I used to go around sniffing the trunks when I was a kid. I loved them—a tree that smells like candy."

Nep wrote this down. "You saw the handwriting, too," he went on. "Can you describe it? Most of the packaging was burnt up in the explosion."

"I'll never forget it. That writing is burned into my brain. All capital letters. Kind of nervous and sticklike, but neat, too, like whoever sent it wanted to make sure it didn't go to the wrong place. So it was kind of funny it got returned."

The description sounded identical to the writing on the Flight 444 bomb. Nep was convinced they were the work of the same careful man. Had he really misaddressed the package, or was it meant to end up in the computer lab? "Was there any extra writing anywhere? Letters or numbers? Initials?"

"Not that I saw." Henry cracked his knuckles and turned to look at the kitchen, waiting for his cheeseburger. "What's this about, anyway?" he asked. "You find some new leads?"

"I can't speak to that," Nep said.

"Well, I hope you find him." Henry grinned, flexing his scarred palm. "I'd like to shake the bastard's hand."

22

The black wolf stood at the rear of the cage with its four paws splayed and its hindquarters lowered, a posture both submissive and threatening, suggesting imminent attack. Outside the bars, Mason steadied the tranquilizer gun against his shoulder and looked into the animal's yellow eyes. The injured leg had healed and the wolf had grown heavy on Hutch's steady diet of venison. It no longer limped. It looked sleek and healthy, and pink scar tissue showed through the chewed black fur. "Sorry to have to do this again," Mason said.

The dart lodged quivering in the wolf's shoulder. The wolf twisted and nipped at the tailfeather, then turned in a circle and slowly sank to the ground. It looked up at Mason reproachfully. The breathing slowed; the yellow eyes closed. Mason raised his watch and counted down from sixty, considering how best to attach the collar. Hutch had refused to help him with the wolf's release because of the collar, and Mason was alone in the hot July sun, dreading the prospect of loading the animal into his truck on his own.

The cage's latch was a complicated childproof design, and took Mason several tries to open. Then he crossed the well-trodden

ground, feeling the wolf's presence in what had become its territory, along with the lingering memory of the grizzly bear. The
collar was surprisingly heavy in his hand. Made of rough synthetic
fabric with a plastic snap, the transmitter was a black box about the
size of a bar of soap. Would you want to wear this for the rest of
your life? he asked himself, kneeling beside the animal. He pushed
the thought away, along with Hutch's admonitions. The ability to
track the wolf was too important; animals got used to all kinds
of things. He unsnapped the collar and lifted the wolf's head. Its
jaws opened, long canines flashing, and Mason leapt away, scrambling toward the gate. He looked back at the wolf. It lay motionless. The movement had been involuntary. Smiling at his own fear,
Mason returned to the animal, wondering again if he was doing
the right thing. He lifted the wolf's head, fixed the collar in place,
and set it down.

Immediately the wolf was transformed. Civilized, technolo-
gized. Like a dog, as Hutch had said. Part of man's world, connected
by radio frequency to the network of antennae and telephone wires
and underground cables that were tightening a net around the
earth. A wave of guilt passed through Mason. The animal had lost
the spirit that had frightened him when he first saw it. He thought
of taking the collar off, but didn't. He heard Hutch's words: *You'll
turn all this into a zoo. . . .*

Using the tarp as a kind of sled, he dragged the wolf from the
cage and through the trees to Hutch's backyard, limping on his
bad leg. He could feel his friend watching through the trailer's rear
window. A distant boom sounded, and Mason looked up to see a
flock of starlings burst from the trees. The entire year had taken on
a bad feeling. The end of a strange decade. He thought of the astro-
logical charts that Jackie consulted. Retrogrades and eclipses and
other harbingers from the stars. Shaking his head, Mason lowered
the lift gate of his truck and paused for a moment, feeling the sweat
trickle down his back. Then he heaved the wolf into the truck bed,

slammed the gate, and hurried to the cab. He didn't want to have to dose the animal again; there was no time to waste.

The Bob Marshall Wilderness only had four entrances: the northernmost at the end of Hungry Horse Reservoir outside Glacier, another above Holland Lake in the Swan Valley, and the last two in the Blackfoot Valley. The only way to get deep in was by packhorse, a trip Mason had taken his first summer in Montana. Today Mason chose Monture Creek because it was the least trafficked. Turning north off the highway, he drove twenty miles down Monture Road to the old guard station. There the road became a faint two-wheel track along the creek. He followed it as far as he could into the forest, bumping over tree roots, then parked at the last turnaround. The trip had taken forty-five minutes. More than an hour had gone by since he'd darted the wolf. Cursing his own recklessness, Mason jumped from the cab and hustled to the back. The guilt he felt over the collar had morphed into a refusal to alter the animal's state in any other way, including administering more sedatives. He looked down at his bare hands; he hadn't even brought gloves. Stupid. The wolf would be groggy when it woke, but could still easily bite off a finger. Mason opened the lift gate and stared in.

The wolf lay still, half wrapped in the tarp. Mason thought he saw an eyelid flutter. He reached in anyway and pulled the tarp forward. Not letting himself hesitate, he lowered the wolf to the ground, feeling its warmth and bulk, briefly aware of the strange intimacy of having such a predator in his arms. The wolf began to stir, one leg pressing weakly against his thigh. "Not yet, big guy, you're almost there," Mason murmured, dragging the tarp around to the front of the truck. Once he had it ten yards away, with forest on three sides, he set it down and jogged back. He grabbed the tranquilizer gun from the front seat and held it protectively in front of his chest, blinking the sweat from his eyes. The wolf's mouth opened lazily. Its pink tongue searched, then the eyelids rose to slits, revealing the yellow irises. Unsteadily, the wolf righted itself and stood knock-kneed like a newborn colt. It lurched forward, regaining its senses. It snapped at the collar but found it impossible to reach. Then it looked at Mason one last time, turned, and loped into the trees.

After watching it disappear, Mason retrieved the radio collar's receiver from the passenger seat. He raised the tri-pronged antennae in front of him and looked into the woods. He felt ridiculous, like some kind of wilderness KGB agent, and wondered what his heroes—men like Edward Abbey and Jack London—would think of him now. He adjusted the knobs. The *beeps* faded as the wolf moved away. He triangulated them. The location was accurate. The collar worked. Its range was approximately five miles, and Mason felt comforted that at least he'd maintained some connection with the wolf.

MASON WAS NEARING ARRASTRA CREEK ROAD when Jim Miller flagged him down from the side of the highway. A buck had gotten its antler caught in the rope swing in his front yard. A small crowd had formed by the time Mason arrived, and Jackie was watching from her front porch across the street as the buck jerked and twisted its head, throwing the rope around.

"Cut him loose before he hurts himself," Jackie called.

"What do you think I'm here for?" Mason answered, instantly reminded of her habit of telling him to do things rather than asking. Maybe that was why she liked Duane: he was obedient. The rope was looped around the main beam of the buck's antler below the crown. It only tightened as the animal struggled. Growing more hysterical, the buck leapt into the air and jerked its head down with such force that it looked like it might break its own neck.

"Be careful," Darlene Miller called, bustling down from her porch in a flour-covered apron, holding out an ax. "He'll kick your ribs in." Mason looked uncertainly at the ax. The haft wasn't long enough to reach the rope while staying out of the way of the buck's flashing hooves. Reluctantly, he took it anyway. More neighbors appeared, and the buzz of their chatter increased.

"Just when you think you've seen it all," Jim said.

"Stand back," Mason advised. "He's going to be in a hurry when I cut him loose." The crowd tittered and backed away. Mason approached the buck, wary of the black tips of its flailing hooves, which looked sharp as knives in the sunlight. He was considering the best angle to take when he saw Preston Carter's old pickup approaching from the west. The once-red truck was unmistakable, bleached pink by the sun, with rusted wheel wells and a Confederate flag painted across the hood. The crowd fell silent. Mason reached back to make sure the .45 was holstered at his hip. He clicked off the safety as the truck pulled to a stop. Then he straightened, adjusting his grip on the ax. Preston and Billy were inside the cab, with a scoped hunting rifle racked behind their heads. The door creaked loudly when it opened. Preston stepped out onto the dry grass on the edge of the Millers' lawn, wearing a bobcat-pelt vest and torn jeans. He leaned back and stretched, looking around in amusement. Thin and rangy, his eyes were narrow above high, slashed cheekbones. "Looks like you caught something, Jim," he said loudly.

Jim smiled nervously.

"You know, if you trap something, you've got to put it down, too. Some people don't like that part." Preston glanced at Mason, who felt a familiar, burning itch. Ever since seeing the dead huskies on Hutch's carpet, he'd been wanting to hit someone. Throw his fist as hard as he could, break bone. Billy got out of the truck and came around the hood to stand beside his brother. He plugged a wad of chew beneath his lip, spat into the grass, and leaned against the side mirror, looking bored.

"Nice-looking three-year-old," Preston went on. "Not much of a rack, but I don't suppose you were hunting for trophies." He grinned at Jim. "Plenty of meat, though." The buck became more panicked as Preston circled. Long strands of slaver hung from its jaws. Its eyes rolled back, the whites showing. The muscles in its thighs quivered and twitched with each powerful jump.

"I never knew they could jump so high," Darlene said, trying to break the tension in the air.

"One jumped over our truck once," Billy answered. "On the way back from Great Falls."

"We clipped him, though," Preston added. "He didn't get far."

"Why don't you just cut the branch?"

"Then what?" Darlene said. "There'll be a buck running around the woods dragging a branch and a swing."

"That's a nice branch, anyhow," Jim said.

Mason gritted his teeth. He watched the buck, feeling similarly rigged up. He hated the way the townspeople tolerated Preston. He was a familiar bully on their small playground, and knew just how far he could go, particularly with a soft, nervous man like Jim. The animal paused for a moment, its brown eye looking back into Mason's, then leapt as high as it could into the air and wrenched its head. The entire branch groaned in protest.

Slowly, Preston unsheathed the bowie knife from his belt. "This here is a mercy killing," he said, directing his words at Mason. "Wounded animal, all caught up." He nodded to the drops of blood running down from the antler's burr. "Like when you see one by the side of the road."

"No." Mason flipped the ax upright. "I'm cutting him loose." A part of him was glad Preston had taken out his knife. Since he was armed, Mason was well within his rights as a federal agent to take whatever means necessary to defend himself. He held the ax's haft lightly, gauging the distance. He knew he had the advantage over Preston at arm's-length. Any closer, the quickness of Preston's knife would prevail.

"You planning to chop my head off?" Preston grinned, then narrowed his eyes. "Town or not, I know my rights." Billy pushed off of the side mirror and straightened. The townsfolk backed away, giving Preston and Mason a wide swath of grass. Mason felt sweat on the back of his neck in the afternoon heat. Jackie's door slammed shut behind him. He smelled the buck's fear also, a sour, pungent musk.

"Did you kill Hutch's dogs?" he asked.

Preston flipped the knife into his right hand and lowered his shoulder, preparing to strike, and Mason saw exactly where he would swing the ax down into the center of his body, sure to hit him even if he dodged. "No," he said. "But I'm glad someone did. That old man had it coming."

"You have a thing or two coming as well." Mason stepped forward. "All the poaching you do. Your goddam cows."

"You the sheriff now?"

"I'm a federal agent. Drop that knife."

Without warning, Billy lunged for the truck door, going for the hunting rifle. Mason watched with a rush of disappointment. He'd wanted so badly to swing the ax. "Stop!" he yelled. "I'll shoot." He dropped the ax and drew the .45, leveling the gun at Billy's back. The boy froze with his hand on the door handle, then slowly turned and raised his arms.

Relief flickered in Preston's eyes, and he sneered once again. "I knew you weren't up for a fair fight." He slipped his knife back into the sheath and turned to the crowd. "This is what the Forest Service is now. Yankees threatening people in their own homes, saying what we can hunt on our own land."

Seeing agreement on some of their faces, the tension snapped inside Mason. He stepped forward and smashed the .45 into the side of Preston's head. The blow caught him above the temple and the gun discharged. The shot was so loud Mason barely heard his neighbors' screams as they threw themselves to the ground, covering their heads. Preston crumpled to his knees. Blood ran down his face. Billy looked at Mason in shock, his hands still over his head. For a moment, the ringing in Mason's ears was so piercing he couldn't think. He stumbled backward, wishing that Molly was nearby to comfort him. Instead, he felt Jackie's hand on his shoulder.

"Put it down," she said firmly. Her voice cut through the ringing and Mason lowered the gun, surprised to find it still in his hand. His fingers trembled as he clicked on the safety and returned the gun to his holster. He turned and saw that Jackie was holding a can of bear spray; she'd been preparing to blast Preston. Desperately, he looked around. No one seemed hurt. Jim crawled over to Darlene, who was sobbing in the grass.

"Where'd it go?" Mason whispered.

"I don't know," Jackie answered. Panicked, Mason searched for damage from the bullet. He scanned the neighboring houses and trucks in the road for broken windows. Finally his eyes landed on the buck. A trickle of blood ran down the white fur on its chest from a single bullet hole in its throat. *No.* All the moisture left Mason's mouth. He moved his lips and felt something dry and hard catch in his throat. The buck stared at him, then its legs gave out and it collapsed, dangling from the rope, its head held upright.

Clutching his bleeding head, Preston staggered to his feet and began to laugh. Softly at first, then wildly, like a madman. "You got him," he wheezed, through tears. "You surely did." He stumbled to the side, nearly falling, and Billy caught him beneath the shoulders and helped him back to the truck. Then Billy went around to the driver's side, started the engine, swung the truck around, and sped down the highway, leaving Mason stunned in the sunlight.

THAT NIGHT, MASON STOOD BELOW one of the tall ponderosas in his yard, trying to remember the tree-climbing strategies he'd employed as a boy. It had all seemed so simple then: you picked a trunk, jumped on, and started climbing. Now his body was tired and the gunshot still rang in his ears. He knew he might be fired in the morning. "Oh hell," he muttered. He gripped the rough bark with both hands and found a foothold. Then he pulled himself up. Molly watched anxiously from between the roots. Mason's feet scraped for purchase and he felt a jabbing pain in his knee but managed to brace himself on a knot and lever his arm over a thick branch ten feet off the ground. Gasping for air, he dragged himself the rest of the way and crouched on the branch. He paused, and found tears in his eyes. He wiped them away, unsure if they were from exertion or something else. He could still smell the dead buck on his uniform. He'd unwound the rope from its antler, carried it to his truck while the townspeople silently watched, and drove it out to the dump, where he'd left it on an old mattress encircled by flies.

The ponderosa's branches formed a kind of ladder as they thinned toward the crown. Mason climbed higher. With each rung, he felt the distance between himself and his life growing. A lightness entered his chest, as if he were escaping gravity itself. A strong gust of wind blew in from the north and the entire tree swayed. Mason gripped the trunk, nearly thrown off the side. Molly *yapped* far below, and dashed across the grass. He looked down at her, feeling the rough bark against his cheek and inhaling the sweet butterscotch scent. She was all he really cared about. He smiled at his own predicament. Alone, up a tree. Far from home. The townspeople surely hated him now.

When the wind subsided, he looked out over the valley. From this vantage, forty feet up, he could see clear over the treetops to the Swan Range. The vast territory seemed manageable somehow, as if the vastness itself were only a matter of perspective, and the memory of the dead buck was drowned out by birdsong. The pine needles around him seemed to vibrate in the evening sun, a symphony of life and growth. He sighed. All he'd wanted to do was help. How had it all gone so wrong? Molly barked again, and in the distance Clem's old tractor rolled slowly across a hay field. Finally, Mason understood why Everett Ford hadn't come down.

23

Slanting sunlight from the open door filled the single room of Ted's cabin. He'd built the structure without windows for privacy and to keep the heat in, and it was a relief to leave the door open on warm summer evenings. Handmade shelves lined the far wall. They were full of books on plant and animal identification, as well as philosophy, mathematics, history, and a few novels by Joseph Conrad. Specimens of mushrooms, sap, and moss that Ted collected were stored in labeled glass jars. His knife lay atop a row of canned meat beside his snowshoes and a rack of dress clothes. A gun rack held a deer rifle and .22 over the bed. Beneath the bed, his coded notebooks were stacked beside a nearly completed bomb. All in their right place. Ted looked around in satisfaction, then settled down at his desk to read. He cultivated the appearance of a dirty hermit in town, but at home he kept the cabin pin-neat.

The Technological Society by Jacques Ellul lay open beside his notebook. Ted had found an unlikely compatriot in the French philosopher, and underlined long passages in each chapter. He was particularly fascinated by the idea that people had come to serve technology, rather than vice versa. It confirmed what he'd seen in computer labs at Michigan and Berkeley, and on assembly lines in

Chicago: man's utility was now based on his ability to operate and care for machines. He'd become the tool and they the master—a form of slavery too degrading to be believed. Ted returned to the passage he'd been reading the night before, attempting to formulate the opening line of an essay.

"The Industrial Revolution has been a disaster for the human race," he wrote. Then he amended, "The Industrial Revolution and its consequences. . . ." He set the pen down, distracted by the warm summer air. It had been a fine day. His new detonator was working perfectly and the test blast he'd performed that afternoon was so powerful it completely eviscerated the deer carcass he'd strung up on the far side of Strawberry Ridge. He tapped his pen against the desk, trying to regain his focus. "Technology has destabilized society, made life unfulfilling, led to widespread psychological suffering, and . . ." He read the sentence back. "And inflicted severe damage on the natural world." He nodded to himself. Generally he thought of environmentalists as weak-minded fools, and he didn't hesitate to poach animals or litter in the woods, but their movement aligned with his own. The clarity of his intellect was his greatest pride. If he was caught, his worst fear was that he'd be declared insane and dismissed as a lunatic like the serial killers who dressed up in women's clothes.

At dusk, he returned outside and climbed the rungs of his lookout tree, a tall Doug fir in the corner of his property. He sat in the small plywood roost he'd constructed high in the branches and looked out over the valley. Hutch's driveway lay empty. The blackened circle of the pyre in the yard was all that remained of the huskies. The road was thankfully quiet. Ted spat and watched the gob fall to the ground between the branches. To the east, Duane and his son Hudson sat on camp chairs outside Duane's canvas army tent. Smoke drifted up from their small fire. They'd been nailing studs in the walls of the partially framed cabin all afternoon. Behind them, Ted saw the checkerboard pattern of clear-cuts on

Tom McCall's logging claims. He turned northwest to the Bob
Marshall Wilderness, where great stone formations—granite peaks
and cliff walls stretching to the Canadian border—rose from the
pine canopy like the turrets of an ancient castle. The sight of this
wilderness comforted Ted. Mountains and rocks operated on geo-
logic time. They eased his impatience and made him meticulous
in his work, and he dreamt of one day finishing and walking alone
into that immensity with no intention of coming back.

Darkness spread across the valley, and lights blinked on one
by one in the houses of Lincoln far below. Ted sighed, imagining
the lives behind these windows. He ran the long nail of his index
finger along the pattern of the bark. He thought of his brother
David, the only human being for whom he maintained affection.
As young men, they'd been united in their hatred of industrial
society, and David shared his vision of a world reformed by fire.
For a time, David had even moved to Montana to be close to Ted.
But now he'd met a woman in West Texas and taken a job teaching
at a local high school. His mind wasn't as strong as Ted's, and such a
menial existence wore a person down. Ted worried that his brother
had become another slave in the machine of modern society. Once,
he'd fantasized about taking David on as an accomplice. Now his
brother was leaving him truly alone.

It didn't matter, he told himself. He'd always been alone. He
climbed down from the tree and walked to his garden, opening the
gate of the tall deer-proof fence. He knelt in the rich soil, checking
the progress of his crops. He fertilized the garden with his own
shit, carried on scraps of newspaper from his cabin—a practice he'd
read about in a book on rural India—and a rich, fecund scent hung
in the air. He pulled up several carrots for dinner.

After eating, he put on a pair of latex gloves and took the
nearly completed bomb from beneath his bed. His irritation with
his brother redoubled his determination. He poured soybean oil
and salt into a small bowl and soaked the igniting wire to obliter-

ate any fingerprints. When the wire dried, he soldered it in place and dabbed the first layer of his new C4 mixture beneath it. Combining the chemicals was a delicate process that took a number of days. He would slowly add more of the black powder mass, letting it dry completely each time, until the mound touched the end of the igniting wire. Then he would cover the wire itself, and over the course of more days apply layers of epoxy and paraffin. Finally, he would add the pipe and lid to seal the entire device. He suspected that improper sealing had hampered his previous efforts, and intended to add several extra layers of paraffin around the entire exterior.

As Ted prepared for bed, he ran through the additional steps he needed to take: buying a bus ticket, assembling a disguise, choosing a target. He whistled to himself as he rinsed his face in the washbasin. Choosing a target from the long list of names in his coded notebook was his favorite part of the process, and he savored it until the very end. Where to direct the package . . . who to destroy. . . . The months before he sent a device were the most focused of his life. His headaches went away. His nightmares lessened. His stress and anger were assuaged by the prospect of direct action, and his previous failures diminished in magnitude as he imagined his imminent success. He was sure that this bomb would finally accomplish the goal he'd pursued for more than a decade: it would take a human life.

24

In early August, Mason was awakened by the phone ringing just before dawn. A hiker had been mauled on Stemple Pass. He dressed quickly in the darkness, rummaging through a pile of clothing on the floor to find a clean shirt. He stuffed several pieces of jerky in his pocket, along with his badge, unlocked the gun safe, and withdrew the .30-06 and a box of thirty-five-caliber ammo, or "thumpers," as the other rangers called them, for the way they knocked down even the biggest game. Molly followed him out to the truck. Ten minutes later, they were outside of Lincoln, traveling up Stemple Pass Road.

The sheriff, two deputies, and another ranger were waiting at the small campground on the pass, their lights flashing. One of the deputies held a roll of caution tape, looking sick. A fire lookout stood on the rise above them, with the first rays of sunlight streaming through the wavy glass of the many-paned windows. Behind it, the full moon faded into the lightening sky. Several campers sat wide-eyed in cars in the parking lot, their faces pale, staring into the middle distance. Mason got out, told Molly to stay, and went to meet the sheriff.

"Hell of a thing, worst I've ever seen," Sheriff Kima said,

motioning for Mason to follow him. Warily, Mason nodded. His relationship with the sheriff had always been strained, and he knew Kima wanted him fired for discharging his gun during his confrontation with Preston—rather than the four-week suspension he'd served—but now the sheriff appeared badly shaken. "We've had a couple bear attacks in my time, and they're all bad, but I've never seen anything like this."

Four tents were pitched around the campground loop, and at first Mason couldn't tell which one had been hit in the dim light. Then he saw the blood. It was spattered over the top and as he approached he realized the nylon itself was askew, one of the front poles snapped and mangled. "Tore right through the front," Sheriff Kima went on. "She was a through-hiker, on the new Continental Divide Trail. None of the other campers knew her, but they say she was real friendly, talking to everyone. They saw the bear earlier, at dusk. It had a limp and was nosing around at the edge of the woods looking for food. It ran off when they shouted, then . . ."

The Continental Divide Trail had been completed the year before, and the first through-hiker—a quiet, leathery little man—had arrived soon after, surprising Mason, who thought the trail was too remote to compete with the Pacific Crest and Appalachian trails. "Then it came back," Mason finished.

"Around three this morning."

Mason stopped beside the tent. Nausea flooded his stomach and he had an intense desire to turn away and retch, but he held his ground. The bear had ripped open the front flap and dragged the woman halfway out. Her left arm was gone completely, as was her left thigh. The contents of her stomach were strewn around the grass. Her neck was broken, but her face was strangely untouched, her features contorted into a rictus of shocked suffering that Mason immediately wished he could unsee. He drew his palm across his forehead and gazed up at the jack pines below the peak.

"You said the bear had a limp?"

The sheriff nodded, looking down at the woman. "That's what they said."

"It won't have gone far after a meal like that, especially if it's hurt." Mason turned away, afraid the guilt would show on his face. He remembered the young grizzly caught in the leg-hold trap on Strawberry Ridge, snarling and furious, ready to chew off its own paw. Rescuing it had seemed right at the time, even heroic. Now Mason wondered if he was a murderer. Wounded animals were always the most dangerous, and he and Hutch had acclimated the bear to humans. Had it only been a matter of time before it killed someone? He took a deep, ragged breath.

Vividly, he remembered walking with Jackie in the snow around the old Glory Hole Mine the first winter after they were married. Her face tipped back to the winter sun, her expression one of pure belonging, a part of the landscape itself. He'd spent ten years chasing this quality. Now he feared he'd only made things worse.

"With all the new logging, I reckon the only way for it to go is north up around the peak," he said. "It'll be looking for a place to sleep for the day."

"You want to take one of my deputies?" Sheriff Kima asked. "Pearce is a good shot."

Mason shook his head. He felt something ending and he couldn't see beyond it to what might begin. His guilt was like a smothering hand. "I'll move faster on my own."

25

A hushed electricity filled the Ponderosa Café. Customers streamed in and out, nearly the entire town showing their faces, everyone whispering about the mauling. Jackie moved between the counter and the booths, trying not to succumb to the lurid rumors. No one knew the woman hiker, which seemed to make it easier for them to speculate on the condition in which her body was found. The wife of one of the deputies said her husband had come home so pale she'd thought someone in his family died. "Ate her right in half," Vern Floyd said, shaking his head over his coffee, clearly pining for the days before the Endangered Species Act when he and his buddies could go out and shoot the grizzly themselves. The undercurrent of excitement reminded Jackie of the aftermath of the death of Dan Delaney, the owner of Delaney Lumber Mill, who'd fallen into the augur when Jackie was a girl. His death had harkened the beginning of the end for the mill, and Lincoln as a timber town, and provoked a strange combination of grief and excitement in the townsfolk, many of whom had been jealous of his wealth and influence. For Jackie, it was one of the first glimpses of the dark, incomprehensible aspects of adulthood.

Emergency vehicles rushed by on Highway 200. Jackie looked

for Mason's truck among them. Finally someone told her: He'd gone after the bear alone. Hearing this, Jackie excused herself, stepped into the bathroom, and locked the door. She leaned over the sink and looked in the cloudy, yellowed mirror. The lines around her eyes and a single deep wrinkle in her forehead marked the history of her sadness. For a moment her heart felt so heavy she had to grip the porcelain. Mason was the closest she'd ever come to true love. During those first fervent years, even the smell of his sweat awoke a blinding passion. She'd wanted to have his children, with the same deep cleft in their chins, and the same stubborn bravery.

Wiping her eyes, Jackie turned on the faucet and ran her hand over her black hair. Slowly, she returned to the service area. The rush of customers trickled out, and by late afternoon, near the end of her shift, Jackie was able to sit on the stool by the register looking out the window at the pines over the Alpine Motel. Having grown up in nature, she saw it not as such a fragile thing as Mason did, balanced on the knife edge of disaster, but a force like a wave or a storm that might be beaten back temporarily but would never be controlled. She knew that men who spent their lives hacking away at trees would one day feed the roots of the growth that would cover everything they'd built. It would be the same with Mason, whether he stayed or went or saw a thousand wolves return to the valley: inevitably, the place would change. She felt sad for him, and the futility of his anger, and she felt sad for the bear, whose life would soon have to end just because it had done what every living creature did each day: hunt down its next meal.

The vacancy light flickered across the parking lot. Jim Harwood leaned over the ledger at the check-in desk, his stubbled face shrunken and gray. Thirty years before, he and his brother Walt had killed a grizzly for eating calves at the Company Ranch, and displayed its massive corpse in front of the ranger station. They strung it up so people could see its full length, and the sight of its head sagging forward over its chest had sickened Jackie so deeply that she and Rita snuck out one night and cut the bear down. They'd wanted to bury it, but the corpse was much too heavy for the two girls to move, so they'd left it there, a mounded shadow on the ranger station steps, the golden eyes shining glassily in the moonlight.

Lost in these memories, Jackie didn't see Duane's small blue pickup until it was nearly to the parking lot, with Duane and Hudson inside. Duane took the turn too fast, screeching the tires and sending his collection of rocks and bones sliding across the dash. Hudson's eyes went wide as he tried to catch them. Duane parked and father and son jumped out, hitched up their jeans, and jogged into the café. Their mannerisms were so similar it was almost comical. Both were long and lean and mournful, with awkward, loping strides and expressions of slight overwhelm at whatever was in front of them.

Duane burst through the glass door. "You hear about the bear?"

Jackie stared at him.

"It got someone on the pass," Hudson chimed in, his shaggy blond hair hanging over his eyes.

"Of course I heard," Jackie said, pushing the hair back from Hudson's forehead. "It's all anyone's been talking about." She looked down at him affectionately. She wasn't sure she and Duane would've lasted if it wasn't for the boy. Having a son made a man of him, and for two months each summer she got to be a mother herself. All three of them stayed at her house on her days off, watching movies and playing games, and sometimes she joined them to camp on Duane's land on the weekends. She wanted to cut Hudson's shaggy hair, but there were limits to her role.

"They say it ate a woman," Hudson went on. His eyes held an awestruck combination of fright and fascination that transported Jackie back to her own childhood. "Can you imagine that? Being eaten by a bear?"

"I can't, and neither should you," she answered.

"We saw all the flashing lights on the road. We were out hiking." Duane shook his head. "My God, it must have just passed us by."

"Mason is up there now going after it," Jackie said.

A puzzled expression crossed Duane's brow. "Mason is?"

"What do you think the Forest Service is for? It's his job when something like this happens."

Duane chewed on his lip thoughtfully, then crossed the linoleum and leaned against the register by Jackie's elbow. She smelled his peculiar woodsy scent and observed several newly white chest hairs poking from the collar of his threadbare T-shirt. He ducked his chin toward her and glanced furtively into the kitchen and then back at his son, before dropping his voice to a low whisper. "Remember how I told you about the bear with the wounded foot on Hutch's property, right after I got to town?"

Jackie nodded.

"I've seen that bear a few times over the years, around my property and up on Stemple Pass. It's a grizzly for sure. The only one I've seen. It walks funny, too, kind of dragging that back paw. And I wonder . . ."

The ramifications took a moment to clarify in Jackie's mind, and when they did, she felt the breath leave her chest once again. Life in the Blackfoot Valley never failed to surprise her, the way it brought every man around to face themselves. She couldn't imagine what Mason must be feeling. She worried that in his guilt, he might be more intent on letting the bear kill him than in killing the bear. "My God," she murmured.

Duane nodded slowly.

"Don't tell that to anyone else, not a soul."

"I won't," he replied.

"Don't tell them what?" Hudson asked, staring up at her.

"It's nothing, hon," Jackie said. "You want a cinnamon roll?" She reached below the counter for the one she'd hidden behind the stale coffee cake nobody ordered. "I saved one for you."

The boy nodded eagerly, the bear momentarily replaced in his mind. Setting the plate in the microwave and turning on the timer, Jackie thought again of Mason. She saw him walking away from her, his back growing indistinct, a dark speck disappearing into memory as he climbed into the mountains after the bear. He wasn't hers to save, and never had been. No more than he could save the valley. Life was so much bigger than that. It nearly made her cry.

26

The dusk was luminous. The full moon rising in the pink sky cast an iridescent glow, bringing out the glimmer of quartz in the cliff face below Ogden Mountain. Black smoke from a distant sawmill threaded upward like the exhalation of the earth's interior furnace. Vultures still circled the campground to the west, where the woman's body had been. Mason had tracked the bear for the entire day. In his guilt and hunger, the quest had taken on biblical proportions. He limped after Molly through forests and across shadowed clearings, haunted by his past. The bear had not stopped and rested as he'd thought it would, as if it knew it needed to retreat deep into its territory. The distinctive tracks it left—the left front paw favored, the dragging imprint slightly deeper—led around Ogden Mountain, keeping to the jack pines at the timberline, then descending through a draw on the far side of the ridge. The bear had stopped to drink at the mouth of Deadman Creek and Mason had stopped also, sharing his jerky with Molly. Now night was closing in, and both man and dog were famished, exhausted, and cold. But Mason sensed the bear was close. He couldn't let it escape. His mistake had led to a woman's death.

Shadows flickered in the periphery of his vision. He picked his way across a field of scree and paused to rest against the charred trunk of a lightning-struck pine. All around him, similar blackened spear trees were driven into the earth. Fingering the bark, he felt something soft and withdrew a tuft of warm brown fur. He tilted his head back and sniffed the air. He could smell the bear: a strong, musky, earthen scent. It had stopped here and rubbed its back. Mason knew he was in danger—the bear was tracking him just as surely as he was tracking it—but he wasn't afraid. After a month of looking over his shoulder for Preston or one of the other Carters, the idea of facing the bear was almost a relief. He wondered what it would be like to be eaten. If at some point the pain would be replaced by curiosity, revelation. His only concern was for Molly, who watched him with glinting brown eyes, wondering why they weren't going home.

"Soon," he said, patting her head. "I'm almost done."

The woman's death had caused him to reevaluate his entire concept of right and wrong. By arresting poachers and running old trappers out of business, he'd cleared the way for rich tourists to build second homes around the old Mike Horse Mine. They'd used easements for an eighteen-hole golf course at Smith Pond. Their contracting crews killed animals by the score with bulldozers, and the cement they poured left no way for the trees to grow back. They parked their fancy cars outside the Lincoln Hotel and walked beside the river at night. Their children fed deer. A sadness filled Mason that he could not shake, for the Montana he'd first come to ten years before, with its trappers and speculators and violence at the Wilderness Bar every Friday night.

When Mason turned, he saw the bear behind him atop the scree field. It had flanked him and circled back, and now stood upright, watching him like a sentinel in the dusk. Smart, Mason thought, but it didn't matter. He had a gun. Slowly, he unslung the heavy rifle and braced the stock against his shoulder. The safety was ice-cold and it seemed to take a great amount of energy to click it off. In his exhaustion, he wasn't sure he could pull the trigger.

The bear's golden fur shimmered in the moonlight. It shifted its weight, sniffing the air. The hump on its back seemed to grow. It was a magnificent, towering creature, and Mason felt the whispered memory of a time when human life was defined as prey, before houses and cars and high-caliber weapons. Cavemen raising flaming torches against saber-toothed tigers, sharpening sticks, learning to launch arrows. On and on, until technology became a god of its own and all the predators were vanquished, leaving men to turn on themselves, with napalm and nuclear bombs. But we're still prey, Mason thought, thinking of his mother spending her days alone in the big house in Charlestown, the TV blaring, a slave to desire, shackled by commercials for new appliances and hi-fi equipment, afraid of all the things she might not have. He steadied the rifle, beginning to count down from ten, a tactic his uncle had taught him during their first hunting trips in Maine when he was a boy. Each number slowed his breath and focused his mind. He thought of all the pathways that had led to this moment, his disdain for his father, his love of the wild, his divorce.

Prey. he mouthed the word, shifting the interior vowel from *e* to *a*. He thought of the woman in the tent, how stunned she must have been that in the last half of the twentieth century her life could end in such a way. He thought of the black wolf, alone in the Bob, unknowingly transmitting its signal back to the receiver in his living room. He wished he could snap his fingers and make the collar fall off its neck. Of course Hutch had been right. *Pray.* Mason couldn't remember his last prayer. If he did now, it would be to the bear he was about to kill. This ancient giant at home in the unfeeling web of the universe. Mason's hands trembled. He peered through the scope. Magnified to fill his vision, the bear's eyes looked back into his, two golden pools, expectant, as if waiting for the debt of its life to be repaid.

On the final exhale, Mason squeezed the trigger. The recoil of the rifle slammed into his shoulder. Molly cowered by his leg.

The shot was so loud that Mason half expected flames to shoot from the earth, his damnation complete. The bear twitched and swatted its chest, rending the fur. Its claws came away wet with blood and it stumbled backward. Mason ejected the shell and slotted a second round forward into the chamber. The bear rose on its hind legs and bellowed a final wounded call across the valley. The sound echoed over the parks of Doug fir that lined the ridges, each one successively lighter in the starlight, forming waves along the shoreline of a lost antediluvian lake. Mason fired again. The impact knocked the bear back, twisting, before it collapsed on its side on the broken rock.

The night was silent. The moonlight seemed to tremble. Everything it touched was so pale and delicate that tears filled Mason's eyes. He set the rifle down. He patted Molly's head. He took the bronze Forest Service badge off his uniform and left it beside the gun.

"Come on, girl," he said. Then he began the long hike back to his truck, looking east toward what he knew would be the last sunrise they'd see over the Blackfoot Valley.

Salt Lake City, December 1981

*Pat Garret lived alone in a large gabled Victorian house that he'd paid for
with his inheritance. Every morning before leaving for work, he fed his beta
fish, typed a command into the* Colossal Cave *game on his Commodore
VIC-20 computer, and waited for a response. He'd played the game for
years, navigated every possible course for collecting the treasure, died in every
conceivable way, and now considered it a kind of friend, taking pleasure in
the odd singularity of its voice.*

YOU ARE IN A VALLEY IN THE FOREST ABOVE AN
OLD MINE.

"go in," he typed.

YOU ENTER THE MINE. IT IS DARK. YOU FALL
DOWN A SHAFT AND BREAK EVERY BONE IN YOUR
BODY!

*Pat smiled, gathered up his keys and wallet, and locked the front door
behind him. For the first time that winter, he had to scrape the frost from
the windshield of his sedan. As he traveled south to his store in Fairpark,
the morning traffic on the interstate was light. He listened to a talk show,
the hosts arguing about whether they could find Seychelles on a map, then
throwing it over to a new pop song about a woman dancing in the rain.*

*Rent-A-Tech was in the far corner of a strip mall on Lehi Avenue.
Pat had chosen the location because it was cheap and easily accessible to
the freeway. Rent-A-Tech was the first computer rental store in Utah,
and he'd figured, correctly, that though his customer base would be small,*

they'd be willing to travel great distances. He locked his car and walked around the front of the shop, scanning the empty lot. None of the neighboring businesses—Kirby's Shoes, Thrifty, Mario's Peruvian Restaurant—were open yet. He unlocked the door and flipped on the lights, shivering. Heather must not have left the heat on overnight. She was careless; he'd told her many times he didn't like his machines getting cold. Pat would have fired her if he didn't secretly dream of marrying her on the shore of the Great Salt Lake. He walked down the aisle between the display models: several Apple Macintoshs, the older Commodores in back, a brand-new sleek Amiga by the counter. Each one wiped clean of dust as if it had just emerged from the box.

In the back room, he turned on the heat and the sound system, and found a radio station playing Christmas music. He hated the saccharine songs, but it was what customers wanted this time of year, and it made them feel generous. He straightened the invoices and receipts on the table, stuck a pen and notepad in his pocket, and walked back up front to switch on the OPEN sign. "It's the most wonderful time of the year."

Thirty minutes later, late as usual, Heather showed up, and together they spent the morning assisting the slow but steady stream of customers: walking them through each machine's capabilities, the daily versus weekly rates, and insurance options. Most were small business owners looking to calculate their year-end books, but the Macintoshs brought in more and more dads who wanted a new toy "for the kids" at the holidays. These were Pat's favorite customers; they were interested in the games, and watched, impressed, as he demonstrated how entire worlds could open up on the glowing screens with a few simple keystrokes.

Pat had studied math at UC Berkeley, and while the free speech and antiwar protests raged outside, he'd spent most of his four years in the computer lab working as a lab assistant. At night in his dorm room, he wrote code for the open-source games that he and his friends passed around on floppy disks. The store had seemed like a logical choice when his academic career stalled and he found himself back in his hometown, dealing with his parents' estate. Now he found it oppressive, and he longed to move away *and create his own game.* Auguries, *it would be called, a game of potential futures, apocalypses interspersed by a few glittering utopias.*

Through the front window, he noticed a man in aviator sunglasses and a hooded sweatshirt hurrying away from the parking lot toward the bus stop on Lehi, his shoulders hunched against the wind. He moved oddly, like he was trying to hide his face. Pat glanced up at the clock. It was almost noon. "I'm heading out for lunch," he said to Heather. "Make sure the door stays closed. It lets the cold in."

Heather nodded impatiently as he left the store.

Bitter wind blew from the northeast. It smelled faintly of snow coming down from the Wasatch Mountains. Pat turned up his collar, trying not to fixate on his frustration. His infatuation with Heather left him feeling constantly provoked. He was unsure of how to deal with women, having spent most of his life alone. He reminded himself to bring his snow shovel from home the next day, so he wouldn't have to borrow one from Mario. Then he stopped.

A paper bag was sitting in the center of the empty parking space in front of his store. Pat stared at the bag. It was clearly full of something, since it didn't blow away in the wind. Shaking his head, Pat approached and bent down. Inside was a wooden box studded with nails. The nails had been hammered out through the wood so the sharp ends stuck up at different angles. It could easily puncture a tire. In fact, it looked like it had been designed to. Was someone trying to sabotage Rent-A-Tech? Pat looked around nervously, craning his neck to see if the man in aviators was still on the corner, but he had disappeared. The only possible enemy Pat could think of was another of the game designers he exchanged code with. Had he slighted one of them somehow? The thought pained him. He always tried to give credit where it was due. He had few friends, and the nascent community was sacred to him. Plus, the design of the wood was vicious. At least thirty nails bristled inside the bag. The malevolence was almost comical. Perhaps it was meant as a joke, a command-prompt taken into the real world. YOU'VE BROKEN EVERY BONE IN YOUR BODY!

Curious now, Pat reached for the bag. He felt a strange sense of vertigo as he did, the same as he'd experienced in temple as a boy waiting for the sacrament. The paper crinkled in his fingers and he lifted the bag. A ball of fire ignited in the center. The fire spread outward, enveloping his hands, and bearing the nails into his chest on the crest of a flaming wave. Pat felt pain, terrible pain. He heard a tremendous deafening crash. The entire lot shook. The percussive blast blew out the front windows of his shop. The sign above Mario's Peruvian Restaurant crashed down and Pat watched the remains of his lower body, blackened beyond recognition, scatter across the pavement. That's my body, he thought, overwhelmed by horror. I need it.

TED

The last thirty years have been witnessing
the active disintegration of Western
civilization. . . . Everywhere the machine
holds the center and the personality
has been pushed to the periphery.

—LEWIS MUMFORD, *THE CONDITION OF MAN*

27

Slow down, dammit, Ted cursed his feet, which were propelling him rapidly down the sidewalk away from Rent-A-Tech. Panic made it hard not to sprint. The explosion had nearly knocked him to the ground from three blocks away. A blast that powerful must have killed someone, maybe several people. And the girl in the store had seen him. He knew she had. Their eyes met after he placed the bomb in the parking lot. It was too late to pick up the bomb—it was armed—so he'd fled. It doesn't matter, he told himself. She can't identify you. He hunched his shoulders and tucked his chin into his hooded sweatshirt. Aviator sunglasses blocked his eyes, and he'd rubbed bootblack into his cheeks to darken his complexion. A fake mustache was pasted over his upper lip. Still, he felt a crushing terror, fearing agents in pursuit.

Waiting pedestrians were clustered at the bus stop on the corner of Lehi Avenue. Ted pushed his way between them. Their gaunt faces looked tired in old caps and earmuffs. All races, all ages. A hopeless crowd. His people, he thought, listening to them chatter nervously about the explosion. Often, when he rested in his favorite clearing at the foot of the ancient Douglas fir, he imagined such an army rising up to finish his work. Planting explosives of their own, burning down factories, shooting up universities. This was why he stamped F C, for Freedom Club, on all of his bombs, pretending to be part of an eco-anarchist collective. Coded messages for keen eyes.

"Gas line must've blown," a construction worker said authoritatively, and Ted felt the crowd give a communal sigh of relief. It wasn't the Russians. Ted imagined the entire mass of them subsumed in flame. Cigarette smoke mixed with the exhaust in the air. He avoided eye contact, stuffing his hands into his pockets and leaning into the street, hoping to see the crosstown bus. He'd left his belongings in a locker in the central station and was desperate to get back and change his clothes.

Beside him, a little girl in a pink coat clung to her mother's neck. Sirens wailed and more pedestrians elbowed in around Ted, talking breathlessly. "Wasn't it last Christmas that the whole electrical grid blew out?" "What are we paying taxes for?" Finally, the bus arrived, lurching to a stop as the driver cranked open the door. Ted was the first to board. Keeping his head down, he paid his fare and found a seat in the back. Only when he was wedged in tightly did he allow himself to look out the window.

Black smoke twisted over the strip mall in the distance. The cloud grew, obscuring the entire roof. Police and ambulance lights flashed around the parking lot. Ted clasped his hands together, suddenly overcome by a wild excitement. Gleefully, he pulled the hood tight around his ears. Finally. He'd done it. He knew he had. The bus rocked forward and merged back into traffic. Looking down at the other cars below, Ted felt an electric tension in his veins and thought back to the first bomb he'd built—little more than a firework—that he'd tossed from the Anderson Bridge at Harvard and watched pop uselessly over the Charles River. How far he'd come. And what was possible now?

In the shaking of the earth, he'd felt a power more profound than any he'd ever experienced before, akin to what a god must feel, if there was such a thing. He thought of his old friend, the grizzly who'd been shot down by Mason after killing the woman on Stemple Pass two summers before. Ted had climbed up to the fallen beast in the moonlight, and now wore one of its claws as a necklace on a leather cord. He could feel the cool, curved shape beneath his layers of clothing. Glancing around at the other passengers, registering their faces for the first time, he felt welcomed into a lineage of predators. He no longer saw them as fellow civilians, but as prey. It was a marvelous feeling. He was a bear moving invisibly among deer, and as the bus bore him past grocery stores and gas stations thronging with people, he knew he could reach out and destroy any one of them without ever revealing his true face.

28

A mile away, Tracy heard the blast as a dull *thud*. The dirty dishes vibrated in the sink. She yanked her hands from the soapy water, spraying droplets across the counter, and leaned forward. Through the window, she saw a thin column of smoke in the distance. Fear made her spin around, looking toward the bedroom where her two-year-old daughter Kit was asleep. What was happening? An explosion here in her neighborhood? Lately, Fairpark seemed like it was on the verge of chaos. Drunks and bums slept in the alleys, hippies crowded the freeway on-ramp, and shortages led to fights at the gas station. Now what? A bomb?

Bombs were supposed to go off in foreign countries, not Utah. Tracy wiped her hands on her shirt and ran outside into the yard. It was a cold, clear day and the winter sun hurt her eyes. Faintly, she smelled melting asphalt. A cop car sped past, lights flashing. She watched it until it disappeared around the corner of Lehi. The empty street unsettled her. The silent houses were a facade, a veneer of safety that had never been real. What if there were more bombs? In grocery stores, on street corners, in schools? Her children. . . . Her heart rattled her rib cage and she thought of Pete's gun in his sock drawer. She could get it, wake Kit from her nap, go to the school and find Hudson, and drive them into the mountains.

Calm down, Tracy told herself. It could have been a gas line, faulty wiring—any of the explanations they always gave for disasters on the nightly news. But with crime rising, Russians on the march, and terrorists blowing up embassies in the Middle East, it seemed stupid *not* to worry. She returned inside, cradled the phone against her ear, and dialed the number for Hudson's school, looking out at the rising smoke.

The school secretary didn't know anything about the explosion. She assured Tracy that classes were continuing as scheduled. "But Hudson hasn't been here all morning, and that's the second time this week."

Tracy's hand trembled as she hung up the receiver.

She leaned her forehead against the cool wall, forcing herself to breathe. Sometimes life was just too much. Ever since starting seventh grade, Hudson had constantly been in trouble. He refused to do his chores, talked back, and cut classes. With Kit and her job, Tracy couldn't keep track of him every minute. She'd been promoted to manager at Walgreens. Along with the twenty-cent-per-hour raise came extra hours and making the schedule every week. Looking over the list of names, all of whom wanted the holidays off for ski trips and parties, she'd realized she was a thirty-year-old woman doing a teenager's job. It was enough to make her scream.

The front door opened and Tracy spun on her heel, relief briefly overwhelming her worry. She confronted Hudson in the living room, grabbed his shoulders, and pulled him close. She held him until he pushed her away. Then she forced herself to keep her voice down so as not to wake Kit. "Where the hell have you been?"

At twelve, the boy was already almost a foot taller than her, with his father's mournful eyes and sloping shoulders. Sometimes she felt she was in the presence of another version of Duane, and had to force down her distaste. "Did you hear that?" he asked.

"Answer my question."

"It sounded like something blew up. There are cops all over."

"I called the school. The truant officer is looking for you."

He shrugged and brushed past her to the fridge, emerging with a block of cheese and a package of ham. "It's lunchtime. Shouldn't you be at work?"

Tracy battled the urge to grab a fistful of dirty forks from the sink and launch them at her son's chest. Hudson spent the majority of his time sulking or eating. Complaining about school, saying how he wished he lived in Montana with his dad, and devouring everything she bought without a word of thanks. The quantities he consumed astounded her. Entire boxes of cereal and gallons of milk would disappear in days. Pete called him "the Black Hole." "Sit down," she said. "I need to talk to you."

"I'm hungry." Hudson moved toward his room.

"Sit!" she commanded.

Reluctantly, the boy sank into a chair at the kitchen table. He set the ham and cheese in front of him, awkwardly adjusted his long legs, and crossed his arms. Tracy took a deep breath. It exhausted her trying to talk to her son, like moving rocks across the freeway. Her father would have slapped the hell out of her if she skipped class. The boy had no discipline, that was the problem. He didn't know what it took to survive in the world. "The secretary said you weren't in class earlier this week. Where'd you go?"

"Nowhere. I just walked around."

"Walked around?"

"The neighborhood."

"You think it's safe to walk around the neighborhood alone? You're twelve. There are *serial killers*." Tracy stopped herself. She watched the news every night, and it caused her a near-hysteric anxiety to compare the faces of murder victims to Hudson's. So often they were thin, sandy-haired boys. She'd wake deep in the night convinced that he'd already been taken, and blaming herself.

"I'm almost thirteen," he said.

"You're still a boy." Tracy looked at her son. His wispy innocence was falling away by the day, replaced by pimples, sullen moods, and the first straggly whiskers above his lip. Cleaning his room the week before, she'd found a stack of comics with bare-breasted women and leering bikers—*Killers on Wheels, Race with the Devil*—in the drawer where his coloring books used to be. "I'm trying to keep you safe," she said.

Hudson shrugged.

Tracy reminded herself not to lose her temper. If Kit woke, she'd be fussy all afternoon. "How about this: If you stop skipping school and pass all your classes, you can spend the whole summer with your dad in Montana this year. Three months, June, July, and August." Hudson had never been away for more than two months before, and Tracy hadn't cleared the plan with Duane, but she didn't intend to give him a choice. He'd finally finished his cabin and had room for the boy. Lord knew he owed her at least that much in child support.

Immediately Hudson's face brightened. "Really?"

Tracy nodded.

"The whole summer?" The change in his disposition was so dramatic Tracy wondered if he was being bullied at school. Was that why he cut class? Fundamentally, he was a gentle boy, and she suspected that some of the older kids picked on him.

"You have to pass all your classes," Tracy repeated, feeling a weight leave her shoulders as well. Three months without Hudson in the house would be good for her. It would be good for Pete, too. She tried to remember the last time they'd had sex, and had to count in weeks.

Through the window, the black smoke thinned out to a gray haze above the distant strip mall roof. No more explosions shook the duplex, and Tracy's nerves began to calm. Maybe it had been an accident, a gas range or transformer blowing out. Beyond the smoke, the I-15 freeway curved south, raised on concrete pylons leading out of Salt Lake to Las Vegas, Los Angeles, San Diego. Watching the freeway during slow hours at work, Tracy felt entire planets passing her by. Some days she wanted to get in her car alone and drive until she hit the ocean.

"Can I go to my room now?" Hudson asked, looking at her with a crinkle of worry on his high forehead.

"Yes." Tracy sighed. "Finish your lunch and then I'll bring you back to school." Hudson nodded, his face still lit with excitement over the prospect of a full summer in Montana, and disappeared into his room with the ham and cheese. After he was gone, Tracy sat at the table and tried to reassure herself that she'd made the right choice. Not only for Hudson's summer but her whole life. She thought of Pete, her kids, her job, the duplex. . . .

You do the best you can with what you have, she told herself.

Not entirely convinced, Tracy stood and finished washing the dishes. Then she took the chicken she'd picked up from the grocery store that morning out of the refrigerator. She had to work the evening shift, so dinner had to be made now, or else Pete would waste money on takeout. She rinsed the chicken and slopped the slimy white body onto the cutting board and sawed off the legs. She split the chest and flattened it in the Pyrex baking dish so it would cook faster. What an ugly bird. She lay the legs around the severed neck and sprinkled it with salt. She didn't even particularly like chicken, but Pete, Hudson, and Kit did, and it was cheap. Tracy poured oil over the chicken's breast and tossed a few garlic cloves into the chest cavity, then put it in the stove. Was this all there was to life? Cooking dinners you didn't want while you waited for disaster to strike? Tracy idly thumbed through a fashion magazine, listening to Hudson thump around in his room. Life wasn't what they pretended on the glossy pages, that was for sure. The models all had eating disorders and actresses were killed by their stalkers.

Sighing, she pushed the magazine away and turned on the

radio. She scanned the channels until she found a report on the explosion. In rushed tones, the announcer said that a bomb had gone off in front of Rent-A-Tech, killing the shop owner. Tracy knitted her brow, remembering the small store in the corner of the strip mall by the weird Peruvian restaurant. Passing by, she'd wondered what anyone could possibly need a computer for. She imagined the shop owner walking to his car and then, *bam*, blown to pieces. It really was like a war zone. She drummed her fingers on the edge of the table. Maybe Hudson would be better off in Montana with his dad. It had to be safer there, in the woods.

29

That night, the campus of Brigham Young University lay silent by ten-thirty. Only a few lights still glowed in the dormitory windows, and these were blocked by curtains. Ted walked down the shrub-lined path to the campus post office carrying his backpack. The power he'd felt earlier in the day had dissipated into fear. A radio report had confirmed that the computer store owner, a man named Pat Garret, was dead. Ted had even seen Pat's face on the news through the window of a TV store. Flaccid, nominally intelligent-looking. Repeating the name, Ted shivered. A line had been crossed and he couldn't go back. He reassured himself that it had been a painless death, merely blinking out of existence, but he still felt frightened. Police were out looking for him, the FBI. . . . He longed to be out of the city, but his work wasn't done.

The December night was cloudy and still. Ted wore a collared shirt, slacks, thick-framed glasses, and black gloves. He'd removed the metal frame from his pack in the hope that, if confronted, he could pass for a doctoral candidate, like he'd been a decade before. The pack was heavy; the straps dug into his shoulders. He walked with an odd shuffling gait to keep it from jostling. Extra soles—

two sizes too small—were glued to the bottom of his shoes to obscure his footprints. He passed a janitor and ducked his head.

The post office was in the far corner of the student center. An empty fountain stood in the courtyard. Through the plate-glass window of the campus shop, purple sweatshirts proclaimed COUGAR PRIDE. Shouldn't they be the missionaries? The proselytizers? Ted wondered. His hands were sweating beneath his gloves. He tugged them nervously. He knew people made mistakes when they were anxious and rushed. Gently he pushed open the post office's glass door. Walls of numbered mailboxes surrounded him. The counter was shuttered, but a night-drop bin lay on the floor below it. Kneeling, Ted eased the pack from his back and set it down. A strange-looking metal apparatus rested on top of a stamped and addressed package inside. He removed the apparatus, then lifted out the package. He held it affectionately for a moment, like a child, then placed it in the night-drop. It was addressed to Lionel Cass, chair of psychology at Vanderbilt University. Ted had calculated the postage using a lab scale, then soaked the purple Eugene O'Neill stamps in lacquer and applied them with tweezers. He intended to keep using the mail even though leaving packages was a more effective method. He wanted to make people afraid of the postal service, to shake their faith in the pillars of industrial society.

He returned the apparatus to the pack, lifted the pack carefully onto his shoulders, and left.

The moon was barely a sliver. He'd chosen the night of the new moon for its darkness. The winter solstice was two weeks away, and while the Blackfoot Valley had already been frozen in snow when Ted left, here in Salt Lake the ground was dry. Dead grass lined the walk. The bare branches of maples reached up like gnarled claws in front of the dining hall. Being on campus raised painful memories, and Ted hurried on. Breathing rapidly, he crossed the quad, seeing only one other figure in silhouette moving in the opposite direction. Brigham Young himself stood in bronze inside a paved circle where the north-south and east-west paths converged. A cape hung from his shoulders; his chest was thrust forward. He held a cane in his right hand, driving it down into the granite stand. Ted felt a twinge of jealousy for the age when you could come to Utah and find a vast, barren landscape, free of houses and cars.

The Computer Science Building was a huge brutalist structure with cement columns and only a few small windows high up on the walls. Ted remembered the windowless carrels where he'd spent his mid-twenties as a young professor at Berkeley, grading student papers and preparing lectures on boundary functions. He briefly wondered if he might blow up a young version of himself, but he dismissed the thought: none of his peers at Harvard or Michigan or Berkeley had been anything like him. They were all followers, fools, without an original thought in their heads. Time to burn them out. He found an unlocked side door and entered a dimly lit hall. The classrooms on either side were closed. Paintings of scientific innovators lined the walls: Galileo, Archimedes, Humboldt, Einstein. Forefathers of the industrial age. Ted would have liked to send a bomb to them all.

The clack of keyboard keys and the soft murmur of voices drifted from the computer lab at the end of the hall. Ted's heart sped up. If someone emerged, he worried he might panic and run, detonating the device in his pack and blowing himself to pieces—an end too humiliating to contemplate. The last thing he wanted was to die inside a building like this.

The extra soles on his shoes squeaked on the linoleum floor as he tried each door. Finally, just before the lab, when he was considering giving up and leaving the apparatus by a drinking fountain, a door swung inward. He slipped inside. Standing in the darkness, he smelled the peculiar combination of cleaning supplies, chalk, and textbook paper common to academic buildings. The smell infuriated him. He wished for a moment that his bomb was big enough to flatten the entire campus.

He knew now that Henry Murray's study at Harvard had been funded by the CIA. Murray was developing interrogation tactics to break prisoners of war, and had used Ted and his class-mates as guinea pigs, asking them to submit an essay about their core beliefs and values, then giving the paper to the interrogators before the first session so they had all the information they needed to shred the subject's self-confidence. They berated Ted using his own words against him. Then they forced him to watch a video recording of his increasingly hysterical responses. He could still see his body cowering on the hard stool beneath the spotlight in the grainy footage, flinching at each question like a beaten animal. Ted wished he could send a bomb to Murray himself, but knew that would put him on a list of suspects. His eyes adjusted and the fur-niture took shape: Couches, tables, a bulletin board holding a class schedule. A refrigerator hummed in the corner. A coffeepot and microwave sat on the counter. It was a faculty lounge.

Perfect. All professors were colleagues of Murray's, in a sense, with the same craven self-importance. Ted took off his pack and set it gently on the floor. He unbuckled the straps and carefully lifted out the apparatus. Heavy and bulbous, the strange shape was cast in shadow, the welded joints glimmering. It had been a lot of work, his most complex device yet. He'd incorporated gasoline, hoping fire would spread after the initial explosion. The main body was a metal tank with rounded sides two feet long and one and a half wide. A gauge was attached to the front. A handsaw grip was welded to the lid. The gauge and grip had no function save to cause someone to attempt to open the lid and trip the trigger. The gasoline filling the upper chamber made it heavy and Ted exhaled when he set it on the counter beside the microwave. He backed away, lifted his empty pack, swung it on, and stood for a moment in the darkness, imagining the flames, the smell of burning hair, and the screams that would soon fill this room. Smiling to himself, he hurried out into the night.

30

Duane had found an old pair of skis and boots, miraculously his size, at the church rummage sale. He couldn't afford any of the nearby resorts, so he strapped the skis to his back and skinned up the long gentle grade of the old logging road on Strawberry Ridge above Hutch's property. He made sure to keep his tracks on the left, then skied down the virgin powder on the right. He couldn't turn without falling but found he had a knack for keeping the tips straight in front of him. It pleased him immensely to see the forests and mountains sweeping by and his own tracks neatly in the snow.

On his way home, he passed Hutch and Pastor Younger standing on the icy driveway in front of Hutch's trailer. Hutch waved him over.

"I've got something you'll want to see," he said.

"It's incredible," Pastor Younger added. "Like looking into the eyes of God."

Duane stared at them, confused.

"I won't say anything else." The pastor raised his hands. "I don't want to spoil it. See you tomorrow, though, Duane?"

"Sure thing," Duane replied. He was halfway through splitting another load of wood at the Blackfoot Valley Church. Pastor

Younger had started a wood ministry the year before, delivering split wood to families in need throughout the valley, and trying to keep up with the orders occupied Duane through most of the winter. The muscles in his shoulders had grown hard from wielding the ax, and callouses marked his palms; Jackie told him he might make a woodsman yet. He'd tried his hand at ranching as well, hiring on for haying season at the Company Ranch, but discovered he was terrified not just of cows but of horses, too. Cows in general after his encounter with the Carter steer, and horses for riding. He didn't mind a horse in a pasture, but with a saddle they turned skittish and malevolent, Duane thought. He'd only lasted two days at the ranch and the foreman still joked that he was the worst cowboy who ever cowboyed, a statement Duane found both hurtful and unnecessarily hyperbolic.

"What was that about?" Duane asked, when the pastor's truck had disappeared.

"He's an owl man," Hutch said, chuckling. "Owls and blondes."

Unsure of what this meant, Duane leaned his skis on the side of the porch and followed Hutch inside.

The shades were drawn and it took Duane's eyes a moment to adjust to the dim light. When they did, he saw a huge domed cage in the center of the living room. A great horned owl was perched inside, motionless, the size of a toddler, much bigger than any bird he'd ever seen, with a broad white chest and mottled brown markings on the wings. The tip of the left wing was wrapped in gauze bandages. Its talons and bill were gunmetal-gray. The eyes, under threateningly slanted brows, were so bright and yellow they felt physically sharp, like knives piercing Duane's chest. The owl stared directly at him. Not a feather trembled on its body. Duane felt his mouth go dry and looked away. "Where the hell did that come from?"

"He hobbled right onto my land over by the sawmill, like he knew I'd help." Pride filled Hutch's voice. "I sometimes think the animals talk about me, let each other know I'll fix them up if they get hurt."

Duane had occasionally been helping Hutch with his animals ever since Mason left the valley two years before, but he'd never considered their opinions of him one way or the other. It opened up a new realm of insecurity, having to worry what hawks and coyotes were saying.

"Something got into him bad, bit his wing so he can't fly. I'm keeping him in here until he heals. It's too cold for him outside."

The owl swiveled its head and fixed its stare on Hutch. Duane was relieved to be free of the piercing glare. Dixon Sleepingbear—back in the valley after a stint driving logging trucks in British Columbia—had told him it was bad luck to see an owl in the daytime, let alone make prolonged eye contact.

"Where'd you get the cage?" Duane asked. Gilded with gold spray-painted flowers, it looked like something out of a French palace.

"It was Mrs. Didriksen's. She kept cockatiels. Show birds, apparently. After she died, Mr. Didriksen gave it to me. Said she'd want it put to good use. I've had it out in the shed for years."

"He looks like royalty in there," Duane said.

Hutch nodded, clearly pleased.

"Does he do much hooting?"

"Every hour or so. Wakes me up all night. Hopefully I can move him outside soon, he's eating half his weight in mice." Hutch cleared his throat and Duane noticed the exhaustion on his friend's face. Hutch had never quite recovered his manic energy after the death of his huskies, and he was prone to bouts of sudden quiet, in which his eyes searched the past. "I have to slide them in, in a little tube; he'd hurt himself trying to catch them otherwise. He won't eat anything that's already dead."

"Lots different than what goes on in my cabin," Duane answered. Bone-filled pellets littered the floor of the cage. The owl unsettled him and he wanted to leave, but he felt obligated to his friend to give the bird more consideration, so he pushed down his unease and knelt in front of it. Its eyes locked on to his, following them while Duane bobbed his head back and forth. "Does it watch you wherever you go?"

"Even in the pisser I can feel him watching through the door," Hutch answered.

"Jesus."

Walking back to his cabin, Duane remembered an owl that had frightened Hudson the summer before when they were camping on Monture Creek. It had flown low over their fire, its immense wingspan a gliding shadow, causing the boy to press himself against Duane's shoulder. The memory filled Duane with melancholy. It had been four months since he'd seen his son, and he missed him badly. He felt like a stone skipping across the surface of Hudson's life, finding his son dramatically changed each summer when he touched down.

As Duane rounded the bend, his property came into view. His pride for the finished cabin pushed away his melancholy. It was a simple split-log structure with a bedroom and bathroom in the back and a small loft over the living room. The eaves were slightly uneven and nail heads poked out around the window frames, but it was solid and held heat, and Duane had had a hand in building every part of it, even the plumbing. It was the greatest accomplishment of his life, outside of Hudson. A chain-saw-carved bear that Hutch gave him stood by the door. The trailer he'd bought from Vern Floyd—where he'd lived for the four years it took him to build the cabin—was parked on a flat spot ten yards away. He was trying to sell the trailer, and, finding no buyers, used it as storage. It amazed him how much junk he'd managed to accumulate, even though he never had any money. Sighing, he leaned the skis against the corrugated side and went inside the cabin.

An old woodstove stood in the corner. The leather couch,

chair, and coffee table all came from the sale the Lincoln Hotel had after it was sold to new developers. Jackie had helped him pick out the sky-blue tile in the bathroom. The tile gave the room a brightness even in the depths of winter, and an electric heater kept it warmer than the rest of the house. Duane often lingered on the toilet in the mornings, feeling a deep satisfaction. He had a home, land, and a woman. In the summers when Hudson was visiting, his life seemed just about complete.

Taking off his boots at the kitchen table, Duane considered the pastor's proclivities. Owls and blondes. He knew about the pastor's years-long affair with Joni McCall, Tom's wife. Everyone did, but what business was it of theirs? Duane surely hadn't wanted anyone to know when Tracy was running around with Pete. He sighed. But maybe Tom didn't mind. Back in Salt Lake, Duane had heard of a contractor who *paid* other men to sleep with his wife. And that was in Mormon country. The world was a strange place. Duane took off his hat and ran his hand back over his receding, close-cropped hair. At thirty-five, he figured he was getting old, and wished he had more wisdom to show for it.

Cracking a beer, Duane leaned against the stove and looked around his small kitchen. The particular affection he held for his truck had spread to the cabin, and he often found himself speaking to it as if it were a friend. "What's for dinner tonight?" he asked.

The walls offered no answer, and, opening the fridge, Duane was disappointed to find a few slices of bacon, a crusty bottle of mustard, and a wedge of old cheese, along with some bread. He didn't feel like driving into town. He took out the cheese and a piece of bread and glanced out the window at the end of Hutch's driveway, thinking of the owl with its gunmetal talons and dagger eyes. He quickly drew the blinds in case the bird was still watching.

IT WAS A CLEAR DAY, and the Swan Range rose craggy and white to the west. Duane drove slowly from the Food Town parking lot, drumming his fingers on the steering wheel to keep them warm. Impatiently, he looked up at the snowy peaks. It wasn't yet Christmas and already he was tired of the cold. He had to invent ways to keep his spirits up over the long, dark winters. Jackie had encouraged him to cook, so he'd bought tortilla chips, beans, a pound of ground beef, cheddar cheese, and salsa from the grocery store to make her nachos when she got off work. Now that his cabin was finished, she sometimes stayed over during the week. He smiled at the thought.

A familiar figure was sitting on his pack on the snow by the side of the road in front of the Wilderness Bar. Hunched forward with his arms wrapped around his knees, he looked pathetic and exhausted in the shadow of the tinsel-wrapped pine, which Liv decorated for Christmas every year, and then neglected to un-decorate until spring. Duane pulled over. "Hey, Ted, you need a ride?"

Ted nodded and picked up his pack. Duane was surprised by his shaved face, khakis, and collared shirt. Generally, his neighbor's appearance ran from dirty to filthy, and he kept his beard long and wore the same pair of canvas trousers and green army coat all winter long. Because Ted was his closest neighbor, Duane often gave him rides, but still knew very little about him. The only private information he'd been able to extract was that he'd grown up in Chicago and had a brother in West Texas. Private, Duane figured, like many men who sought refuge in the woods of northern Montana. He'd heard rumors that Ted had gone to Harvard but dismissed these, figuring no one with such a big brain would live in the squalor of a one-room shack. Duane leaned over and opened the passenger door, swatting an empty Styrofoam cup off the seat. "Where you been?" he asked.

"Visiting family." The high nasal quality of Ted's voice always startled Duane, as if it were being forced through a narrow tube. Ted climbed into the cab, set the pack—which had a loaf of bread poking from the top and clanked with soup cans—between his legs, and stared straight ahead through the windshield. He was generally quiet when Duane picked him up, though sometimes he asked a series of questions in rapid succession: "What's the date?" "What's the temperature?" "Is there a storm coming?" Now he seemed nervous, as if he didn't want to be seen in town.

"Didn't miss much here," Duane said, glancing again at Ted's collared shirt, which on closer inspection had the rumpled, sodden look of multiple days of wear. He was surprised by the heaviness of his jaw without a beard. His neighbor could've been handsome if he took better care of himself. "Hutch has an owl in his living room and it's been snowing every damn day."

"Do you mind if we stop at the library?" Ted replied.

"Sure," Duane answered. Ted had never asked him to make an extra stop before. "You looking for a book?"

"There's a history of ecology. The librarian ordered it for me."

Duane felt his cheeks redden. He didn't know exactly what ecology was, but it had to do with the environment, and he still felt guilt for clear-cutting the forest each summer. "Did I tell you about the bobcat Hutch and I rescued up Hogum Gulch after that cold snap in the fall?" he said, hoping to balance out his logging. "Hutch held the dang thing right against his chest the whole way home to keep it warm. I kept thinking the tranquilizers would wear off and it'd bite his face off."

"I'm just glad those dogs are gone," Ted said. "They never used to shut up."

Surprised, Duane glanced at his neighbor. Ted was staring out the window, as if thinking about something else. He'd never mentioned Hutch's huskies before. They'd been dead almost three years. Uneasiness spread through Duane's chest as he pulled into the library's small parking lot.

"I'll be right back," Ted said, climbing from the cab.

Duane watched him disappear inside and then looked down at the pack on the floorboard. He thought again of how little he knew about his neighbor. He admired Ted's self-reliance, how he made it through winter without a vehicle, and the sizable garden he harvested in his yard. On several occasions, Duane had asked him for directions to some new part of the territory, and he always obliged in painstaking detail with instructions of where to go and where to avoid. He'd even spent several days helping Duane roof his cabin before winter set in. Now Duane wondered if he could have killed Hutch's huskies simply for making too much noise. No, impossible. It had to be the Carters or some other rancher, mad about Hutch disarming their traps.

Still . . . Duane peered into the library. He could see Ted talking to the librarian. Without thinking, he reached down and opened Ted's pack. Inside was a pair of aviator sunglasses wrapped in black gloves, along with the bread, soup, canned olives, and a stack of mail. A bus ticket from Salt Lake City was tucked between dirty undergarments. The underwear smelled fairly of gasoline. Duane closed the pack and straightened, wondering why Ted's ticket was from Salt Lake—hardly on the way home from Chicago. The door of the library opened and Ted reappeared, carrying a thick cellophane-wrapped book.

"Thanks," he said, settling into the passenger seat.

Duane bobbed his head and continued the drive, turning off the highway onto Stemple Pass Road. "Where's your family, again?" he asked casually.

"Chicago," Ted answered.

"That's a long trip."

Ted nodded silently.

"They ever come out here?"

"No." Ted stopped. "My dad did once. Not anymore."

"My mom's never come, and she's just down in Salt Lake." Duane glanced at Ted, whose expression didn't change. "She doesn't like the bus."

"They don't understand my life," Ted said.

"I guess most people wouldn't." Duane looked out the window at the tall, snow-covered, sentinel trees on either side. He remembered how he'd wondered what they'd look like in winter the first time he'd driven the road. Now they were garlanded in snow just as he'd imagined, with tiny icicles clinging to the upper needles, ready to be shaken free by a strong wind. "Are they retired there?"

Ted nodded silently.

The road was freshly graded and plowed and gravel embankments lined the edges. Two new cabins were under construction, one for a dentist in Helena and the other for a retired couple out of Boise. The dentist was building a gaudy stone mansion, and had trucks delivering supplies almost every day. "I reckon this new road will be a lot easier on your bike come spring," Duane said.

"Why'd they do it?"

"The road? You didn't hear? A new timber company got a contract to harvest up near the pass. Some big German outfit. They'll start as soon as the snow clears."

Ted's body tensed. Duane could feel it even in the driver's seat, like a caged animal was suddenly in the truck.

"You shouldn't hear much but some big trucks going by," Duane said. "I know you like your privacy."

"How much are they taking?"

"Oh, I don't know the stumpage. I only work for Tom. . . ." Duane trailed off.

"They should leave these forests alone."

"I reckon I agree with you there. I hate to think of the big outfits coming in."

The two men continued the drive in silence, gazing at the corridors of pines on either side of the road. The Doug-fir needles looked blue in the winter light. Duane's uneasiness made him run through all the strange things about his neighbor: the scrap metal he was always hauling from town, the way his hands and clothes were often blackened with soot, how he muttered to himself when he rode his bike, carrying on conversations as if the rest of the world didn't exist. "How'd your garden come out this year?" Duane asked, to mask his discomfort.

"Carrots, onions, parsnips, potatoes," Ted said, looking straight ahead.

The forest deepened, long shadows stretching across the snowy ground. Tangled branches blocked out the sun. Duane pulled off onto the shoulder in front of Ted's property. His shack was barely visible through the trunks. It was little more than a ten-by-ten frame surrounded in plywood and tarpaper and propped on concrete pillars. One corner of the steep green roof was patched with sheet metal. The wall studs were plank wood, hastily banged together. Bits of insulation poked out at the corners. Duane couldn't imagine how cold it must get. Some nights in Lincoln the wind chill went down past fifty below. Odd bits of trash littered the yard: bottles, scrap metal, a pair of rusted bike wheels, a pile of burnt cans. "You grow enough to last for the winter?" he asked.

Ted nodded.

"How do you store them?"

Ted looked at his home, then back at Duane impatiently, clearly wanting the conversation to end now that he was home. "Root cellar. Five feet in, it stays forty degrees all year-round." He pointed toward the hillside, where Duane saw a wooden door planted in the dirt. Ted gathered up his book and pack, got out, and walked to his cabin without looking back.

Well-traveled paths crisscrossed the yard. One of them led directly to a tall gnarled Doug fir with several boards nailed to its trunk below rung-like branches leading up to a plywood roost below the crown. Duane had the sudden suspicion that Ted climbed the tree to surveil the road. Shaking his head, he swung the truck around and headed home.

31

Ted spent the afternoon in his cabin resting and recovering from his trip. He was still out of sorts from the long bus ride, with his nerves jangling and Pat Garret's name repeating in his head. The conversation with Duane had irritated him as well. Why had he said so much? Luckily his neighbor was a fool.

At dusk, he realized he'd forgotten to change clothes. Immediately he took off the collared shirt and khakis and hung them on the rack by the door. Then he unpacked his pack, setting one of the soup cans aside for dinner and dropping his undergarments in the wash basket. He returned the aviators to the chest with his other disguises and burned the bus ticket over the stove.

Three bombs. One at Rent-A-Tech, one at BYU, and one on its way to Vanderbilt. His most successful mission yet. Pride mixed with Ted's concern over his own absentmindedness, particularly with the long winter ahead. He heated the soup and sat eating by the fire, finally beginning to calm in the familiar setting. It was natural, he supposed, to feel agitated after killing someone. He remembered the first deer he'd shot and how adrenaline had kept him up most of the night. The deer had suffered, though. The bullet pierced its lung and he'd tracked it through the woods for an hour before it died. Pat Garret was incinerated instantly.

The soup didn't satiate Ted—he'd barely eaten in two days—and he used his knife to open a can of preserved deer meat. He'd learned more about Pat from newspaper stories: thirty-eight, single, and by coincidence a Berkeley grad. Ted wondered if he'd ever seen him on campus when he was teaching there. He was pleased that Pat had no children or spouse. A neatly closed loop. It all felt preordained and right, though he wished the visiting professor who'd picked up his bomb at BYU had died as well. He sat at the chair at his desk finishing the meat and flipping idly through his mail—mostly letters from his mother and subscription offers for garish magazines—until he came to a large pink floral-scented envelope. Unable to imagine what it could be, Ted tore open the flap and removed a folded piece of ivory stationery. He stared down at the ornate script. The gold writing was so flowery it took a moment to decipher: his brother was getting married in San Antonio the following June. Shock made Ted lean back in his chair. He hadn't spoken to David in almost two years, since an argument in which Ted accused his brother of letting his romanticism compromise his ideals. *Married.* It seemed his downfall was complete. Angrily, Ted stood up and paced back and forth in front of his bed. Why hadn't his mother said anything about this in one of her rambling letters? She must've known it would upset him.

Still pacing, Ted resented how the news had returned him to the trivial world of his family. He should be celebrating the success of his mission. Hadn't he told them not to ever disturb him? He tried to imagine David buying furniture sets and matching china, cooking dinner for his new wife, teaching high school history. It was so pathetic he wanted to punch the wall. Perhaps as a wedding present Ted could give David the old leather dog leash he'd found in the woods the month before. It would fit him. Ted grinned mirthlessly, then sat down on the edge of his bed and rubbed his forehead.

Such a waste. In Salt Lake, he'd realized how helpful an accomplice would be. His own panic had put him in danger as he fled Rent-A-Tech. An accomplice could have brought him his extra clothes and planted one of the other bombs. Frustrated, Ted stood, picked up the empty bucket by the door, and walked through the cold moonlight to the creek. The idea of being put in jail was too terrible to consider. The torture of the concrete box. His freedom in the woods kept him sane. He knelt on the icy shore and filled the bucket, listening to the rushing water. He resolved to wire a fail-safe bomb to the door of his cabin. With his brother gone, his last connection to society was severed. He'd rather die than be caught. He ran through the supplies he'd need to make the booby trap. It pleased him to think of three or four or even more agents blown to pieces along with every scrap of evidence.

Back inside, he stoked the fire and then impulsively dropped the pink envelope and invitation into the flames. Good riddance. He watched the paper curl to ash, wondering if his brother had actually expected him to come. He returned to his desk and opened his latest coded notebook. He reread the opening line of the essay he'd begun two years before: "The industrial revolution and its consequences have been a disaster for the human race." The piece had ballooned to over fifty pages, with no end in sight. It was his legacy and call to arms, and he knew it had to be comprehensive when it was published.

Ted cracked his knuckles, rubbing his thumb along the burn calluses on his index finger. His hands were completely transformed from his days as an approval-starved student being manipulated and abused at Harvard. Now they had taken a life. Feeling reinvigorated, he opened the new book on ecology and skimmed the introduction, amused by the overwrought language it employed in its defense of the continuing fad of interconnectivity, which had started twenty years before with the weepy treatise *Silent Spring*. In it, he detected a hatred for corporations and technology that mirrored his own, and yet had found an acceptable context demanding the protection of lakes, rivers, forests, black-footed ferrets, and so on. But its proponents were too feebleminded to realize that the endgame of their beliefs was the extinction of the human race: a happy, mindless planet full of plants and beasts living in so-called "balance." Ted's formulation was superior. By cutting off the head of the technological snake, man would be liberated, and return to his natural position as the apex predator, using only tools he made with his own hands.

All the national newspapers had carried stories on the bomb at Rent-A-Tech and Pat Garret's death, but their conclusions had varied between breathless and confused: a mad bomber, a jealous lover, an act of anti-Mormon hate, even an organized crime hit over unpaid debts. Why couldn't they understand? He'd left so many clues. Ted sat back in his handmade chair, fuming. Reporters and cops were even more foolish than he'd imagined.

He uncapped his pen and began to write. "Threats to the modern individual tend to be MAN-MADE. They are not the result of chance but are IMPOSED on him by other persons whose decisions he, as an individual, is unable to influence. Consequently he feels frustrated, humiliated and angry." Pleased, he looked down at the paper and tapped his pen against the edge of the desk. He wouldn't allow his brother's downfall to distract him. It was time for people to understand his work.

The room was warm, the heat preserved by the fresh insulation he'd stuffed between the wall studs that November. He'd have to begin his next bomb from scratch, but the new detonator was the breakthrough he'd been working toward. With it, he could mail a device to the White House and know it would explode. Now it was just a matter of increasing the power of his explosive mixture. This was the most delicate and dangerous part of his work, but destiny seemed close at hand. One day he'd receive the recognition he deserved. Technological society would crumble and fall. Perhaps not in his lifetime, but soon after. It didn't matter what his brother or anyone else did. Looking forward to summer, Ted felt a deep, wintry sense of satisfaction.

32

"If the idiot hadn't filled the gas to the top it would've blown the entire room. There wouldn't have been any of me left to bury." Professor Amthor Loos was sitting behind the large desk in his study near Temple Square in Salt Lake City; his swaddled right arm hung in a sling across his chest. His hand was gone and when he spoke, the stump of his wrist moved, attempting to gesture. "It needs air to ignite."

Nep nodded, glancing around the room, careful to avoid staring at the stump or the agitated-looking stitches on Loos's face. Three bombs had gone off in the past week. By far the most deadly of the bomber's attacks. Nep had tracked the Vanderbilt package—which had nearly killed a secretary—back to BYU, where he'd learned of the bombings in the Computer Science Building and at the computer rental store. That made five in total now, and one death, all linked by technology. It shocked him that he was the one to discover this connection. With all their resources, the FBI hadn't even considered it. The last Nep had heard from Symes, his unit had a list of over fifteen thousand suspects and no real leads. Names on names, as many as the needles on a pine tree. The other postal inspectors laughed at the growing mountain of papers on Nep's desk.

"It was just a welded-up piece of junk," Loos went on. "Had a gauge on the front. I thought it might be some kind of measuring device, or a joke." The wall behind him was covered in pictures of herons. Great blues, blacks, goliaths, lavas, mostly in Audubon-style drawings, but some more stylized, Japanese, winging in front of layered calligraphic sunsets.

"A joke?"

Loos shrugged. "Grad students and professors sometimes have a weird sense of humor. Like rigging up a big old pump scale to test processor speed."

Nep thought of the green smoke. Were they dealing with a comedian? "These birds," he said, nodding to the wall.

"I have what my wife and therapist call a nervous mind. Some days I can't get anything done, then I come in here. Have you ever seen a heron take flight? It's the most graceful thing in the world. Their whole body gusts up into the air, smooth as a sail in the wind."

"I used to watch them on the lake in the summers in Iowa." Nep thought back to those trips with his mother and father as if they were something he'd seen in a movie. It seemed strange to him that he'd ever been a child at all, the experience was so distant and foreign. "Have you ever had an affair?"

Loos turned from the wall and blinked. "What kind of question is that?"

"Or your wife. Has she?"

Loos leaned forward. "Look, I've only been at BYU for a year. I'm a visiting professor. You should talk to Martin, he's the department chair. At first we thought it could be a student, someone who flunked out, looking for revenge, but after we heard about the bomb in Fairpark . . ."

Nep stared at him.

"No, I've never had an affair. And neither has my wife."

"Do you know Lionel Cass, who the other package was addressed to?"

"We've met, actually. At a conference, but I wouldn't say I know him."

"He's quite prominent in the psychology world."

"Yes, he knows how to get attention," Loos said.

"Where were you in 1976?"

Loos frowned. "Stanford, finishing my dissertation. Teaching as well. Does my losing a hand not eliminate me as a suspect?"

Nep knew Loos had nothing to do with the bomb—anyone in the Computer Science Department could've opened it. He was simply curious about this man who'd lost his hand. He often interrogated people out of curiosity, to get a sense of who they were, and what this knowledge might lead to, each illumination a stepping stone to the next. "Do the letters F C mean anything to you?"

"No. Why?"

"They were stamped into one of the pieces of shrapnel," Nep paused, aware of the cuts on Loos's face. "We think it might be a message of some sort."

"F C?"

Nep nodded. "Maybe an activist group."

"You know what you're dealing with here?" Loos asked, leaning forward across the desk and wincing at the effort. "It's pretty simple. Some recluse, some pathetic lonely loser who hates progress, hates the future, hates what the world is becoming. He thinks he's funny. He's probably holed up somewhere all day remembering how much better the world was back when he was a kid playing in the woods." He sighed, falling back in his chair and raising his stump. "He's playing a game. It took my hand, and I'm lucky, unlike that poor sap from the computer store." He paused. "We're all lucky, really, that most of the people who want to blow us up are too stupid and careless to pull it off."

AFTER LEAVING LOOS'S HOUSE, Nep drove north through Salt Lake to Heather Logan's apartment in Bountiful. It was his first time in the city and he was struck by the way the entire metropolis was built around the huge central temple—a modern iteration of ancient design. The tall white turrets and golden trumpet-playing angel were a vortex around which the whirlpool of commerce circulated. Passing by, he wondered what the bomber thought of all this. Had he chosen the location because it exemplified religious superstitions? Or did he long for a return to those traditions, and want to purge modern influences from sacred ground? Did he simply live nearby? His new, more powerful bombs had left little in the way of physical evidence. Nep had counted twenty FBI agents in the Rent-A-Tech parking lot that morning combing over the pavement. They reminded him of insects, with their matching suits and the way an order rippled down the chain, slowly shifting the entire swarm. For five years they'd been bumping their heads together, and now suddenly there was a witness. He hoped they hadn't ruined her.

Logan's apartment glowed like a firefly in the March dusk. Every room lit up. Even the small outdoor light over the balcony. Nep was used to this behavior in witnesses. He remembered one who'd placed knives on every windowsill in her house and nearly stabbed him when he rang the doorbell. Heather had watched her boss die, and then spent two days being interrogated by the FBI. It was natural to be frightened. The apartment building was built like a motel, with stairs on the outside and a long open walkway fronting the numbered doors, leading to her unit on the far corner of the second floor. Nep thought of his mother as he climbed the stairs. He'd left her in the care of a nurse while he was away. Her health had declined and the doctors said she didn't have much time. An akimbo regret, like a thin branch over water, reached toward him: a wife, a family.

It was strange to Nep, shocking even, that the bomber had been seen in person after five years. Up until now, what he'd lacked in execution he'd made up for in patience and care. Waiting years between attacks, spreading them out geographically, meticulously sanding away any identifying marks on his bombs. Then to just walk up and drop a bomb off in a parking lot in the middle of the day? Nep wondered if it wasn't the bomb maker himself who'd left the package, but a lackey, a fall guy. This would explain the sudden carelessness. F C could be the name of an organization, a collective of radical ecoterrorists with a Manson-type figure at the top, dispatching his followers.

Nep rubbed the cold, dry tip of his nose. The theory didn't feel right. Everything about the attacks suggested a lack of resources, from the handmade wooden boxes to the scrap-metal shrapnel. A man with followers could simply send someone out to buy blasting caps and C4. He agreed with Loos: This was a loner, a woodsman, constructing his bombs out of kindling and scrap. Had he finally gotten tired of being alone? Nep had seen it time and again: criminals were caught when they were ready to be caught, making mistakes that begged for handcuffs. But the bombs themselves didn't suggest the perpetrator was losing interest. They were getting stronger, more compact, better made. Even Symes had looked impressed. Loos had survived through dumb luck. Heather's boss Pat Garret hadn't been so lucky.

"Who is it?" Heather called through the door, after Nep knocked.

Nep held his badge up to the peephole.

"What's that?" she said.

"Postal Service inspector, ma'am."

"I didn't know the post office had inspectors," she said.

"I didn't, either, until I became one."

"I have a gun." Sure enough, Heather held a .38 Special protectively over her stomach as she inched open the door.

Nep held up his hands. "You won't need that."

"I told the FBI everything I saw," she said.

"May I come in?"

Heather nodded reluctantly, backing into the kitchen and setting the gun on the counter within easy reach. People always retreated to the kitchen when they were scared. Nep wondered why they felt the safest there among the saltshakers and hand towels. Was it the knives? The food? The bright light? The comfort of appliances? He looked over Heather's shoulder into the small, colorful living room: a floral couch, silk tapestries hanging from the wall, a stack of sci-fi novels, a wood-paneled TV set. All of it hippyish and bohemian, not what he'd expected to find in Salt Lake. "No computer?" he asked.

Heather shook her head. "What would I need one for?"

He shrugged. "I haven't figured out what anyone would need one for. I just thought, since you work in a computer store . . ."

"I didn't get paid enough for that."

"Were you close with Mr. Garret?"

Heather sighed. Her tired eyes had a greenish tint and Nep realized how pretty she was, petite and small-featured, with shining auburn hair. She looked like the smiling wife on the cover of the pamphlet a Mormon missionary had given him in the airport. Behind her, a sliced apple lay fanned across a yellow cutting board. "He was fine, for a boss."

"Did you know he was coming in, the morning he died?"

"Of course," she nodded. "He came in every day. An hour before opening until an hour after closing, like clockwork. I was the only other employee."

"Did he have any enemies that you knew of? Debts? People he might have crossed?"

"No, the guy just left the . . . the bomb on the ground. Anyone could've moved it. I thought he was trying to pop some tires. A jealous husband or something. I could've . . . I should've . . ." she stopped and wiped her eyes. "Pat was a nice man."

"The bomb was left in front of your store on purpose. You must know that."

Heather looked away. "I guess so. But I don't know why."

"No angry customers? There are some strange people interested in computers."

"Sure, we had some weirdos, but I'd never seen this guy before. I know that."

"Did you and Pat always get in by eight-thirty, before the store opened?" Nep had his notebook in his hand, but he wasn't writing. He watched her face.

"Yes, I was supposed to, but I didn't usually get in until around nine. There was nothing to do before then and Pat always wanted to stand around and chat."

Nep smiled. "He liked you, you mean."

"I guess. But it doesn't matter now, does it?"

"Do you have a boyfriend?" Nep asked.

Heather's eyes narrowed. "No, not that it's any of your business."

"No jealous exes?"

"I've never dated any terrorist bombers, if that's what you're asking."

Aware she was losing patience, Nep softened his voice and changed tactics. "The man you saw leave the bomb, if you had one word to describe his face, what would it be?"

"Nervous," she said. "Like he was doing something wrong. That's why I noticed him. He was shifty. Normal people don't wear those big sunglasses."

"Aviators?"

She nodded. "I've only ever seen them on cops and criminals."

Nep had to keep himself from smiling. He was surprised to find he liked Heather. She was sharp as well as pretty. He wondered how she'd avoided marriage in this Mormon state for so long. "Did his clothes have any brand names on them?"

She shook her head.

"Nothing you could identify?"

Exasperation tightened her lips. "Can't you talk to the FBI? I spent days telling them all this."

"Are you an outdoorswoman?" he asked, his eyes flicking back across the living room. On this second look, he saw more intimate details: a pair of jeans and a sweater were draped unceremoniously over the couch, a red lava lamp bubbled by the TV, and wild horses thundered across a field in front of a snowy mountain range in a framed poster over the mantel. Their sorrel bodies were sleek, muscles rippling, something undeniably charged in the way they moved. He imagined Heather on her couch, unsnapping her bra, gazing up at these horses.

"No, not really. I mean, I ski."

"What about trees?" he turned to face her. "Do you love trees?"

33

That spring, when the high country had begun to thaw and the warmth of late May brought new buds to the chokecherry bushes, Ted shouldered on his pack and set out through the woods on a sunny afternoon. He climbed toward Stemple Pass. Following the creek at first, then cutting across the glacial till above Florence Gulch toward Weyerhaeuser's new logging claim. He paused at Heavy Runner Rock to look north over the valley at the white peaks of the Swan Range, feeling a tingling rush of vertigo. Tom McCall's most recent clear-cut scarred the mountainside to the west. Behind it, the striated cliff face rose above Deadman Draw, sparkling with ribbons of meltwater. Everywhere he looked, the land glowed with the relief of spring. Sighing to himself, fighting the weakness in his limbs after the long winter, Ted continued on toward the cliff.

At dusk, he arrived at the waterfall above the deep blue pool. Wildflowers dotted the shore and rainbows of mist shimmered over the water. This was Ted's sanctuary, where he bathed in the summer and spent peaceful hours drowsing in the sun. He'd built the small bone altar between the roots of the ancient Douglas fir and considered it sacred, his version of a church. Secretly, he called the tree the Old King, and imagined it presiding over the entire valley. He scrambled down the steep trail by the waterfall, stopping at the bottom to look at the familiar pattern of red and yellow stones beneath the pool, then turning his gaze upward to where the Old King's crown rose over the surrounding forest. It was by far the tallest tree Ted had ever seen. He named it after Ed Youderian showed it to him his first summer in Montana. Youderian claimed it was the oldest in the valley, and along with its fellows around the clearing had been called the Council by the local Indians, who'd met here to trade and settle disputes. Old King was a sapling when Christopher Columbus landed in the New World, reached maturity in the time of Shakespeare, and grew to its full height at the beginning of the first gold rush. In its presence, Ted felt the closest thing he ever had to spiritual awe.

Ted stopped in the shade at its base and placed his hand on the trunk, greeting it after the long winter. Then he took off his pack, knelt, and dug the silver button from his pocket. He thumbed the smooth surface, bringing out the shine, and placed it on the altar. He'd clipped the button from the coat of one of the Weyerhaeuser executives while the man was in the bathroom in the Ponderosa Café. Offerings from previous years were strewn around the base of the altar: a broken computer key, an airplane pin, the faded pages of a psychiatry textbook. . . . For Ted, the altar was a place of self-fulfilling prophecy. He decided where he was going to send his bombs, then he brought a representative offering to augur their success.

Satisfied, he retreated to the flat, mossy rock by the pool and ate dinner, watching shadows overtake the light around him. The woods rustled with life as daylight hunters returned to their dens and nocturnal creatures stirred. At midnight, Ted climbed from the clearing and met up with the new logging road. It was disturbingly close, less than a mile away. The dirt road was heavily chewed from the skidder's metal treads. Snapped branches and bark chips littered the shoulder. It smelled of wet mulch. Ted swore vengeance on the forces threatening his sanctuary. He moved quickly, his steps as soundless as a deer's. He pictured his next bomb destroying the headquarters of a logging company—incinerating the executives and their secretaries, blowing out the windows, collapsing the walls—the deaths he'd caused multiplying exponentially.

The logging site appeared suddenly through the trees in the moonlight. The huge skidder and loader and the smaller Cats, their scoops raised to the stars. They were like relics in the dark, but Ted knew them in the day: the hack and roar of their engines, the churning of the giant treads, the stink of exhaust, and the scream of wood as the infernal machines ripped through the forest. He'd been listening to them for weeks—they'd come as soon as the snow melted—a man-made devil loosed upon his home.

He crept slowly from the trees, making sure the company hadn't hired anyone to watch the camp, like Tom had hired Duane to do years before. But it was early in the season, and Ted knew from scouting that only a basic crew was working. The big corporations were arrogant, careless. He stood for a moment in the center of the machines, then he went to the skidder. He unscrewed the gas cap and tossed it aside. He opened the front of his pack and removed a pound of sugar. Shaking it vigorously, he poured the contents into the gas tank. Then he took his hunting knife around to the front. He opened the hood and cut everything he could: hydraulic hoses, wires, tubes, the gas line. At first he worked almost cheerfully, but the stubbornness of the machine frustrated him and he stabbed the plastic coolant tank viciously until blue liquid spilled over the carburetor.

As he looked around at the other machines, his anger grew. He picked up a thick branch and bashed off the mirrors of the loader, then attempted to smash the windshield. The reinforced glass sent shock waves up his arm, and when it finally caved inward it did so gently, like a sail, thoroughly unsatisfying. He hammered at the tires and doors, denting the yellow metal until exhaustion made him dizzy. Then he climbed into the skidder and tried to dislodge the steering wheel, but couldn't gain enough force in the narrow space. He rammed the end of the branch into the instrument panel, splintering the glass. Finally, he lifted one of the large rocks the men had left behind the rear wheels, and smashed it down into the engine, breaking the rods and crankshaft, hoping to mangle it beyond repair.

A faint, crackling buzz filled his ears. Adrenaline made his heart pound. He stood back in the darkness panting, bathed in cold sweat. He realized that what he really wanted was to blow the machines up. Watch them leap into the air and burn, like the structures he built in the woods to test his bombs. If he incinerated the entire camp, what would they be able to cut? He was elated by the image of the great tires lifting from the ground, shrapnel flying, flames engulfing the yellow metal in a bright, cleansing cacophony, and saw himself dancing naked in black shadow around the periphery, a vision so pagan and carnal it frightened him.

Exhausted, he gathered up his pack and headed home.

A KNOCK ON THE DOOR woke him late the next morning. He scrambled to wrest the deer rifle from the wall above his bed, panic replacing the groggy confusion of sleep. He hadn't wired a bomb to the door yet. If it was the FBI or the sheriff, he'd have to go down shooting. "Who's there?" he called.

"Duane." The voice was soft and apologetic.

Cursing his neighbor under his breath, Ted replaced the rifle and looked around the room. "Just a minute." When he first started making explosives, he'd been careful to hide all signs of his bomb-making, but it had been years since someone knocked on his door, and he wasn't as diligent as he once had been. Luckily everything seemed to be in its place: the books, the canned goods, the hunting supplies. His newest device was tucked under his bed behind his spare boots. He pulled on his pants, buckled his belt, and opened the door.

Duane stood on the plywood porch with his hands stuffed in the pockets of his jeans. He wore an old flannel shirt with holes in the sleeves and was bent forward, as if trying to make himself less tall. His face was irritatingly submissive. "I've got a favor to ask," he said. "My son's coming up for the whole summer this year and I was thinking of putting in a garden, now that the cabin is done. I thought I'd see if you have any advice, since yours does so well." He looked over Ted's shoulder into the dim room and Ted felt himself tense. He wanted to run Duane off his property, but he pushed down the desire, knowing he had to be neighborly.

"Sure, come and see." He stepped onto the porch and slammed the door shut.

The soles of Ted's feet had lost their calluses over the winter and he winced crossing the rocky ground. "I hear this is tough soil," Duane said, following him to the high barbed-wire-topped fence that surrounded his garden.

"The soil's not the hard part. It's the deer," Ted answered, nodding up at the fence. "Has to be eight feet high, at least." He showed Duane how he'd positioned the plot on a south-facing slope to maximize sun exposure in an old wash where the ground held moisture from snow runoff each spring. "I brought fertilizer up from the hardware store for the first couple years, but I haven't had to since." He didn't mention that he now fertilized the soil with his own shit. "You'll want tough plants: radishes, beets. Ones that can survive a frost. I wasn't able to get tomatoes until my third year."

Duane nodded, squinting in through the fence. "You water it yourself?"

"Buckets from the creek," Ted said. "I thought about trying for irrigation but it's too much digging."

"A little digging might be good for Hudson." Duane grinned, glancing around at the rusty equipment in the yard. "You know how kids are, they get bored, even in a place like this."

Ted didn't know how kids were, nor did he want to. As the eldest son of Polish immigrants, his childhood had been a time of constant pressure—to earn straight As, win prizes, graduate early. He didn't have time to be bored, or pay attention to his half-witted classmates. "When's he coming?" Ted asked, already dreading the noise the boy would make on the road. The previous August, Hutch had given Hudson lessons on his old dirt bike and he'd spent the final weeks of his visit driving up and down the road, revving the engine. Ted had had the impulse to shoot him off the seat.

"Tonight," Duane said. "At midnight," he added, ruefully. "I've got to drive over to Butte to pick him up. Helluva time for a bus to get in."

Ted knew the trip well. He'd spent many nights in Butte's cold, drafty bus station, waiting for dawn to hitch home, sustained only by the lightness of his pack and the thought of one of his bombs making its way across the country. He'd carved the letters F C into the wall of one of the bathroom stalls, in case an investigator was ever smart enough to track him there. "I can come by next week to help you choose a spot," he said, wanting Duane to leave and not make any more unannounced visits.

Duane's face brightened. "I'd appreciate that."

Ted nodded and crossed his arms to demonstrate that the conversation was over.

"All right, then." Duane wiped his palms on the front of his jeans and stuck out his hand. Ted stared down at it. It had been so long since he touched another human being that he'd nearly forgotten how. Quickly, he clenched Duane's fingers. The touch brought on a disconcerting feeling of tenderness, and he thought of his brother preparing for his wedding. He wondered if his parents were driving down from Chicago. His mother was afraid to fly, so they'd be in their old Chevy, fighting over where to eat and which hotel to sleep in. He dropped Duane's hand and looked away. Down below his garden, buried in the dirt, were sealed jars of explosives and an untraceable gun he'd assembled himself. Crows squawked back and forth in the branches of the pines, and the warm spring sun shone on the green shoots in the furrowed rows of dirt. Ted turned and quickly went back inside.

34

Duane walked back to his cabin more confused than ever. It was true that he wanted to start a garden with Hudson, but more than that he wanted a better feel for Ted. His uneasiness hadn't left him since their trip to the library. It wasn't good to have a neighbor you knew nothing about, especially with Hudson around. He figured if Ted got to know them both, and they to know him, they'd all be better off. He'd even planned to invite Ted over for dinner, but something in his demeanor stopped Duane. A menace, as if his neighbor didn't want anyone else around. The feeling had lessened in the garden, where Duane could sense Ted's pride, but then he remembered the cold, clammy grip of the man's hand.

Pride was a fairly new emotion for Duane, and he paused, looking at the split-log walls of his cabin in the spring sun. He loved the way the afternoon light made the patches of raw wood golden where the bark was stripped away. It still amazed him that he'd built the whole thing himself. He knew the townsfolk had laughed at him for taking so long, but there it was: a home all his own. The walls kept out the wind and the roof kept out the rain. Duane rapped his knuckles against the doorframe. Sturdy. He'd make friends with Ted in the long run, he was sure of it. Life just put things in your way to keep you from getting too comfortable, whether it was your neighbor, an owl, or your ex-wife.

After shaving and combing his hair, he patted cologne onto his neck—as he always did before visiting Jackie—and glanced at his face in the mirror. "If you can't look good, at least you can smell good," advice his mother had given him when he hit puberty, which still rang in his ears. He was going to Jackie's house for dinner and then straight to Butte. Jittery nerves made it hard for him to be still, as they did every year when he went to pick up Hudson.

The little truck's old engine took three tries to start, coughing each time. The thought of replacing the truck saddened Duane. He felt he'd replaced enough things in his life, he didn't want to have to replace any more. As he drove down Stemple Pass Road, the sentinel trees stood commanding watch, as they had on his first visit. Duane knew there was a chance these trees would be cut one day, too. In Washington, D.C., the new President was opening national forests to logging. Big corporations had already lined up, forcing Tom to scramble to compete.

Duane's thoughts were interrupted by Sheriff Kima's cruiser driving by on his left, followed by a deputy in a Forest Service truck, and a shiny black Ford with Colorado plates, all of them clearly in a hurry, their tires kicking up dust, heading toward Stemple Pass. Duane looked after them curiously, wondering what business they could have.

At Jackie's house, she greeted him with a plastic package of cookies from Food Town. "Peanut butter chocolate chip," she said. "Hudson's favorites. He'll be hungry when he gets in." It pleased Duane that she took such an interest in his son. Her devotion had surprised him at first, until he realized that her own lack of children was a deep, concealed wound that she'd carried for most of her adult life. During Hudson's first summer in Montana, when he was only eight, Duane was still living in a tent at the logging camp, and Hudson had spent most nights in Jackie's spare room, too frightened by the rustling noises in the dark woods to sleep next to Duane. Ever since, she'd been like a surrogate mother to him.

"I just saw the sheriff heading up toward Stemple Pass," Duane said.

Jackie nodded. "Someone monkey-wrenched the new Weyerhaeuser camp. Busted it up real good. A whole truckful of suits is in from Denver."

"How'd they get here so fast?"

"Apparently they were already in Helena setting up an office."

Duane furrowed his brow. A local office meant they were planning to stay long-term. Would he have to find a new job? He didn't want to have to deal with a big corporate outfit, and it seemed safer to stay local. He'd heard plenty of stories of spiked trees and sabotaged equipment from Dixon and the other men in the crew, but over his years working for Tom he had yet to experience it firsthand. It made him nervous to think of it happening so close to his home.

"Been a few years, but, my God, back in the early seventies, before you came, not a week went by without some piece of equipment getting messed with. It got so bad Tom had a whole crew quit on him. They just up and left."

"Did someone get hurt?"

"Someone died. Tipped the skidder and went off the road, though it's more likely they were hungover and being careless."

"Why do you think it's starting back up?"

Jackie shrugged. "Probably some redwood tree in California got cut down or the last condor killed or some such. People in the diner are talking about big protests in San Francisco." She paused. "Take off your boots if you're coming in, I just vacuumed."

Obediently, Duane removed his boots and followed her into the kitchen, feeling slightly vulnerable in his socks. It pained him sometimes how casually Jackie treated him even after six years. She kept her distance, maintaining her own life and space, and laughing it off when he hinted at marriage or moving in together. The only time the distance between them disappeared was when Hudson was in town. Then they felt like a family. But she never ran around on him or spoke to him cruelly, which was more than Duane could say for his ex-wife.

Watching her make coffee at the stove, he remembered the hardness of her face when they first met and she tried to send him on to Canada. She'd softened since then, her center of gravity lowering to the ground. The silver streaks in her black hair caught flashes of sunlight when she walked around the old Glory Hole Mine or in the hills above Hogum Gulch. Duane loved to watch her in nature; she stepped softly like an animal, reminding him of the sure-footed coyotes in the cages behind Hutch's trailer. She was beautiful to him in a way he couldn't quite express, like the trees that grew around his cabin. He cleared his throat and rested his hand affectionately on top of his old microwave.

Jackie glanced over at him. "I still don't know if you come to visit me or that microwave."

"If it wasn't for this microwave, I might not get to visit you at all." Duane wiped a smudge from the chrome finish with his thumb.

"I've had men try to seduce me all kinds of ways, but never with an old Touchmatic." Jackie smiled. "I don't know what I was thinking."

"Well, it's hard to find a reliable machine these days." Duane grinned and crossed the linoleum. He slid his arm around Jackie's waist and looked down into her eyes.

Jackie reached up and plucked a stray hair from his eyebrow, making him wince. "I guess it is." Her eyes danced. They hadn't changed. In the amber irises, she was sixteen, forty-five, a thousand. He clasped the small of her back, pulling her waist in to his.

After dinner, Jackie and Duane lay together on the couch watching the sunset. The last light didn't disappear over the mountains until after ten. Then Duane kissed her goodbye and returned to his truck, carrying the package of cookies. Memories overwhelmed him as he drove south to Butte in the darkness: the first time he'd bathed Hudson in his and Tracy's apartment on Kensington, astounded by the tiny perfection of each foot, the smell of his soft hair; Hudson's first words, a constricted and astonished "Baba," which Duane had interpreted as "Daddy." He became so flustered that he mistook a shadow for a deer and nearly went off the highway.

Rounding the last curve at the truck stop in Rocker, he took the exit between the hills into uptown. He often came to Butte on errands for Tom, and he knew the roads, but at midnight the city was altered, no longer a fading ghost town but a sprawling metropolis filling the valley. Floodlights dotted the hills around the Berkeley Pit and shone from the tops of the headframes. He pressed down on the accelerator, pushing the little truck as fast as it would go. Tracy had warned him not to be late picking up Hudson. In her tone he heard a whole paranoid diatribe about drug dealers and serial killers, one that he remembered well from their marriage. Something had caused his ex-wife to lose her faith in people, and at one time he'd wanted desperately to know what it was, thinking he could mend it like a busted fence.

The bus station was on the east side of Butte directly below the Berkeley Pit. Duane passed the old Copper King Mansion and the Dumas Brothel, the red light glowing dimly over the door. He wondered if Dixon or any of his other crewmates were inside. It was Tuesday and the streets were empty. Finally, he saw an old man sleeping on the doorstep outside the M&M Bar, and was relieved not to be entirely alone.

The Salt Lake City bus was already parked in front of the station. Pale clouds of exhaust rose from the tailpipe. A few cars idled behind it and a small crowd of passengers were huddled in the light of the glass doors. Hudson stood apart from them in the building's shadow, tall and thin, his shoulders hunched, unmistakable. Duane recognized him before he could make out any features, as if by scent, some ancient bond. My son, I would know you anywhere. His heart pounded as he pulled to a stop. The boy began to walk toward him.

"My God, you've grown," Duane said, stepping out of the truck, the first words he uttered every summer. Now it wasn't only the boy's size that had changed. His entire demeanor was different, self-conscious and aggrieved, teetering on the painful edge between boyhood and puberty. "Shit, I'm sorry you had to wait."

"It's okay," Hudson said. "Hi, Dad." Duane opened his arms and wrapped the boy in a hug. His mind raced as he tried to assimilate all the emotions scrambling in his chest. Love and fear and doubt and more love. He felt so rattled that he wanted to drive off and return when dawn spread its comforting light over the valley.

"I'm hungry," the boy mumbled into his shoulder.

"Jackie got cookies for you. They're in the truck."

"Isn't there a burger place or something?"

"At midnight?" Duane stepped back. He'd forgotten such things existed in cities.

The boy frowned, and Duane was struck by the heaviness of his features, his blond hair and broadening shoulders. Perhaps he wouldn't be skinny for long. Tracy's father was a short, bull-chested cudgel of a man. "I reckon there's a gas station we can stop by on the way, they'll have a hot dog, at least."

Hudson hefted his bag into the back of the truck. He sniffed the air, then sat down in the passenger seat. His tired, bloodshot eyes slowly followed the stream of traffic departing the station. "It smells funny here."

"That's the Berkeley Pit," Duane said, inhaling the sweet cyanide scent. "It's full of poison."

Hudson nodded, seeming to take this in stride. "I'm just glad to be out of Utah."

"I know that feeling." Duane looked at him one more time and smiled, then put the truck in gear and pulled away from the station into the night.

THE NEXT MORNING, Duane awoke to the sound of his son's voice. "Dad, there's nothing in here." Groggily, he rolled out of bed. Sunlight streamed through the open window. It was after nine, but they hadn't gotten home from Butte until three in the morning and he'd tossed and turned for another hour, too excited to sleep. He pulled on a shirt and staggered out to the kitchen. Hudson stood in front of the fridge staring in at the two cans of beer and crusty bottle of yellow mustard. He'd already finished the entire package of cookies.

"I figured we'd go shopping together this morning," Duane said. "Get whatever you want. Check the freezer, though, there's some stuff in there."

Hudson opened it. Frozen meals were stacked in two rows to the top of the freezer.

"Got half of those for you."

"Great," Hudson said, taking out a beef stroganoff. "Just what I feel like for breakfast."

Embarrassed, Duane rubbed his forehead. "Why don't we go to the diner? Jackie wants to see you." He paused. "Aren't you teenagers supposed to sleep in?"

Hudson shrugged. "I'm starving. There was nothing to eat on the bus, and all I had for dinner was a hot dog."

"Just give me a minute, I'll get dressed."

Hudson was silent on the drive into town. He'd been quiet coming home from Butte as well, which Duane had written off as exhaustion. Now he began to wonder if something was wrong, or if it was merely the sullenness of puberty that Tracy had warned him about. "Hutch'll sure be glad to see you," he said, to break the silence. "He needs the company. He's spent most of this spring talking to an owl in his living room." He paused. "You going to help with his animals again this summer?"

"I guess so," Hudson answered, looking straight ahead through the windshield.

Now Duane knew something was wrong. The previous summer, the boy had been so excited about feeding coyotes and bobcats and riding Hutch's dirt bike that it was impossible to get him to stop chattering. But Duane didn't know how to dig the problem out of him. No one had asked after his troubles when he was a teenager.

The Ponderosa Café was busy for a Tuesday. The same shiny black Ford that Duane had seen on his road the day before was parked in front. Clean-shaven men with snap-button shirts tucked into suspiciously clean Wranglers filled two tables by the window. One wore a watch with elk-turd-sized chunks of turquoise studded in the silver band. "If it doesn't get done, I'll talk to the governor," he said.

Jackie smiled broadly when she saw Hudson, reminding Duane of the first time he'd made her laugh. "My God," she said, reaching out her arms. "You're taller than me now."

Sheepishly, Hudson accepted her hug, awkwardly at first, then leaning over and burying his head in her shoulder. He remained there until Jackie looked over his head at Duane in concern.

Duane shrugged helplessly.

"Both of you sit down," Jackie said. "I'm going to bring some pancakes and then we'll talk. Hudson, you've grown so much I expect we have a lot to catch up on."

Duane took his usual booth by the window and sat across from his son, trying to think of something to say that didn't involve the weather. Finally, he gave up. "Been a real nice spring here. Snow all melted by May."

Hudson didn't respond.

Thankfully, Jackie returned and slid into the booth next to the boy.

"Can I get a refill?" the man with the turquoise-studded watch asked, holding up his coffee cup.

Jackie turned and glared at him. "I expect you can," she said. Then she shifted her attention back to Hudson. "Tell me about seventh grade. From what I can remember, that was when math stopped making sense and boys started sniffing around." She glanced at Duane. "But that was a long time ago."

Hudson lowered his eyes. "I hate school. I'm no good at it."

"What do you like?" Jackie asked.

"Motorcycles." Hudson glanced up from beneath his shaggy hair.

"Well, we've got plenty of those around here. I bet Hutch will let you ride his dirt bike again this summer."

The boy nodded, brightening slightly. "I want to ride on my own this summer. It's legal now that I'm thirteen."

Duane didn't know if this was true, but he didn't want to discourage his son. "I reckon that's okay, as long as you stay off the highway." He sensed the boy was having the same problems he'd struggled with as a teenager: tall but no good at sports, failing in school, clumsy, picked on.

Hudson lowered his eyes again and Duane trailed off. Jackie studied Hudson closely for a moment, then leaned toward him conspiratorially. "You see those guys in the fancy shirts?" She nodded toward the table where the man still held his empty coffee cup accusingly.

Hudson glanced over at them.

"They work for Weyerhaeuser. Big shots, right? Coming into town acting like they own everything?"

He nodded. "That's how the eighth-graders are."

"Well, here's the secret: They're just pretending. They don't know more than anyone else. They'll buy up the whole world and end up right back where they started, more pissed off than ever."

She looked affectionately at the boy. "Once you realize that, life gets a lot easier."

"I'd rather just be on my own," he said.

"Time alone helps, too," Jackie answered. "Outside, where you can see how things really are."

A plate crashed to the floor in the kitchen and the cook swore loudly. Duane looked up, startled. He'd been so engrossed watching Jackie and his son that he'd nearly forgotten where they were. Jackie paused before sliding out of the booth. She put her hand on Hudson's. "Don't forget you need other people, too, though. I've known men who went off to live alone in the woods, and none of them turned out right."

35

Ted had planned to spend the afternoon at one of his camps, testing a new technique for packing shrapnel, but now with the headache, his plan was ruined. He went inside his cabin and shut the door, immediately relieved by the darkness. Climbing into bed and thinking of Duane's visit the day before, he was surprised by a pang of melancholy. He wondered if in a different world he and his neighbor could have been friends. Hutch also. All three of them living together on this road, helping one another. Briefly, he was pained by the harsh solitude of his life. A thousand years earlier, he wouldn't have had to dedicate his days to fighting technology, making bombs, and writing out his thoughts in elaborate code.

The question bothered him and he lay his pillow over his eyes. He felt a wash of self-pity. Why had he chosen such a lonely path? He thought of his brother, assimilating into the world of microwaves and dishwashers and TV sitcoms. He thought of Duane clear-cutting the woods in his idiotic red, white, and blue cap. And Hutch, keeping an owl in his living room, pretending his rescued animals were friends.

Don't wish yourself a fool just because they are, he told himself. He conjured up painful memories—the interrogations at Harvard, his thin-walled room in Ann Arbor—to drive the desire away. But a part of himself wanted an ordinary life: to be a fool among fools, watching sports at the Wilderness Bar, working mundane jobs, going on dates. He envied the most pathetic men for their simple pleasures. "It's too late for that," he said, out loud. Much too late. He pressed the pillow down on his forehead and burrowed into the pain and darkness, resolving that when he emerged, he'd leave all such self-pity behind.

BUZZING PENETRATED HIS SLEEP, and in the dream the interrogator was a giant fly, pursuing him through the dark halls of a university basement. The fly's bulbous head was grotesque: black bristles surrounded its compound eyes, its proboscis wavered, searching out his scent. Ted couldn't escape. He was too frightened to kill it and awoke in a cold sweat to the sound of a dirt bike on the road outside his cabin. He swung his legs onto the floorboards and staggered to the door. He poked his head out in time to see Duane's son Hudson disappear around the bend on Hutch's old white Husqvarna.

Dammit all. The boy had just arrived, and already he was destroying Ted's peace. The buzzing of the bike was worse than Hutch's huskies. At least their barking had been a natural sound that alerted him when someone was about to pass by. The grating chirr of the engine made his brain vibrate against his skull. Ted slammed the door and stood in the middle of the cabin, rubbing his head. He had no way to play music or otherwise cover up the sound. Even shouting wouldn't help—the buzzing had wormed its way into his brain.

Finally, the noised faded out. Ted paced back and forth, his fists clenched, thinking of bludgeoning the boy off the bike with a metal bat. Hoping to calm himself, he took down his garden journal from the top shelf. In it, he carefully recorded the dates that he planted each type of seed, the number he planted, and the resulting harvest. He discovered that on this day the year before he'd begun his radish crop. He already had several trays of tomato seedlings on the porch, which he brought in each night. Another hard frost was unlikely. Gardening would do him good. He rummaged through his shelves, found the jar of Lady Slipper radish seeds, took his straw hat from the hook by the door, and walked barefoot into the yard. The afternoon sun coated the trees like honey, and he paused, raising his arms and letting the warmth make its way through his skin. He was pale and thin after the long winter. He took off his shirt, soaking in as much sunlight as possible, wishing for a moment that he were a plant himself.

A branch had fallen on the far side of the garden fence, causing it to sag, and Ted reminded himself to fix it. He unlatched the gate and knelt on the soft dirt in the garden bed. He used his hands to turn the soil in three neat rows lengthwise along the fence. Then he spread compost and his special fertilizer across the top, patting it down and working his fingers through as if he were kneading bread. Pink worms squirmed away from him and ants ran up his wrist. Wiping the sweat from his brow, he watched the ants navigate between the hairs on his forearm, searching for food in their mindless, obedient industry. If only he had such an army planting bombs across the country. The revolution would be over in a week. He brushed them off. Then he poked a row of holes a quarter inch deep in the soil with his index finger, and laid a single seed at the bottom of each hole. He'd found that the Lady Slippers sprouted so reliably multiple seeds were unnecessary. He appreciated the durability of radishes and spoke encouragingly to the future plants as he covered up each seed. It was easy for him to interact with vegetables because they never talked back. They asked for nothing but water and light.

He was nearing the end of the row when the buzzing started up again, coming back down from the pass. Hudson's white bike reappeared, joined by a neon-green Kawasaki with an older teenage rider in a black helmet. They revved their accelerators as they passed, kicking up dirt, the tires fishtailing on the loose gravel, as if they were mocking Ted. He watched from beneath his straw hat, his teeth clenched, his hands in the damp soil. His temples began to throb, and he felt a seething hatred.

36

The composite sketch was a simple charcoal rendering of a man in large aviator sunglasses and a hooded sweatshirt. White but with something faintly Hispanic in his shaded features. Young, average height, average build. The only distinguishing characteristics were his gaunt cheeks, which the artist had carefully emphasized in shadow, and the pencil mustache drawn above his thin down-turned lips. A sad face, Nep thought, leaning over his desk to study the drawing more closely. A trapped and angry young man.

Agent Symes had sent a sketch artist to sit down with Heather Logan and produce the portrait. Soon it would appear on the nightly news and wanted posters all across America. The FBI was preparing to go public with the university and airline bomber story, asking for help with any leads. Nep had been bitterly disappointed when the sketch arrived in his office. It seemed uselessly vague—the face interchangeable with every truck driver's in the Southwest—but now in the dim light of his office, with the sound of the hospice worker moving around downstairs in the bedroom where his mother lay dying, Nep found clues in the portrait. This was no gleeful chameleon, like the serial killers on the news, with the ability to kill in one moment and charm in the next. No, here was a loner, an outsider, unable to blend in or be a part of society, and forced to the undernourished margins. Lashing back at the universities and technology that had spurned him.

Radical thought had a way of getting frothed up on university campuses. Nep remembered this from his own time at Northwestern, groups of Communist students railing against America's postwar boom. Perhaps the bomber was a thwarted assistant professor, disillusioned by the protests of the sixties, and determined to act. But leaving a bomb in front of a cut-rate computer rental store in Salt Lake City? The crimes didn't make sense. Nothing did anymore, Nep thought, rubbing his eyes and looking at the newspaper lying open on his desk. Race riots, serial killers, assassinations, superfund sites. The great ship of America going down with all the lights blazing.

The teakettle began to whistle in the kitchen and Nep sank back, sighing. It was pointless to stare at the drawing. Sketches derived from a single witness were notoriously unreliable, and Heather—sharp as she was—had only glimpsed the bomber; she was too far away to make out the details of his clothing or mark any identifying features. Even the acronym the FBI had chosen for the case—UNABOM—seemed misplaced. Nep knew he should leave the study and go down and sit with his mother. Each remaining second with her was precious. But the wracking effort of her breath, in a chest as frail as a bird's, tore at his heart. And when he held her cold hand, he felt only bones.

Are you hiding out in here, at the end? he asked himself, glancing around at the certificates and diplomas on the wood-paneled walls of his office. Accolades for what suddenly felt like a useless life. Who had he helped? What had he learned? He'd seen the worst of men— their darkest perversions and desires—yet nothing had prepared him for this: to watch his mother wither away, each inhale shallower than the last. Within this space, questions arose. His life of logic teetered on the brink of the inexplicable. His mother was frightened also, he could tell. She'd been the second woman to graduate from the University of Chicago with a degree in mathematics. Now she was faced with both zero and infinity, an equation that didn't add up.

Nep was deeply grateful for the hospice worker, a recent refugee from Yugoslavia who muttered prayers in her own language and seemed to move as easily between realms as she did between the kitchen and the bedroom. She sat with his mother for hours, their eyes gently closed in communion. When he interrupted them, they both looked up, startled, and he felt like an explorer in a pith helmet tripping over idols in an Aztec temple. A bumbling buffoon far outside of his depth.

He'd spent the previous week looking at maps. He was amazed by how much wilderness was left in America. Even with the environmentalist movement in full swing and talk of saving the rivers and forests constantly on the evening news, thousands and thousands of miles of unbroken terrain remained along the Continental Divide, from New Mexico up to Montana. It would take lifetimes to explore, even with Symes's horde of bumbling agents. Nep ran his finger up the rocky spine of the mountains, whispering the town names along the way: Pagosa Springs, Rawlins, Lander, Dubois. You're out there somewhere, he thought, picturing the bomber kneeling in a clearing tinkering with his newest creation. Nep had eliminated the coasts purely on instinct. This was a crime from the interior, he believed. You could feel large in the woods. On the beach you were nothing but a grain of sand.

Nep wondered if the man in the sketch had his own experiences with death. Was he lashing back at the unseen force that had taken from him, broken him? No. This man was selfish. Cruel. Nep closed his eyes. He saw the shrapnel scars on the face of Amthor Loos, the passengers streaming from Flight 444, and Henry Leck holding up his mangled hand. He tried to imagine what Pat Garret must have felt in his last moments, the terror and despair. He smelled ponderosa bark and saw green smoke disappearing in the ether. Mother, he thought. Please don't go.

37

The border of the Carter Ranch was delineated by a decrepit amalgam of fencing, beginning with the buck-and-rail put in by the original homesteaders and culminating in barbed wire the brothers had strung sagging loosely and bunched in coils at each precariously leaning post. A porous border at best, and Ted often came to scavenge for supplies of which he wanted no record. The Carters had all manner of scrap on their land, from old cars to artillery shells. Plus they were invariably drunk or passed out by nightfall, and the two German shepherds were too old to roam far. Their cows were the most dangerous, unpredictable occupants of the ranch, and Ted kept an eye out for them. Often one would appear in town, bearing the outsized Double C brand on its bony flank, picking fights with stray cats and knocking over trash cans.

The July night was warm. Always cautious, Ted waited until almost midnight before crawling under the fence. His shirt caught in the barbed wire, tearing at the cuff. Twisting and cursing, he finally ripped free and straightened in the moonlight, clutching his rifle and listening for cows and dogs. His mood was black and he reckoned if he saw man or beast he would open fire. For the entire month of June he'd been plagued by the buzzing of dirt bikes. Hudson's presence seemed to have convinced every delinquent in the valley to bring their machines to Ted's road. They buzzed up and down deep into the night, tossing beer cans and shouting curses at one another. The noise was so bad it even bothered Hutch, who told Ted on a ride into town that his animals were growing agitated by the commotion. *You could stop letting him use your bike*, Ted wanted to answer, but kept his mouth shut.

The foul smell of hogs wafted up from the converted sheep shed in the ravine by the ranch house. A single light glowed inside the house. Ma Carter most likely, watching television. Billy had been arrested earlier that spring for building a raft and floating it down Monture Creek, robbing the new summer cabins along the shore. Ted was continuously amazed by his neighbors' idiocy. Rusted machinery and metal detritus were scattered behind the trailers, along with piles of animal skulls and stretched furs tanning on handmade racks.

Crouching low, Ted jogged north along the fence toward Cade's trailer by the highway, where old fifty-gallon drums and fencing supplies lay in a field of weeds. A semi truck rolled past, its distant headlights like the faint memory of civilization. Cade's dark trailer seemed deserted. Ted was nearly upon it before he saw Preston slumped in a rocking chair on the porch. With both his brothers locked up, he'd been working the door at the road house in Ovando to help his mother pay the bills. Ever since his run-in with Mason and the caught buck, he'd been a less conspicuous presence in Lincoln. He snored softly, his chin resting on his bare chest, his belt unbuckled, his fingers dangling above an empty whiskey bottle and a pump-action shotgun on the porch boards. Ted froze, holding his breath, cursing to himself, and began to tiptoe away. Behind him in the ravine, one of the German shepherds barked, and Preston sat bolt upright.

"Who's there?" he slurred loudly, picking up the shotgun and swinging it from side to side.

Ted crouched in the shadow of the woodpile. He was barely twenty yards away and had no idea if he was hidden, but Preston would surely see him if he moved. The waning moon was bright in the night sky. The few pale clouds were wraithlike and menacing, offering no cover. What a stupid way to die, Ted thought. Preston's eyes glittered in the dark as he levered the gun around. The muscles in his shoulders were corded with a jittery adrenaline that Ted recognized from the junkies he sometimes encountered in the woods. Preston peered into the night, jabbing the shotgun barrel as if it were a bayonet. "You come to take me away, too?" He stumbled forward and bumped his hip against the rail. "My brothers not enough? You want all of us gone?" His eyes were crazed, and for a moment Ted thought he'd pull the trigger. Then Preston let the barrel drop and leaned over the rail, his eyelids sagging. "Come and take it, then," he muttered. He turned and lurched inside, slamming the door shut behind him.

In the sudden silence, Ted could hear the blood pounding in his ears. He remained motionless for several seconds, then dashed behind the woodpile to the scattered array of old fencing equipment. He knelt in front of a coil of razor wire, gripping the rifle to stop his hands from shaking. Why was he taking such stupid risks? Coming onto the Carter Ranch. America was full of lost, violent men like Preston, with no reason for existing. A brave new world of speed freaks with shell shock passed out on trailer porches, and unemployed factory workers waiting to blow their own heads off.

Ted carefully picked up the razor wire, left over after Cade strung the wire around the windows of his trailer before going to prison. Avoiding the bladed edges, he stuffed it in his pack. The wire was all he needed for his plan, and if it was somehow traced back to the Carters, all the better. Like a rock dropped in a pond, a single provocation could upset the entire workings of a community, a state, a nation. . . . The ends justified the means. Nodding to himself, Ted zipped up his pack, then crept back along the fence and off the Carter Ranch, looking back once at the empty rocking chair and the whiskey bottle glinting in the moonlight.

38

A silver banner hung above the couch in Jackie's living room: WELCOME TO THE EIGHTIES. Duane stared up at it, holding a six-pack of beer in one hand and a tub of ranch dip in the other.

"It's 1982," Hutch said, coming up beside him.

"She got it on sale," Duane replied.

The two men regarded the sign a moment longer, Duane wondering at the fact that he'd been born in the 1940s—did that make him old?—then he handed Hutch a beer and snapped one open himself. It was ninety-five degrees outside and the beers were already getting warm.

"You set loose that owl yet?" he asked.

Hutch looked uncomfortable. "Maybe next week, after this heat wave passes."

Duane didn't see why an owl needed to rely on indoor shade and ceiling fans to survive the summer, but he was relieved that the bird would soon be off his road. It had been in Hutch's living room for six months now and unnerved him every time he passed by, knowing it was watching him through the window. Peeing in his yard under the moon, he'd experienced the terrible, helpless sensation of a predator plunging down on him in the darkness, gunmetal talons outstretched.

"Where's Hudson?" Hutch asked.

"Out back with Jackie. They're putting up the lights." Jackie had been planning the Fourth of July party for the past two weeks. Her friend Rita was visiting from Phoenix and she wanted an event like those she remembered from their childhood, when the dancing in Hooper Park lasted until dawn and unruly cowboys were handcuffed to trees.

More guests arrived, crowding in around Duane, the men in jean shorts and baseball caps, women in tank tops and cutoffs with their permed hair teased high off their foreheads. The smell of hair spray made his eyes water. Bottles clinked together and hors d'oeuvres accumulated on the long folding table he'd helped Jackie set up against the far wall: pigs-in-a-blanket, buffalo wings, small greasy meatballs skewered on toothpicks with tiny American flags on the ends. Red, white, and blue bunting hung from the ceiling, and one of Cecil Frazier's taxidermy squirrels perched on a stack of country records by the record player. Darlene Miller ladled generous cupfuls of blue spiked punch from a huge glass bowl. The temperature stubbornly refused to drop even as the sun set, and by nine the windows were fogged over in the muggy heat. People wrote messages on the glass with their fingertips: hearts and stars, names, and even one mysteriously large phallus that Joni McCall quickly wiped away. The hot, dim room felt to Duane like the hold of a ship. Vern Floyd told a story of a Fourth of July in his boyhood during Prohibition, when a terrible blizzard forced all the revelers to remain in the old community hall until dawn, and they emerged to find that a pine tree had fallen and crushed Mr. Didriksen's new Model T. "Blizzard like that, you can get lost in your own backyard," Vern finished.

Dixon Sleepingbear joined Duane and Hutch on the couch and resumed his argument with Hutch over the owl. "You've got to set it loose. It's a wild animal."

"I'm healing him. I thought you Indians were all about healing nature."

"Don't you Indians me. You healed him three months ago. Now you're making a pet."

Hutch sighed. "I forgot how nice it was to have someone else in the house."

Duane let their voices fade into the background and watched Jackie. She was across the room in the kitchen doorway laughing with Rita. Both women held highball glasses full of punch and their cheeks glowed. Jackie had put on rouge and matching red lipstick—the first time Duane had seen her in so much makeup—and her high-waisted jeans fit snugly around her hips. He thought how lucky it was to know those hips both in and out of jeans, and did his best to toggle the image back and forth in his mind. Through the window, Hudson was throwing a football with two older boys in the backyard. Duane had watched his son's confidence grow over his month in Montana. Salt Lake City was an exotic metropolis to the teenagers of Lincoln, and Duane overheard them asking Hudson questions about music and parties. A group came to ride dirt bikes with him almost every day, and usually he was gone for hours, venturing clear over Stemple Pass. Duane knew it worried Tracy, but he wanted Hudson to feel strong in something, and let him go as long as he wore a helmet.

The Kenny Rogers record that had been playing ended, and Jackie put on an old disco standard. Several people groaned in protest, then Rita began to dance, raising her tanned arms above her head and shimmying to the center of the room, her hips swaying, her dyed red hair bobbing back and forth. She had an anxious, lively grace.

"Now, that's a woman right there," Dixon said. Rita's solo trip to Lincoln was maybe evidence of a marriage on the rocks, and Duane could tell his friend had ambitions. Jackie followed Rita onto the dance floor, swaying her own hips, and a dancing crowd closed in around them. Seeing her disappear, Duane was overcome by a yearning so powerful that it pulled him from his seat. Hutch looked up at him, surprised. "You a dancer, Duane?" he asked.

"No," he answered. Then he crossed the room and pressed in next to Jackie. The swaying crowd held them together and he found her punch-flavored lips. Summoning every drop of his newfound bravery, he shimmied his hips back and forth, trying not to concentrate on his stumbling feet, and thinking instead of the clean white lines his skis made in fresh powder when he glided down from Strawberry Ridge. The rhythm of the music traveled up through the alcohol in his bloodstream and animated his shoulders and chin. As the tempo picked up, he ducked his head and kicked out his legs, letting his arms fly. He nearly clobbered Darlene. Music ran all through his body. The other dancers backed up and he suddenly found himself in space, his long limbs unencumbered, a feeling of freedom that reminded him of releasing the brakes on his bike as a boy and zooming down the long hill in Poplar Grove. He spun and raised his arms so his fingertips brushed the ceiling.

"Why, Duane," Jackie shouted, smiling up at him.

The song ended and a hot red blush overtook his cheeks. Someone hooted and someone else clapped and he nearly tripped over himself getting out of the crowd. He pushed through to the back porch and leaned on the rail, sucking in fresh air, wondering what had come over him. The night breeze cooled his cheeks. Mosquitoes whined lazily around the twinkle lights strung overhead. Hudson and his friends had abandoned the football and were wrestling in the dirt by the shed, kicking and pummeling each other.

"You hungry?" Duane called. "We're going to have cake soon."

"Yeah, Dad." Hudson slammed his elbow down and twisted free from the smaller boy around his waist. Then he jogged toward Duane. His jeans and shirt were caked with mud. "Jackie said I can set off the fireworks, too. The big ones."

"All right." Duane smiled. "You wait for me, though. As soon as it gets dark we'll go out in the street away from all these trees."

The boy nodded, wiped a streak of dirt from his forehead, and turned back to his friends. Watching him, Duane gripped the railing, wanting to hold on to the moment as if it were a physical object he could carry in his pocket, like the rocks and bones he found in the woods. It had taken him a long time to get here, to a place that felt like home, and sometimes he felt like he was perched on a narrow ledge, with untold darkness below.

39

Halfway Creek was at its lowest point in the heat of July, gurgling loudly over the rounded rocks in the creek bed. Deliberately, Ted picked his way across. Fireworks popped faintly in the distance, illuminating the treetops in the silver moonlight. He was in no hurry. With everyone in town for the festivities, he could move safely through the woods. The coil of razor wire was heavy in his pack. He knew exactly where he wanted to string the wire. Every evening Hudson and his friends finished their ride by zooming down Florence Gulch all the way to the old Didriksen homestead, seeming to go faster each time, picking up speed as they neared the bottom, racing one another. Two sturdy ponderosas faced each other there across the trail. The trunks were spaced four feet apart, ideal for Ted's trap.

Stars were scattered across the black sky like an explosion of broken glass, each shard glowing with vestigial heat. Ted paused at a rock outcropping, looking down at the valley and then up at the Milky Way, thinking how an explosion had created all of this. Every atom, every rock, every living being, every galaxy blasting out from a single point. Nature was the original bomber, he was only continuing its work. He tried to picture the party at Jackie's house and was reminded of the final clubs at Harvard; he'd ducked his head as he passed by coming home from the library late at night, afraid of the taunting jeers of the soused pledges. Grimacing to himself, he continued on. The game trail he followed was a pale thread in the starlight. He passed a herd of mule deer sleeping in a swale of matted grass. One raised its head to watch him but made no move to flee—a strange, quiet intimacy. An owl hooted in the distance. At times, Ted sensed another presence trailing just behind him, but when he turned around there was nothing there.

Finally, as showers of red, white, and blue light revealed the peaks of the Lewis Mountains on the eastern horizon, he came to the head of Florence Gulch. He located the dirt-bike track in the darkness and shuffled quickly down the steep decline, the pack bouncing against his back, to the two trees he'd picked. The boys were at their fastest here, and Ted hoped the shadows of the needle-laden branches would hide the glint of razor wire until it was too late. He set to work, wrapping the wire around one trunk, then stringing it across to the other, as tight as he could until the trap vibrated like a guitar string. It crossed the path four feet off the ground; low enough to be hidden and high enough to slice the rider in half.

Pleased with his handiwork, Ted climbed back up the gulch to a grassy clearing in the pines. He stretched out on his back, smelling the pine needles in the night air and listening to the rustle of the breeze in the branches and the distant pop of fireworks. Soon he planned to return to his cabin. He'd sleep late, then work in his garden for the morning, and come back here in the afternoon to hide and watch. He wanted to remove the wire immediately after it served its purpose, leaving no evidence.

But first he needed to rest. The encounter with Preston and the long hike the night before, coupled with this hike into the gulch, had exhausted him. Beginning to doze, he felt the futility of such piecemeal actions: a dirt-bike trap, a few pieces of sabotaged logging equipment, poisoned huskies, random bombs sent here and there, but it was as much as a solitary man could do when faced with the full machinery of Western civilization. He hoped that one day fellow revolutionaries would recognize the disruptive pattern of his actions and rise to burn the entire corroded mechanism.

In his dreams, he saw cities on fire, dams bursting, and planes falling from the sky. The creaking groan of a riven bridge plunging to a canyon floor, while survivors, dazed and bloody, walked away from the wreckage of civilization into the forest.

40

Hot, dusty pine-smelling air blasted Hudson's cheeks. He raised up off the dirt bike's seat and leaned forward. The landscape bounced and careened through the orange visor of his helmet. The passing trees blurred together into a single continuous trunk. His breath was loud beneath the bandanna he wore to keep the dust out of his mouth. He was alone—his friends were too hungover from the Fourth of July parties to join—and occasionally he spoke to himself. Or, more properly, sounded. Emitting long, low hoots, like the cry of a night bird searching for a mate. Rocks pinged off the bike's white plastic fender. He punched the throttle. The engine roared. He knew he was going too fast but this . . . this was heaven.

The dirt bike—a white and green 250 Husqvarna that Hutch had restored—reacted to his most gentle touch. A nudge with his left hand, and he shot around the wide curve at the base of Ogden Mountain. Then he was back in the woods, on the straightaway hurtling down the new trail in Wildcat Gulch, bouncing over a root and sending a spruce grouse rocketing into the sky. In his month in Montana, Hudson had traversed nearly the entire mountain, riding clear over Stemple Pass to the ruins of Silver City to the east, north on game trails to Flesher Lakes, and south to where Monture Creek marked the boundary of Old Lincoln and the Carter Ranch. He'd seen moose and elk and once in the distance a great golden bear, which reminded him of the hiker who'd been mauled three years before. This fact still fascinated him. Here was a place where you could be *eaten*.

Hudson spent most of his waking hours either biking or on Hutch's property. Hutch's animals—the coyotes, bobcat, badger, and one huge gray wolf—captivated him with their ruthless inner lives. At feeding time, Hudson lingered outside their cages with the meat bucket in his hands, looking back into their unblinking eyes, suspended in the knowledge that they would rip his arm off if they could. He liked Hutch's stories also, and the way the wiry old man coiled up like a spring as he exaggerated his history in the valley, all the animals he'd rescued. Hudson didn't even mind cleaning the cages. He'd found a two-inch-long talon in the wolf's shit the day after Hutch rescued it, and he now wore the talon on a cord around his neck.

The best, though, was to be alone in the woods on the bike. Riding, he felt invincible. The first time he'd gone out he rode nearly a dozen miles on rough terrain—learning almost instantly, as if the dozens of biker movies he'd watched had formed years of training—pushing the throttle faster and faster around the curves. The only injury he'd sustained was a nasty burn to his calf when he stupidly let the exhaust pipe tip into him after a long ride. He went so fast and hard he often found himself flying past the other teenagers, even the older boys, literally flying off an unexpected jump and then slamming back down on the dirt with a great exhilarating bounce to the shocks.

He discovered he had a knack for working on the motor as well, and it occurred to him that he could be a mechanic and have a whole stable of dirt bikes and four-wheelers and snowmobiles to tinker with. Hearing this, Duane had brought him to Ricky's Auto, introduced him to the mechanics, and left him for the afternoon to watch how the cars were raised on the electrical lift and admire the showering sparks from the welder's blowtorch. The shop reminded Hudson of the days he'd accompanied Duane to construction sites as a boy, and he felt a pang of sadness for his father, who seemed to have little purpose in his life outside of chopping wood. For the most part, though, Duane seemed content, and Hudson was grateful to Jackie for taking care of his father, in her way.

The only aspect of his days on Stemple Pass Road that he didn't like was Ted, the dirty, glowering hermit who lived up the road from Duane and cursed at Hudson and his friends when they rode by. This daily admonishment so irritated Hudson that he fantasized about sneaking onto Ted's dilapidated property, which smelled faintly sulfuric—especially his mangy garden—and slashing the tires on his rattletrap bicycle.

As the day cooled and the shadows lengthened, Hudson finished his ride by heading toward the ruins of the Didriksen homestead at the bottom of Florence Gulch. The Didriksens had been some of the valley's earliest settlers, and had lost four sons to smallpox. The boys were buried by the creek and their ghosts were said to haunt the property, scaring off ensuing occupants with fires, floods, and strange accidents. The homestead always looked idyllic to Hudson, though. White flowers blooming along the creek, sparrows flitting over the sagging barn. Thinking of it now, he was reminded that soon he'd be on the long bus trip back to Salt Lake, with its strip malls and dirty glass monoliths, days trapped behind a tiny desk, insults and abuse. The prospect of returning home filled him with dread. The older boys at his school picked on him relentlessly. He was already taller than they were, which they took as a personal affront, socking him in the stomach to double him over. He held his remaining time in the mountains like a jewel as he steered the bike into Florence Gulch, looking up at the sunlight filtering through the needle-laden branches. He felt a small part of the majesty around him, an effortless belonging like the fish he saw in the clear current of Halfway Creek and the bald eagle nesting atop the tall ponderosa behind his father's cabin. He was afraid he'd lose this feeling the moment he stepped back onto the bus in Butte.

He paused atop the trail and looked out over the valley. The view was obscured by the pine-furred shoulders of the rolling hills, but he could make out the swooping curve of the church roof like a dropped feather in the distance beside the snaking path of the Big Blackfoot River. To the north, the peaks of the Lewis Mountains in the Bob Marshall Wilderness reared up against the horizon like the points of a massive submerged crown, and Hudson imagined an old king buried deep beneath the earth, beginning to rise.

Visions of his future pulsed in him, synced with the music of the engine as he descended through the clear-cut at the mouth of the gulch. Faster and faster, he found he could cast himself forward into every luster of his life to come—moving back here to Lincoln as soon as he graduated from high school, finding work at the auto shop, riding in the mountains every afternoon. He saw these paths as if time had flattened into a honeycomb and each moment of his past and future were present in a distinct cell across the orange-tinted field of the helmet's visor. He peered down one, seeing a wife and child curled together on a wool blanket, a future of protection and love. In another, he lived alone in a cabin in the woods near his father. The ground shuddered beneath him as he neared the Didriksen homestead, and he looked on in curiosity as the cells blinked out one by one until there was only this, the present moment, trees flashing by as he roared over the final rise. He dropped down from the steepest point and then suddenly, as if the cloth had been yanked from his eyes to reveal the true nature of the universe—capricious, ever-changing, a trickster in holy robes—he found himself separated from the bike, soaring through the air, untethered from gravity, and terribly free.

41

Thrown from the bike, the boy hurtled ten yards, tumbling end over end before coming down hard on his helmet, bouncing once, and sprawling on his back over a rock. He twitched and then went still. A trickle of blood ran down his neck. His legs lay limply to one side. His right arm was thrown over his head. Watching from behind the trees, Ted felt briefly elated, and then nauseated. Smoke poured from the engine of the smashed bike. The wire had caught just below the bike's handlebars—Ted had underestimated its height—flipping the machine and sending the boy rocketing forward.

Feeling none of the triumph he'd hoped for, Ted hurried out from behind the trees. His hands shook and it took him two tries to snip the wire from the ponderosa trunk. He couldn't bring himself to look again at the boy. He didn't know if he was alive or dead. A deep ring was scored into the wood by the power of the impact. Sap would soon ooze forth. Ted's heart pounded. He thought of stripping the bark to remove the evidence but was too panicked. He had to get away.

The bike's engine made a soft groaning noise as it rattled out. In the silence, Ted smelled melting plastic and the sharp tang of gasoline. He stuffed the wire back into his pack along with the cutters, scuffed away his footprints on the path, and ran through the gathering twilight to his shack without looking back. He took the long way around Duane's property, terrified of seeing his neighbor. Once home, he bolted his door.

He leaned back against it and looked around the small room. Everything was as he'd left it: his books, his supplies, the nearly finished bomb. He realized he'd expected to find the room ravaged, destroyed, the punishment he deserved finally meted out. Ted laughed once in relief and then his mouth went dry. He felt dizzy. He had to sit down on the edge of his bed. He gripped his head in his hands. For a moment, his rage was overcome by shame. He'd been a boy once, and he felt the presence of this child now, looking at its future self with horror. "Go away," he mumbled, digging his long nails into his scalp. "Leave me alone."

But the boy wouldn't go and Ted was briefly afraid.

42

The little blue truck had nearly three hundred thousand miles on the odometer. Duane rounded the front bumper and patted the hood affectionately. He turned on the hose at the side of his cabin and began spraying the dust off the topper, smelling the sweetness of the water when it hit, and remembering the many nights he'd slept inside, next to the little antler and the ball-peen hammer. The truck wasn't so much little, as Hutch always joked, but compact. A compact and efficient vehicle, unlike the diesel-spewing monsters that tore up the shoulders on the road. "You'll outlast them all," he said.

As if in response, he heard the distant grumble of a motor and looked up, expecting to see Hudson returning on the white dirt bike. The sound of the engine faded away—it wasn't Hudson after all—and Duane returned to washing the truck. He sprayed the fenders and doors, pleased to see the original powder-blue of the paint shining through, set off by the chrome of the hubcaps. He'd loved the truck since he first set eyes on it at the used dealership down the street from his and Tracy's first apartment, and had bought it on layaway after their marriage. He wasn't worried about Hudson; there was still plenty of daylight left and he was a strong rider. "Never seen anything like it," Hutch had said to Duane, after giving Hudson his first lesson. "Like he was born on two wheels." This evaluation filled Duane with pride, and he'd asked around at the diner if there was such a thing as a professional dirt-biking circuit. He'd been disappointed to learn that it was mostly Evel Knievel–type daredevils jumping bikes through flaming hoops; not the future he envisioned for his son. He wanted the boy to have a successful, happy life, and believed him capable of accomplishments far beyond the meandering lassitude of his own.

After finishing the truck, Duane microwaved a dinner and sat on the porch eating as the sun set, looking up the road for Hudson. Concern began to creep in as the shadows lengthened. Usually the boy was home before dark. He knew better than to ride at night. Maybe he was over at Hutch's, putting the bike away or feeding the animals while Hutch ran some errand. That wouldn't be unusual, though generally the boy let Duane know if he wasn't going to be home for supper. Never having cared for a child, Duane sometimes forgot that Hudson was only thirteen. Now edgy nerves set in. He stood, tossed the meal's plastic tray onto the porch behind him, dusted off his jeans, and walked down the road through the slanting orange light.

Hutch's property was silent. His truck was gone from the driveway and the white dirt bike was gone from its place by the porch. "Shit," Duane said under his breath, feeling the first prickles of true fear. He didn't know how he'd explain it to Tracy if their son had had an accident. He rounded the trailer and walked between the row of cages into the woods, his heart beating faster as he peered in at the coyotes and bobcat and finally the huge gray wolf, which lay in the far corner of the farthest cage, its yellow eyes glinting at Duane with chilling ambivalence.

No, no, no. The word repeated with every footfall as Duane jogged back to his trailer. He's fine, he told himself. He just lost track of time. The phone in his cabin began to ring as he arrived at the property, and somehow he knew it was Tracy. Aware in her psychic, mothering way that something was wrong. Duane ignored the ringing, grabbed his coat and a flashlight, and ran out into the night. The wall of woods atop the escarpment behind his cabin looked like an approaching storm, teeming with black shadows. He had no idea where to begin looking. There were dozens of game trails leading to dozens of gulches along dozens of streams in the woods below Ogden Mountain, and in half an hour it would be full dark. "Hudson!" he shouted, hoping against hope that the boy was nearby. No response. Duane plunged forward into the woods.

Jogging in his work boots and jeans, he followed the first game trail he came to, cutting east toward the clear-cut, gaining elevation quickly through the trees. He knew the boy liked to ride on the new logging roads. Maybe he'd gone looking for a view and run out of gas. Duane yelled Hudson's name hoarsely as he went. Years had passed since he'd really run, and he was soon panting from the exertion.

As he emerged into the clear-cut, the peaks of the Lewis Range formed an otherworldly horizon to the east. The expanse of the wilderness overwhelmed Duane. He leaned against a broken stump, catching his breath. So many places to get lost, so many rocks or branches to run into. Only the whispering of the breeze answered his calls. A sickening fear spread through his gut and into his limbs, making them heavy and weak. Something had happened, he could feel it. He only prayed it wasn't too bad. He clicked on the flashlight and swung the beam in wide arcs across the stumps. He cursed and forced himself to run on. Goddamn it. Don't you lose him.

None of what had gone on between Tracy and him was Hudson's fault, yet he was the one who'd been punished, left fatherless, and now alone somewhere in the woods in the dark. Duane felt a shame he could hardly bear. The greatest gift of his life, and he'd left it behind. For what? For pride? Some stupid need to live alone in the wild. He lurched through the trees, calling Hudson's name. He recognized fewer and fewer landmarks on the shadowed ridges, and when he turned, he wasn't sure which direction he'd come from. Wild panic seized him. Was he lost? Back in the forest, he came to a waterfall above a large pool. He thought it was the same one he'd plunged into years before, but when he searched for the huge Doug fir with the bone altar between its roots he couldn't find it. Driven by the desperate, impossible hope that the boy would suddenly appear in the flashlight beam, Duane ran on.

After crashing through a dense stand of brush, he tripped over a root and fell sprawling on his chest, cutting his knee. Pain shot down his leg as he pulled himself up, and warm blood stuck his pants to his skin. He found that he was in a circular clearing below the cliff face. His lungs were screaming and his leg throbbed. He had to rest. He'd run for miles. He spat dust from his mouth and gasped for air. As his eyes adjusted, he saw a strange lean-to built between two saplings on the far side of the clearing. The ground before the shelter was blasted and pocked with blackened rings, as if someone had been setting off fireworks.

"Hudson?" Duane called softly. He pulled himself up and walked slowly across the blast marks, his boots raising small clouds of black ash. He knelt in the entrance to the lean-to. Two red eyes stared back at him and Duane screamed, falling backward into the ash.

Slowly, he recovered his senses. He sat up, terrified and confused. The red eyes glimmered beneath the bough roof. Duane crept forward, afraid he was hallucinating. Or perhaps it had all been a dream. He wished this were true, but the pain in his leg let him know he was awake.

The snow-white head of the albino moose was propped against the back wall of the lean-to. The white fur glowed ghostlike in the night. Duane had heard stories of the moose from Jackie, the sacred, mysterious totem of her youth, and he knew that the head had gone missing from Ernie Floyd's hunting cabin years before. But how had it gotten here? In person, the animal was even larger than Jackie had described. Four feet from the tip of the snout to the base of the severed neck. The fur was dusted with ash but still impossibly white, arctic, a creature born of ice. It didn't look real. Batteries and nails and odd springs of wire were scattered on the ground around it. What is this place? Duane wondered. An overpowering sense of fear and helplessness overtook him. The dark woods held unfathomable secrets. Hudson could be anywhere.

Duane knelt beside the moose. Not knowing what else to do, he asked it for help. "Please," he begged, appealing to the once-sacred spirit of the forest, shot down at thirty yards by a small-town hardware store owner, and now entombed in this blasted landscape. "Please help me find my son." He set his hand on the snout, and in a flash he knew where Hudson was. His favorite place to ride in the evenings—the boy had told him—was the old Didriksen homestead by the creek at the bottom of Florence Gulch.

The homestead was almost two miles from the lean-to, but Duane sprinted the entire way in the dark without falling, and never took a wrong turn, his feet guided as if by the woods themselves. He arrived gasping and covered in sweat. The boy lay motionless in the moonlight fifteen yards from the mangled dirt bike. His right arm was thrown over his head and his legs bent awkwardly to the side. His dented helmet was still on his head. Kneeling over him, Duane felt the faint rise and fall of his breath. He pulled the helmet off, frightened by the blood on his fingers, and raised the boy in his arms. "Hudson," he whispered.

The boy's eyelids fluttered. He made a faint choking sound.

"You're going to be okay." Duane held him to his chest, wanting desperately for the words to be true. His strength returned, a strength greater than any he'd ever possessed. If a tree had pinned his son to the ground, Duane would have tossed it aside like a twig.

If a bear had threatened him, he would have tackled the beast, sacrificing his life for Hudson's a thousand times over. As gently as he could, Duane lifted him up. The boy felt no heavier in his arms than he had in the hospital after he was born. Duane ran with him toward the road, toward town, toward anyone.

NEP

"Make the sentence bullet-proof, or
bomb-proof. Lock him so far down that
when he does die, he'll be closer to hell.
That's where the devil belongs."

—SUSAN MOSSER, UNABOM VICTIM STATEMENT

Missoula International
Airport, September 1996

A huge grizzly bear, stuffed and mounted on its hind legs with its dinner-plate paws outstretched as if it were about to hug or maul each arriving passenger, greeted Nep in the terminal of the Missoula International Airport. He stared up at it dumbfounded as the other passengers from his Chicago flight streamed around him, oblivious to this roaring behemoth in their midst. Finally, a sour-looking woman in net shorts and flip-flops, carrying a camouflage duffel bag, stopped beside him.

"That's Charlo," she said.

"Who?" he asked.

She grinned crookedly, hefting the bag up onto her shoulder. "They named him after some Indian chief, once he was shot and stuffed." Her grin widened. She fished a pack of cigarettes from the pocket of her shorts and looked Nep up and down appraisingly. Her grin turned to a scowl. "You from California?"

"No, ma'am."

"You look like you are." She sniffed. "If you're thinking about moving here, trust me, you won't make it through the winter." She pointed a cigarette at him hostilely, then turned and walked past the baggage claim out to a waiting pickup.

Nep watched her go, as confused by her as he was by the bear. Was she warning him about the weather or threatening his life? He looked down at his clothes: tan slacks, a navy polo, the watch his colleagues had given him for his retirement. Did it suggest California? He felt a field of disdain directed at him from the cowboy-hat-wearing father and son waiting by the baggage claim and the burly, tattooed janitor leaning against the stanchion outside the restroom. Montana, it seemed, had had its fill of tourists. Warily, he shuffled across the linoleum to the rental car desk.

After hearing he was driving to the Blackfoot Valley, the agent brought him outside and showed him the largest SUV on the lot: a raised cherry-red box on wheels that looked like it could drive through walls and across rivers. "A lot of the old Forest Service roads up there just peter out to nothing," the agent said, folding his arms and nodding up at the SUV. "This one'll get you home no matter where you end up."

Nep sensed that he was being up-sold, but the few extra dollars a day didn't matter, and it was true: he didn't know what kind of roads he'd end up on. "I'll take it."

"You a reporter?" the agent asked, as they walked back inside to retrieve the keys and sign the paperwork.

Nep shook his head. "Just on vacation."

"For a couple months, there were so many reporters heading up to Lincoln I wouldn't have had a car to give you," the agent said. "You sure you want to go there for your vacation? We have lots of prettier spots around here. You head north to Glacier, now, that's something you'll remember when you're old." He stopped, as if registering Nep's gray hair for the first time. "I mean really old."

"I have friends there I'm visiting," Nep lied, though in a sense the townspeople had come to feel like his friends. He'd read every article written about Lincoln over the past ten months since Ted Kaczynski's arrest, every interview, every profile, and some of the names were repeated over and over again: Hutch Smith, Vern Floyd, Pastor Kim Younger, and one man in particular, the bomber's closest neighbor, the subject of a long, odd, in-depth article in a glossy magazine, "The Killer Up the Road," which detailed the nearly twenty years the man had spent logging and building a cabin, oblivious to the bombs being constructed less than a mile from his door. The article's author was also a novelist and had added apocalyptic flourishes to the end of each section, using the man's oblivion as a microcosm for America's decline—the evil that creeps in when neighbors stop looking out for each other amid the disconnection of modern life. It was over the top in every way, but the portrait of the neighbor had struck a deep chord with Nep, and he wanted to find the man. He had the magazine tucked carefully between two shirts in his luggage.

Interstate 90 was cut from the flank of the dry, golden hills above Missoula. Peering over the SUV's high steering wheel, Nep passed the university, a patchwork of old brick and newer industrial buildings with the Clark Fork River rushing by the football stadium. He imagined a different life in which he'd been a professor here, living in one of the brick houses at the mouth of Rattlesnake Canyon. His mother could have spent her last years in the mountains. Even though she'd been dead for more than a decade, rarely an hour went by when Nep didn't think of her, and he often wished they'd seen more of the world. Too much time had passed in the old house in Evanston; somehow their lives there had gotten stuck. He'd been taken off the UNABOM case in 1992, five years after Symes was reassigned. "It needs new eyes," his boss had said, and Nep had been surprised to feel only relief. He'd accepted an early retirement soon after, thinking he'd travel and read and perhaps learn what it had all been for.

The Interstate split in Bonner and he followed the overpass for Highway 200 across the Milltown Dam and around the lumberyard, where stripped pines were stacked into pyramids several stories tall. Huge burn piles lined the reservoir and black smoke belched from the mill buildings. Workers carried planed boards to waiting trucks. Above the mill, cloud wisps clung to the mountainside over the Big Blackfoot River, and two bighorn sheep stood sentry on a rock promontory. Nep felt a swell of emotion in his chest. The silhouetted sheep were the kind of thing he'd hoped to see in Montana. He imagined the bomber, likewise from Chicago, encountering these mountains for the first time, and understood the wild sense of meaning and possibility they provoked. For a city kid, this territory rose up out of imagination, the crags and spike-rocked peaks like kingdoms from a fairy tale.

Outside Bonner, the canyon narrowed, following the twisting path of the river. Nep had to slow down on the turns to keep the big car from veering into the opposite lane. Not that it would have mattered. At one point, he counted five mile markers before he saw another car. He rolled the windows down and breathed the fresh, pine-smelling air. The place seemed unreal: buck-and-rail fences separated one pasture from another, black cows spotted the yellow plain, and mountains upon mountains layered the horizon. On the hilltop past Garnet Ghost Town, Nep caught his first glimpse of the layered peaks of the Bob Marshall Wilderness, spires upthrust from the earth's crust, stretching north into Canada and beyond to imagination. A place he'd read about in guidebooks as the wildest in the Lower 48, unmapped and roadless, accessible only on foot or by packhorse, with far more bears than men. The hills were summer-browned with heat and in the distance he saw a thread of smoke from a wildfire. Fly fishermen stood in the river outside Ovando casting their lines in shimmering arcs. Nep was happy such a place still existed.

"Modern society caters more to the wellbeing of its technology than to the human beings who live within it," the bomber had written in his manifesto, which had been published in several major newspapers before his capture. "Skilled workers are replaced by machines and it is accepted as progress. No one asks if the workers are frustrated, humiliated, or angry, nor cares what they will do next." Lines Nep found variously prescient and childish. In footage replayed over and over on the evening news, the scowling, bearded man in handcuffs looked nothing like the sketch Symes had commissioned, but very much how Nep had imagined him. Pathetic and smart and angry and alone. An avatar of the back-to-the-land movement's dark shadow. Spiked trees, blown-up dams, and now first-degree murder. By the time the bomber was caught, three people had been killed and twenty-three more injured.

Dropping into the Blackfoot Valley, Nep felt an instinctive kinship with the place, having read so many descriptions of the river and pines. The town's first outbuildings appeared, the slumping trailers of an abandoned ranch and a faded church with a swooping white roof, a relic of the optimistic architecture of the sixties, when even the smallest rural communities wanted to join the space race. The roof was crumbling and looked out of place among the ponderosas. A trading post and the Wilderness Bar marked the beginning of town. All the buildings had log walls and green metal roofs, save for a quickly erected plywood gift shop with the words THE LAST BEST PLACE TO HIDE emblazoned across the window above a full-sized poster of Symes's police sketch. Nep nearly drove into the curb, he was so surprised, remembering the hours he'd spent staring at the inscrutable face beneath the dark hood and aviators. Behind the window were T-shirts, blankets, and coffee mugs, all printed with the same image. Murder keepsakes at a roadside stand. The dichotomy between the store and the mountains made Nep's head spin, and he was grateful when he saw the sign for the Alpine Motel.

Instead of checking in, he walked across the lot to the Ponderosa Café. He was starved from the long journey; he'd left his apartment in Chicago before first light that morning, and the peanuts and withered sandwich they served on the plane had done little to tide him over. The diner was nearly empty in the late afternoon: a pair of truckers in red flannel ate hamburgers at the counter, and the waitress, a broad-shouldered older woman with steely eyes and gray hair pulled tightly back in a ponytail, sat on a stool by the register. The name JACKIE was written across the breast of her apron. She jerked her chin to indicate one of the open booths by the window, and Nep selected the one with the best view across the highway to the mountains, great turrets of stone rising from the green forest.

"We're out of the fish sandwich," Jackie said, slapping a menu down in front of him. "Not that I'd suggest it."

"Just a grilled cheese," he said. "And coffee." She nodded and disappeared into the kitchen without another word.

After eating, Nep raised his hand and called her over. "Do you happen to know a man named Duane Oshun?" he asked.

Startled, she narrowed her eyes. "You a cop?"

"Not anymore. I was a Postal Service inspector."

The waitress softened slightly. "My dad delivered the mail here for twenty years," she said. "And I never knew Postal Service inspectors existed until this summer."

"You probably never needed one."

"There were a lot of things we didn't know we needed around here." She paused. "What do you want with Duane?"

Nep fumbled for words. "I worked on the bombing case for years and I spent a lot of time thinking about where the bomber might live, and the people around him. Then I read the article about Duane and I guess I feel like I know him somehow."

"You don't," Jackie said shortly, and Nep feared the conversation might be over, but then she sighed and raised her eyes to the mountains. "There were about five hundred agents like you here last spring. FBI, ATF, I never knew there were so many kinds of cops. They filled every hotel between here and Great Falls, and tore the hell out of the forest getting that cabin out. Ted would have hated that more than anything: knowing they tore up his land to move his cabin."

"I'm sorry we weren't able to find him sooner," Nep said softly.

"Well, it's too late now." She shook her head. "I hope Duane got paid good for that article. He split right after it came out."

Nep was surprised and disappointed. "Any idea where?"

Jackie's steely eyes followed a passing semi. "Last I heard he was up in Canada."

"What's he doing up there?"

The hint of a smile played at Jackie's lips. "Oh, Duane never did much of anything, but I suppose he's getting by. Chopping wood, carrying water." She paused. "He had a son, you know. Things were never the same after that. . . ." Tears suddenly sprang to her eyes. She blinked them away and turned, and in the rounded form of her shoulders Nep saw a hurt and love that encompassed Duane but was bigger than him, too, covering the whole landscape of her life.

"I'm sorry," he said, setting a twenty-dollar bill by his empty plate. "I'm guessing you've had enough of strangers asking questions." He stood and left the diner, softening the jangling bell on the door with his fingers as it closed.

The next morning, after a long night on the sharp springs of a musty mattress, Nep drove west from town to Stemple Pass Road. The distant fire had grown in the night and the smoke made the horizon hazy, a western dream, like the Technicolor movies he'd watched as a boy. The turn was unmarked and he would have missed it had he not taken note of the mileage when he wrote down directions. The SUV's big tires bumped off the pavement onto dirt washboard. Regiments of huge ponderosas—much larger than the ones in town—leaned over both sides of the narrow lane. Nep was grateful for the car's sturdy metal roof in case one decided to drop on top of him.

New homes were being built in clearings between the pines, including one gaudy log cabin with a massive elk rack above a wrought-iron gate. The garish stone entryway looked like something out of a hunting catalog. Beyond it, the road curved and began to rise, leaving the new construction behind and worsening in condition, with potholes that made Nep's teeth clack together. Finally, he came to an old trailer set back in the woods with a rusty red Farquhar sawmill out front. An old husky lying on the porch raised its silver head to watch him go by. "Hutch Smith," Nep murmured, remembering an interview he'd seen with the wiry old man standing by this same sawmill. In it, Hutch had said he hoped they fried Ted until his feet turned black. "For the victims?" the brunette newscaster asked solicitously.

"For my dogs," Hutch answered. "That bastard killed my dogs."

Nep parked in a pullout on the next rise and walked the remaining hundred yards to Duane Oshun's cabin. A photo of Duane had accompanied the article in the magazine. Startlingly tall, he was leaning against the side of his cabin with his arms crossed and one long leg propped on the log wall, looking uncomfortable, as if he weren't sure what expression to make, his long, mournful face shaded by an old red, white, and blue baseball cap. He didn't resemble anyone Nep had ever met, and he knew they probably wouldn't have been friends, but he still felt a kinship with him, as if they'd known each other in another life. Here on Duane's property he hoped to find some trace of how the men on this road had lived. What life had been like for the twenty years when Nep was trying to imagine himself into it. The morning light was bright and clear, and a great stillness held the woods, the entire landscape poised in anticipation of the first frost of winter. A path cut off to the right into the trees, treaded with tire marks from dirt bikes.

The small cabin wasn't much to look at. Some of the roof joists were longer than the others, red paint flaked from the windowsills, the porch boards were caved in, and the side window was smashed. The cabin looked as if it had been abandoned a long time ago, and Nep wondered if he was in the right place. Then he remembered all the tourists and thrill-seekers who must have come up this road over the summer, searching for morbid souvenirs. Shaking his head, Nep crossed the yard and put his hand on the rough log siding, peering in through the broken window. He saw an empty living room, a dusty rectangle where a couch had been, and, through an open door, the pale blue tile of a bathroom. The color of the tile matched the sky, and Nep felt the edges of Duane's dream for this place.

"Get away from there!"

Nep jumped and turned to find a familiar short, wiry figure in jeans and an undershirt aiming a lever-action shotgun at him from the road.

"That's private property," Hutch said.

Nep lifted his hands, palms out. He felt his throat go dry as he looked down the gun's barrel. It was the first time in his life that he'd had a gun actively pointed at him, and he was surprised and flustered to find he didn't know how to respond, even with all his training. "I'm an investigator for the post office," he said. "I worked the case for years. I just wanted to—"

"I don't give a shit who you are," Hutch said. "You're trespassing."

"Maybe I could talk to you."

"No, sir," Hutch replied. "I've done enough talking, and this road has seen enough people on it for the next thousand years. You just get the hell out of here." He gestured menacingly with the shotgun. "If I have to start counting, I won't get far."

"I'm going," Nep said, edging from the property with his hands raised. His mind raced through half-forgotten lessons on how to disarm an assailant, but any combat in his slacks and polo shirt seemed too ludicrous to consider. Besides, he was sixty years old, with a metal screw in his shoulder and a bad hip. "Did you know Duane well?" he asked, as they moved in single file through the sunlight back toward the SUV.

"Shut up," Hutch said, and was silent until the SUV came into view. "Jesus Christ, look at that thing. I ought to shoot you on principle for driving such an ugly heap of shit."

"It's a rental," Nep replied. He turned by the door to face Hutch, and noticed how thin the old man was, the tongue of his belt flapping far past the buckle. "You sure we can't talk?"

"Oh, I'm sure. Just get on back to wherever you came from, and don't go driving down no more dirt roads. You're liable to get yourself killed."

"I'm not a reporter," Nep said. "I just want to know—"

Hutch raised the shotgun. "I won't say it again. There's nothing for you here."

Reluctantly, Nep pulled himself up into the driver's seat. The big engine started at once, and he slowly swung the vehicle around. He watched in the rearview mirror as Hutch receded, something tragic in his slight, bowed figure, his whiskered face raised to the sun, the shotgun cradled in his arms. The last man at the end of the road. The only one to survive three decades beneath these trees. What was his secret? Nep knew no more than when he'd started out.

The gaudy new cabin reappeared and Nep imagined a not-so-distant future in which the road was paved and mansions like this lined both sides, all the way to the site of the notorious one-room shack. The area's dark history relegated to cocktail gossip and dickering over real estate prices.

Back in town, Nep parked at the gas station and sat staring at the clock on the dashboard, waiting for his nerves to calm. The image of the shotgun barrel refused to leave his mind. His life, for the most part, had been quiet. His mother had worried about him becoming a postal inspector, but other kinds of police were brought in to face down guns and kick in doors. Even the years he spent tracking the bomber had been defined by solitary imaginings, willing himself into darker, wilder worlds than his air-conditioned office. He looked back toward Stemple Pass. The snowy peak of Ogden

Mountain stood proudly over the valley, with the rocky spine of the Continental Divide stretched out behind it. Brown patches of clear-cuts marked the mountainsides like scabs on the hide of an enormous sleeping animal. Nep thought of Duane and the bomber living as neighbors in these woods in the second half of the twentieth century, as technology marched forward and America assimilated the farthest reaches of the globe into a hive of consumption, fast food, SUVs, and Hollywood movies. Personal computers and wide-screen TVs and now the internet, which Nep's former colleagues used to share information across time and space, and which might one day make catching men like the Unabomber as simple as entering a set of data points.

High above, the midday sun neared its zenith, and a hawk wheeled over the large meadow in Hooper Park, searching for prey. Nep looked down at his hands on the steering wheel, the prominent veins and wrinkled knuckles. He'd gotten old somehow, and wondered if he would have been better off spending his life in these woods. Building a cabin, chopping firewood, carrying water. Could he have found some deeper purpose here? He shook his head, ready to be getting home.

On June 10, 2023, Ted Kaczynski hung himself in his cell at the Federal Medical Center in Butner, North Carolina. He'd been in prison for twenty-five years. Most of that time was spent in solitary confinement. He was allowed outside for one hour per day.